THE

GAMMA

SEQUENCE

DAN ALATORRE

THE GAMMA SEQUENCE
a medical thriller

This is a work of fiction. Names, characters, places, and incidents either are the product of the author's imagination or are used fictitiously, and any resemblance to actual persons, living or dead, businesses, companies, events or locales, is entirely coincidental.

Edited by Jenifer Ruff and Allison Maruska

GREAT OAK PUBLISHING
FLORIDA

!!

ACKNOWLEDGMENTS

A book this good doesn't happen by accident; it's a team effort, and I appreciate everyone who helps.

My two editors (who are brilliant authors in their own right and are also and my good friends), Jenifer Ruff and Allison Maruska are absolutely amazing.

My beta readers—too many to list here, but they know who they are—were a huge help.

My terrific Readers Club members fuel my fire to keep making great stories.

All of these great people play a major role in making these books the best they can be.

Thank you!

i

CONTENTS

DEDICATION

To everyone who ever had to consider
taking on the challenge of an "impossible" task,
and those who encouraged them to do it.

.

CHAPTER 1

The murderer pulled a black ski mask over his face and stared at the ornate entry to his next victim's house.

On TV, cops and angry boyfriends can always kick a door open. In real life, it's a little more complicated than that.

He hefted the 40-pound battering ram to gage its balance. According to the website that sold them, these heavy steel rams replaced a swift kick for police officers around 1975, and had been reliably opening the entries of stubborn perpetrators ever since.

Hit the knob with it straight on, and it will do the rest.

Taking a deep breath, he rubbed the knot growing in his stomach. He leaned away from the door and peeked through the large bay window, focusing on the fat old man at the dining room table. The overhead chandelier cast a warm yellow glow over the walls, spilling onto the yard outside in a misshapen rectangle.

The man inside carved a tiny slice of something on his plate, gently lifting it to his mouth, the fork upside down like European royalty. Good posture, too. No doubt that was the way Dr. Faustus Braunheiser demanded the students at Wellington Academy to eat, all prim and proper. Students watching from their tables would see the rigid old man operating as any good headmaster should, a perfect example of stuffy grace and tedious dignity.

But tonight, the old man dined alone.

No gawking teenage boys in matching shirts and ties, no suck-up faculty. And best of all, no family members.

That's no way to celebrate your birthday, Doctor.

A breeze tugged at the killer's collar and brought the stench of the bay at low tide. He peered at the tall hedges lining the driveway.

Thank goodness for privacy.

He reactively went to wipe his hand on his pants, stopping when he remembered the latex gloves he wore. After patting the butt of the big revolver strapped to his belt, he regripped the 40-pound steel battering ram. Its two handles allowed it to swing like a giant pendulum, and according to the website, the concentrated impact at hand speed was somewhere in the vicinity of 6,000 pounds per square inch.

More than enough to do the trick.

He took another deep breath, straining to guide the tip of the thick black ram to the shiny brass knob, but not touch it. He held it there for a moment, lining up his shot, then he let the ram swing backwards. The momentum of its short, stubby mass wanted to carry him backwards with it, off the elegant front porch and down the majestic home's marble stairs, but he forced his arms and shoulders to contain the pendulum.

When the battering ram reached the peak of its backwards arc, he brought it forward once again toward the door.

One.

Exhaling hard, he rocked the ram backwards again. A bead of sweat rolled past the bandage and down the side of his face.

He swung it forward again, nearly touching the knob.

Two.

The ram arced backwards one last time. With a grunt, he squeezed the steel handles and gritted his teeth, heaving the ram toward the door knob.

Three.

The impact sent a jolt up his arms and a thunderclap that boomed down the doctor's long driveway and past the vintage Jaguar parked there, before fading into the night. As the door knob disappeared, a cloud of splinters took its place. The momentum of the ram carried him into the door frame, the ram disappearing up to the handles inside the thick wooden door.

He yanked the heavy steel tool a few times to get it free, then dropped it over the mansion's stone porch rail and into the manicured bushes. It landed with a thump in the thick mulch. The massive front door stood, cracked in several places and with a big hole where the knob used to be, but it inched open.

The killer raised his foot to do the rest. Kicking the door, it swung open and crashed into the mahogany-paneled wall. The old man at the table was already on his feet, his eyes wide and his mouth half open with the next tiny bite of his elegant birthday dinner. He stormed toward the entrance of his home. "What do you think you're doing? Who are you? Get out!"

Heart pounding, the intruder pulled his large gun from its holster and pointed it at the old man. "Shut up and sit down, Dr. Braunheiser."

The headmaster stopped in his tracks, jaw agape. He slowly raised his hands.

"You don't remember me, do you?" The Greyhound said. A tall, athletic-framed man, he knew he cut an imposing figure. The black ski mask was a nice touch, too. It had a way of keeping the victim slightly terrorized and completely focused. Still, the intruder fought to keep the adrenaline from showing in his voice or making his hand quiver.

"This—this house has an alarm," Dr. Braunheiser said. "The police. They're probably already on the way."

The Greyhound shook his head and crept toward the old man. "I disabled that. Your phone wires run right alongside your electric meter and cable lines, over on the pool side of the house. Besides, when you came in, you didn't re-arm the system, so let's not lie to each other, shall we?" He raised the gun to eye level, staring down the barrel to his victim. "Now get on your knees."

4

Dr. Braunheiser frowned, lowering his hands. "I'll do no such thing."

The Greyhound swallowed hard to quell the knot in his stomach. "Yes, you will." He inspected the long, carved wooden mirror hanging next to a massive aquarium in the foyer. A very scary man in a black ski mask and blue jeans stared back at him. Cocking his head, he returned his gaze to Braunheiser. The old man was probably used to a stern tone of voice sending fear down the spines of grade schoolers. Not tonight. The Greyhound squeezed the thick handle of his .45 tighter. "You'll get on your knees and do what I say, or I will catch the next flight to North Carolina and I will kill your daughter Jenifer in the office of her clinic. Then I will track down your wife Sandy at her seminar and kill her in her hotel room." He narrowed his eyes and growled at the doctor. "Get the picture, birthday boy?"

Braunheiser's hands trembled as he held them in the air. "There's no need for any of that. Just . . . just tell me, what do you want? I can—I, I have . . ." His voice trailed off, much quieter now, and not nearly as stern as a moment ago.

The Greyhound advanced and put his gun near Braunheiser's temple. "I already told you. Get on your knees."

The doctor lowered himself with a grunt, easing his hands down to the shiny wooden planks and steadying himself as he slid each foot backward. Hands at his sides, he raised himself to a kneeling position, wincing, and faced his intruder.

"The car keys to the Jaguar," The Greyhound said. "Where are they?"

The doctor glanced toward the entrance. "On the hook. By the door."

"Okay."

"Do you . . . do you want money, then? I can get—"

The Greyhound hooked a thumb under his ski mask and slid it up past his face to rest on his forehead. The air was cool on his skin. "So, you don't remember me?" He glared at his victim. "Well, I was pretty young at the time. It's not like they took class photos at the facility or anything."

Braunheiser blinked a few times. "Facility?"

"Angelus Genetics."

The old man's face went white.

"Oh, now it's starting to come back to you." The Greyhound lifted a finger to the bandage over his eye. He winced, sweat rolling down his neck and along his back. "I'm glad you remember. I like reminiscing. But first, let me tell you how this is going to go." He slid the mask back down over his face.

"I—I can get you money," the doctor whispered, his voice quivering. "Drugs. Medicine. Whatever you—"

"Just shut up!" The Greyhound screamed, leaning close to the old man's head. "You are not running this show, Doctor!" He turned to the mirror, admiring the mask and the way it hid his features while creating an ominous presence. "You know," he wheeled around to the man kneeling in front of him. "It's amazing you got as far as you did. You're just about the worst liar I've met from the facility—and I've met quite a few of your colleagues over the years."

The Greyhound pulled a handkerchief out of his pocket.

"Here's the deal. You're gonna put a few drops of ether on this handkerchief, and then you're going to inhale it."

"I won't."

"You will." He dropped the cloth in front of the doctor. "If you try not to, I'll put a few rounds into your thighs, and you can lay on the floor kicking in pain while I hold the handkerchief over your face." He lowered his voice to a whisper and put his mouth close to the doctor's ear. "Totally your call."

"Gunshot wounds . . ." Braunheiser swallowed hard, sweat appearing on his brow, "tend to get noticed by detectives."

"Coroners, too, Doc." The Greyhound sniffed. The old man's Clive Christian cologne and aftershave filled the assailant's nostrils. "But if you think somebody's going to come poking around in the middle of the Great Cypress Swamp, way out past the Indian reservation, and dig through a bunch of gator dung to find your injuries, well, just remember—those Miami detectives didn't even bother to get their feet wet when ValueJet flight 592 went down in the Everglades. I doubt the deep swamps are the first place anyone would think to look for you, anyway."

The old man trembled now, his whole body shaking. "So . . . you, you do need to kill me?"

The Greyhound righted himself. "Oh, without a doubt. Was that not clear?" He strolled down the long hallway toward the Christmas tree, admiring the vases and statues as the dark floor gently creaked under his feet. "You have a few minutes. Use them wisely. Pray, maybe—to whatever you believe in. Science. Money, possibly. Power. But make no mistake, in a few minutes, one of us will be dead." He swallowed hard. "And since I happen to be holding the gun, I'll bet it's going to be you."

"You'll never get away with this." Anger seeped into the doctor's voice.

"I already have," The Greyhound said, walking back to the doctor. "Several times. But I'm tired of talking to you. It's showtime. Three deep breaths ought to do it—and I'll be able to tell if you're faking, so don't."

With trembling hands, the doctor reached out and lifted the white handkerchief from the floor.

The Greyhound produced a small vial from his other pocket. "Three drops of this. No more, no less. Remember, there are lots of bad ways to die. This doesn't have to be one." He held out the bottle, waving it back and forth like a clock pendulum as he stared into the old man's eyes. "It must be terrible, knowing you're going to die very soon."

The doctor gazed at him, the handkerchief in his shaking hand. "If you tell me what you want, maybe I can help you."

"No! I've had all the help I care to endure from you, Doctor Braunheiser! Now, one last time." He stretched his arm out and leveled the big gun at the old man's head. "Start sniffing or I swear the walls will be painted with your brain splatter."

The old man uncapped the plastic bottle, the lid slipping from his trembling fingers. It rolled across the floor. The Greyhound stooped to pick it up. "Can't leave evidence laying around."

The vial had a tip like an eyedropper. Braunheiser lifted the bottle, squeezing three small drops into the center the handkerchief.

"Over your nose and mouth," The Greyhound said, waiving the gun at the doctor. "Please breathe through your nose deeply, and count backwards from ten." He snorted. "Just kidding. You don't have to do that."

The old man took a hesitant breath.

"Deeper than that. Gun shots hurt really, really bad, from what I hear. First there is the impact—like getting hit with a baseball bat, wham! Knocks the wind out of you. Then there is this sharp, searing pain that rockets up your body and bashes your brain. Then, there's the intense burning feeling. Some guys say they can even smell their own flesh smoldering from the hot lead. Then wave after wave of nonstop agony overwhelms your whole system and sends you into shock—after enduring ten or fifteen minutes of dire pain. Probably put an old boy like you straight into coronary arrest. And at close range, this .45 can take a whole leg off as well. Now, if you can't do it for yourself, think of your poor innocent wife and daughter. Jenifer and Sandy don't deserve to die, too. Think of the rancid, sticky mess of blood and goo we'll be leaving for the maid to find on Tuesday. So, please. Do it right."

The doctor squared his shoulders and inhaled deeply.

"That's more like it. Better go ahead and count."

Trembling, the man nodded. His eyes filling with tears, he spoke through the handkerchief he held to his face. "Ten . . ." His voice wavered. "Nine."

He closed his eyes, tears rolling down his cheeks. "Eight . . ."

Another deep, shaky breath.

"I'll help you," The Greyhound said. "Seven."

The doctor's shoulders sagged as he inhaled a third time. His hand fell to his side, the cloth floating to the floor. His head bobbed, tipping to the right slightly, and then his body slumped. He crashed face-first onto the polished oak planks.

The Greyhound took a deep breath and released it slowly, rubbing the knot in his belly. "That's more like it. Now, if you'll allow my friends to escort you to your car, we'll start phase two."

CHAPTER 2

Hamilton DeShear dabbed his face with a towel and leaned over the canvas camping chair, snatching his phone from the lid of the cooler before it could vibrate into the sand. He never took the phone with him when he ran, figuring he was allowed an hour at dawn to himself. His daily three-mile run on the beach was one of the few pleasures he permitted himself these days.

A nearby fishing pole rested in a half-buried PVC pipe but showed no indication of having caught a fish. He held his towel over the phone to cast a shadow in the bright light, then read the screen.

Unknown number.

Good. It's not Tullenstein again.

He tapped the green icon and raised the phone to his ear. "DeShear Investigations."

The woman on the other end spoke with a quiet but rushed tone. "Hello, may I speak with Hamilton DeShear, please?" Her words wavered slightly, like someone who doesn't quite know how to ask for what they want.

Maybe a wife who wanted her husband followed, but definitely not one of Tullenstein's minions looking to slap another lawsuit on him.

DeShear held the phone away from his face to note the time. Seven-thirty on the dot. "This is Hank DeShear. What can I do for you?" Setting the phone back on the cooler lid, he pressed the speaker button and brushed sand from his taut, shirtless torso.

The caller cleared her throat. "I'm not sure how to say this . . ."

"Okay, well, take your time."

A well-toned young lady—easily half his age—jogged by wearing a sports bra and pink yoga pants. Her blonde ponytail bobbed at the back of her baseball cap, but her eyes stayed on DeShear. She smiled and gave him a wave. He lifted a hand and nodded. Her long legs churned through the soft sand as she turned and continued down the beach.

"I require your services," the woman on the phone said. "But you must start right away. Will you meet with me? I spoke with Mark Harriman of the Tampa police department. You were very highly recommended."

"Well, that was nice of Harriman. What's this about, Miss . . .?"

"You may call me Lanaya Kim. I assume you've read about the death of Dr. Braunheiser last evening?"

"I caught part of it on the news. Wellington Academy. He was the headmaster." DeShear grabbed the phone, thumbing icons in an attempt to find the Tampa Tribute website. The service indicator flickered with one partial bar as it searched for a stronger signal. His laptop was in the trunk of his car, but it wouldn't power up fast enough to let him find the story quickly and read more—if it got a signal at all.

"The news reports say he died in a single-person car wreck. I want to look into a wrongful death case, but you must start immediately. Are you available to meet me tomorrow?"

"Sure." He brushed the sand from his legs. "I can even meet you this morning if you want. What law firm are you with?"

"Tomorrow. And I am a private individual. An attorney of my employ will contact you soon if you take the case."

"That'll be fine. Can I ask what your relationship to the case is, Ms. Kim?"

"As I implied, the death of Dr. Braunheiser was something other than a simple accident. We can talk in detail about that tomorrow. I'd like to—"

"What do you think happened?" He squinted into the calm waters of the bay as they glinted in the morning sun, tiny diamonds dancing with each ripple.

"I . . . I can't discuss it over the phone. If you—"

"Tomorrow it is, then, Ms. Kim. And don't worry, I'm pretty well versed in these types of things. I do excellent trial research, and like Harriman probably told you, I used to be a cop. So if we need to get a wrecked car's brake lines checked, or a power steering mechanism inspected to find a faulty repair or a manufacturing issue, that's no problem. I can locate the best experts, compile all the research, and present it so anyone on a jury finds in your favor. Of course, for it to go anywhere, you first have to show you're an affected party. Can you tell me how you connect to Dr. Braunheiser?"

A few seagulls landed next to his fishing rod.

"The news . . . the news says that Dr. Braunheiser's death was an accident."

"And you wanna sue."

"No. I want . . . my interest . . ." She took a breath. "If an advanced toxicology screen is performed, it will show Propofol in Dr. Braunheiser's system. Enough to where he would not have been able to drive a car."

DeShear rubbed the beard stubble on his chin. "That's a little different. You think the wreck was intentional? A homicide?"

"I really—I don't want to discuss this over the phone. When we meet in person, I can tell you more."

"Okay, but from what you're saying, you— or someone else—thinks the doctor's death was a murder."

"Mr. DeShear—"

"Ma'am, it's an important distinction for me. I don't do murder investigations."

"Mr. DeShear, please listen to what I have to say." Her voice quivered. "Please."

The quiver hooked him. Fear in others had a way of making him sympathetic. He put a hand on his hip. "Okay, I'm sorry. Go ahead."

"Not on the phone. Tomorrow. In person."

He pursed his lips. Something about her didn't feel right.

"You do bail bonds work, correct? Finding criminals who skip out on their bond? And your bail retrieval account is with Mid Florida bank. Check your balance. You'll see a five-thousand-dollar deposit has been added by Credit Suisse, from an account ending in two-zero-one. Would you like to take a moment to verify the funds are there?"

He snapped upright. "I'm, uh, not really at my office right now." Glancing at the car, he regretted not firing up the laptop earlier—and not jogging where there was a better signal.

"Can you check from your phone? I'll wait."

"Yeah, there's not really a signal here. Five thousand, did you say?"

"Do I have your interest now? It's all yours for simply meeting me tomorrow on Bayshore Boulevard. Hear me out and the money's yours, no strings attached. Afterwards, we can see if you'd like to handle my case."

He nodded. "Five thousand dollars will certainly buy a few hours of my time. I'm available later today if you want."

"Tomorrow. I'll be coming in from Texas."

"What time should I pick you up at the airport?"

"Please pay attention. I need you to report the information about the Propofol to the police. It won't show up in a standard toxicology report, so the coroner will specifically need to look for it."

"Okay. They're gonna wonder how I got the information."

"Tell them the truth. You got a tip over the phone. Tomorrow, meet me at noon, at the corner of Bayshore Boulevard and Gandy. I'll be dressed in red jogging gear and stretching on the grass in the median."

He stood and held the phone to his ear with his shoulder. Folding the canvas chair, he grabbed the cooler and fishing rod as he made his way to the car. "A thousand people jog on Bayshore every day. How will I find you?"

"Your picture is on file with the department of professional regulation. I'll find you. I must go now."

"Just to make sure we're on the same page— if we meet, I get to keep the five thousand."

"Correct."

"Well, you just bought yourself a meeting." He smiled. It might be a merry Christmas this year after all. "So how's the weather out there in Texas during the holidays?"

"I don't know. I didn't say I lived in Texas, I said I was coming in from there." She huffed. "I do hope you pay better attention to detail going forward than you have so far, Mr. DeShear."

He shifted on his feet. "Yes ma'am. Sorry. I sure will. As a private investigator, we often need to deduce things, so—"

"Try not to deduce incorrectly, then. One last thing. You are not to try to contact me in any way. For the moment, assume every aspect of your life has been compromised. Your office, your computers, everything. Operate as though your phones are bugged and your home is under surveillance. I'm calling you from a disposable phone, so don't try to call me back on it."

"Don't take this the wrong way, but that sounds a little over the top."

"For five thousand dollars, I get to sound as over the top as I want."

"All right. Fair enough."

"Come alone tomorrow, and don't tell anyone about the meeting."

"No problem." He set down his gear and rubbed his forehead. "Ah, Ms. Kim, this may cost me the job, but I feel obliged to say this again—I can't get involved in an active murder investigation. It's just not allowed. So, when I tell Harriman about the Propofol, if that pans out—that's it. I'll have to step aside."

"I'll be hiring you to handle a missing persons case. You still do that, don't you?"

"Well, yeah."

"As an investigator working for a law firm in a wrongful death suit or missing persons case, you'll be able to interact with every law enforcement agency necessary. Enough discovery motions will be filed in enough cities for you to act with virtual impunity."

"Okay," DeShear said. "But who's the missing person?"

The line went silent. Just as he was deciding she'd ended the call, her reply came.

"The missing person is me."

CHAPTER 3

After driving to the bank and cashing out his newfound five thousand dollars, DeShear opened a safe deposit box and put most of the cash inside. He then got a haircut and a shoeshine, and spent most of the rest of the day alternating between hunching over his computer and pacing back and forth around his living room like he was trying to wear out the carpet.

Lanaya Kim had been right about Braunheiser's accident—as far as what the news and the Tampa police were reporting. A single-car wreck ended the doctor's life, after apparently losing control of his 1968 Jaguar convertible. With no air bags, no shoulder straps, and no roof, the doctor was crushed under the car when it went off the road south of his home. The vintage vehicle dropped the ten or so feet onto the rocks lining the bay, flipping over and crushing the doctor underneath.

Nothing too interesting there; a case of bad luck on the old boy's birthday, maybe after a few too many glasses of wine.

Propofol, on the other hand, was a very interesting drug. Anything with the nickname "milk of amnesia" had to be. A restricted use anesthesia, it was mainly accessible to nurses, doctors, and pharmacists, but it had been known to be a target for hospital break ins. Propofol had the added distinction of being part of pop singer Michael Jackson's demise, which made it a headliner for a while with some illegal drug users. Since it could cause irregular heartbeats, an overdose might appear as a heart attack. Being an injected drug, Propofol would usually be easy to spot if it was the cause of death.

The fact that it was a standard anesthesia in colonoscopies and many surgeries was most interesting to DeShear.

He leaned back in his chair, staring at his computer screen.

It's a knockout drug. It'd be hard to drive at all when you're looped.

Now that he knew a little about the subject, DeShear called the Tampa Police Department. He used the main line so his call would be logged and recorded, instead of attempting to contact Harriman on his cell phone. The information might make DeShear a suspect in a murder investigation. He wanted it all to be on the record.

"Hank DeShear," Harriman said. "Old Hanky Panky. Long time. To what do I owe the pleasure?"

"Work, Officer. It's not a social call today."

"So I figured. If we were still social, I'd probably have seen you at the hockey game last week like we planned. How's your cough?"

"It put me on the couch for five straight days, but I'm all cleared up now—and trying to catch up on work. Maybe we can see a game later this month." Reaching across his tiny dining room table, DeShear grabbed a yellow legal pad and a pen. "What about you? How you managing?"

"Day by day, man."

DeShear chewed his lip. "I need a favor. It's about the Braunheiser accident."

"Okay, sure. Whatcha got?"

He tapped the pen and took a deep breath. This information could go a lot of ways, and most of them would be bad for DeShear. The legal pad was filled with various scripted versions of how to deliver the tip to Harriman so it raised his interest enough to order the tox screen but didn't get anyone brought in for questioning. It was a dicey route. Harriman's ambition blurred his judgement at times, and DeShear had a five-thousand-dollar lunch date the next day. He couldn't risk getting locked up for forty-eight hours if Harriman's boss got a bug up his butt and wanted to press him for more.

Downplay it.

"I got a tip that the good doctor was drugged and that's what caused his wreck. Seems like a stretch, but I thought I should report it."

DeShear held his breath.

"It is a stretch. Our guys checked the scene. He rolled his car on top of himself, end of story."

"I know, but my source says if you do a tox screen for Propofol, you'll find it in his system." DeShear's heels bounced on the vinyl flooring as he waited for an answer. "That's the stuff Michael Jackson was on when he croaked. Can you request one and let me know?"

"Sounds pretty thin. How good is the source? I don't wanna raise a ruckus over a respected member of the community and end up looking stupid. What if you contact the family directly and see if they'll ask the medical examiner?"

Terrific.

Harriman's ambition could make him a jerk, but he wasn't usually this thick. "Mark, old buddy, if you get information that kicks this upstairs to major crimes, it's another step up the ladder for you. Run the screen. It's a legit tip, and it might prove something. How long would it take to get a result?"

"If I request it and there's nothing there, you owe me a dinner."

That was a good sign. The possibility of getting some kudos from his boss might have worked. "Okay."

"At Bern's, and I choose the wine."

Of course it had to be at the most expensive steak house in town, the one known world-wide for its expansive wine cellar. "Steaks at Bern's, and we drink beer. How long until I can hear back?"

"A day, maybe two. I'll call over there after we hang up."

With the fish on the hook, DeShear decided to press his luck. "That's more like McDonald's Big

Mac speed. If you want a steak dinner, I need steak speed."

"Kinda pushy when you're asking me to do work you're getting paid for, but I'll see what I can do. Because you're a friend."

"Thanks," DeShear said. "Good talking with you."

He ended the call, then returned to the business of wearing out his carpet.

* * * * *

His 7 A. M. breakfast at Ihop wasn't as leisurely as he'd hoped. Five grand was a lot to lose if the interview went bad. He'd have stayed home, but his carpet had suffered enough—and there's only so much nervous energy you can vent at the gym. If he ate really slowly, a big plate of pancakes and eggs might fill some of the gap before his meeting.

At 7:30, shoving his untouched breakfast aside, he opened his laptop and returned emails for a while, trying to not look at his phone every five minutes to see what time it was. Then he went outside and bought a copy of the Tampa Tribune from the box in front of the restaurant. He sat down and perused the pages of each section while quietly bouncing his heels under the table like a madman. At ten thirty, after staring at the newspaper without actually reading anything, and surrendering to daydreams about a lavish cruise to the Bahamas paid for with the cash from his safety deposit box, he gave up stalling and headed toward his appointment.

The drive to Bayshore Boulevard was quiet. Morning traffic had already subsided, and things hadn't yet picked up for the lunch rush. But the south end of Bayshore wouldn't be too busy anyway. MacDill Air Force Base lay at the tip of the Bayshore peninsula, and any contractors there who wanted lunch offsite would stay farther south. Downtown Tampa lay at the north end of Bayshore, and office workers there tended to stay north so they could get back to the grind in less than sixty minutes. Bayshore itself was the scenic respite of big houses and old money, back from when Tampa first became a major shipping port over a hundred years ago. The doctors and lawyers who later moved into those mansions maintained the exclusive aura of Florida's very well-to-do.

Along the route, DeShear passed by the Braunheiser residence. A few police cars lined the driveway. Mrs. Braunheiser and her adult daughter would have gotten the bad news and come home, and by now they were probably meeting with the police to answer any questions as a matter of routine.

DeShear reached up and loosened his tie, more from nerves than from being hot. December in Florida was a fickle thing, causing people to run their air conditioners one day and wear leather jackets the next as Canadian winds struggled with Caribbean currents to see whether there would be a frost on Christmas day or swimming and sun tans. Today, Canada was winning—but only barely. The breeze off the bay created a light chop in the water, and it sprayed onto DeShear's windshield when the occasional large wave crashed into the rocks. Whitecaps were visible past the Tampa Yacht Club. It would be rough sailing for anyone who ventured out, regardless of the size of their boat.

Parking a few blocks from Kojack's Ribs, DeShear walked toward the designated intersection in the hopes of catching a few extra details about his mysterious client before she arrived. He shouldn't have bothered.

"You're early, Mr. DeShear."

Lanaya Kim had long legs, and she was a little heavier than he expected. A middle-aged woman with dark brown hair, almost black, but with few other overt Asian features, running didn't appear to be her thing. She sat in the middle of the wide grassy median that separated Bayshore Boulevard's northbound and southbound lanes, her legs in a V, arching herself toward one foot and then the other.

DeShear crossed the asphalt to stand near her. "Yeah, you never know with traffic around here. Nice to meet you, Ms. Kim."

She continued stretching, not looking up. "You came early to see if you could learn what kind of car I drove, or who else might be with me."

He smiled. "That's just good detective work, ma'am. Don't think anything of it."

"I won't. You are younger-looking in person than your online profile." She sat upright, putting her hands behind her on the grass. "Based on the college graduation date you listed on LinkedIn, you're in your mid-fifties. You could pass for thirty-five."

"Thank you. Good genes, I guess."

"Hmm." She narrowed her eyes at him. "Do my questions make you uncomfortable?"

Yes. "No, ma'am."

"Your hair has almost no gray. Do you color it?"

He stepped back a bit, putting a hand to his head. "Color it? No." His cheeks grew warm. This was already a very strange interview.

"Okay, then." She took a deep breath. "Shall we start?"

"Please."

She extended her hand and he helped her to her feet. The running shoes looked new. So did the red workout shirt and jogging shorts.

"Do you mind if we walk while we talk? It may help maintain the illusion that I'm here to casually exercise."

"Sure." He shrugged. "I'm not exactly dressed to work out, though."

"No, you are not. Next time, I'll be more specific—although I thought it would have been obvious after I said what I'd be wearing. Lesson learned. This way, please."

She crossed to the other side of Bayshore and headed north on the big sidewalk that ran several miles along the bay. Whether it was freezing out or hot, the bay always gave a breeze. Sometimes that breeze smelled of low tide, but the joggers didn't seem to care.

"You have questions," Lanaya said, pulling her hair into a ponytail as she walked. "What are they?"

DeShear followed her, gazing at the concrete railing that lined the sidewalk. "Well, I took the five thousand dollars out of my account and put it in a safe deposit box, so if you change your mind after our meeting, you can't grab it back."

She moved at a brisk pace, swinging her arms. "I have no intention of grabbing it back. It's for services rendered. As of a few minutes from now, it's yours. Then we'll see about me hiring you to take my case."

"Okay. You also mentioned some things yesterday that you said you'd explain today." He loosened his tie again. "So I guess I'm really here to listen."

"Fine. Let's pick up the pace, shall we?"

He winced, wishing he'd worn different shoes, but took off his suit coat and swung it over his shoulder. Though he worked out every day, he still got sweaty easily when he did physical activity. The breeze from the bay could only do so much.

Between breaths, Lanaya spoke in short huffs. "I have information about a murder."

"I know. The news and the cops still say it was just a car wreck, but we're running down your drug tip."

"I'm not talking about Dr. Braunheiser. The authorities dismissed the last two murders as well. Accidental deaths in all cases, except they weren't. If Mark Harriman has requested the advance toxicology screen, we'll have the report soon. Like the others, it will show Propofol."

"That'll be big news."

"That's not the big news. If somebody calls up the police and says a prominent physician didn't die in a car wreck on his birthday, but was actually murdered, and three of his colleagues were murdered on their birthdays in the last twelve months, that's big news."

DeShear stopped walking. "If that were happening around here, I'm sure we'd have heard about it."

"No, that's exactly why you haven't heard about it." She ceased walking and came back to him. "It hasn't happened around here. Dr. Braunheiser isn't linked to the other murders because of where he lives. He's linked by where he worked."

"Which was where?"

She looked down. "I'm afraid I can't divulge that at this time."

Leaning against the thick concrete rail, DeShear frowned. His fifty-four-year-old knees preferred the padded comfort of running shoes to hard concrete and the thin leather soles of his dress shoes.

But that wasn't the only reason for his discomfort. He couldn't shake the feeling that something didn't add up with Lanaya Kim. Maybe he was being played. Nobody spends five thousand dollars on a PI for a meeting. Not *just* for a meeting, anyway.

"You're looking at me strangely." She put her hands on her hips, drawing hard breaths. "I'm not crazy, but what if I am? The money is good."

"Well," he sighed. "I can't argue with that."

"See this?" She patted the thick concrete railing. Waves crashed on rocks a few feet below. "It's designed to have cars not go through it, and it runs the entire length of this scenic drive, without a break, for over four miles. Guess where Braunheiser's wreck occurred?"

He hooked a thumb over his shoulder. "The paper said it was south of here, at Ballast Point. Near the park."

"Twenty feet past where this big railing stops. Coincidence?"

"Maybe. Most people don't go for a drive and stay in front of their house."

She folded her arms. "Let me turn the tables on you for a moment. You were highly recommended. I'm not seeing it. You said you were a police officer. Why did you leave your career after so many years? Did you not like it?"

"I'm not sure you want to hear my story. It has a sad ending so far."

"Our future work arrangements end now if I don't hear it."

That got his attention, but it was a delicate topic. His instinct was to stare at the sidewalk, but he forced himself to look into her eyes and be firm and candid. "I got let go," he said. "I received three commendations in two years, and had just gotten my picture taken with the mayor, when they fired me."

The wind lifted a tuft of her long hair. She pushed it from her eyes and tucked it behind her ear. "What was the picture with the mayor for?"

"I was fishing at a marina, and I'm on the dock next to some of the bigger boats. Some guy jumps in this one boat and steals it. Problem is, he didn't realize there were little kids down below. He gets about three hundred yards offshore and stops, and he throws the kids overboard. Now, there's nobody around. The boat owner is in the bait shop getting ice and sodas, and I'm standing on the dock

watching this thing unfold. The thief takes off again, and the kids are drowning in the channel. I don't have a boat, so I jumped in. Swam over, saved the two kids. The waves were pretty good sized that day. The kids wouldn't have lasted five minutes. Anyway, it made the newspapers, and I got my picture taken with the mayor. 'Off-duty cop makes city proud.' That kind of thing."

"Fishing again. Do you do a lot of that?"

"I used to fish a lot with my dad when I was a kid." DeShear stuck his hands in his pockets. "He died when I was in high school."

"I'm sorry." She shifted her weight. Her tone had softened. "What about the commendations?"

"You need the whole bio, huh?" He shrugged. "Okay." He took his hands out of his pockets and counted on his fingers. "I got one for stopping a school shooting. Busted in the door and knocked the kid to the ground when he was still scaring everybody and firing holes into the ceiling. One was for a big drug bust where we saved a hostage. The other was for getting people out when the library was on fire."

She shook her head, tucking another strand of hair behind her ear. "Why on Earth did they let you go?"

DeShear turned around and leaned on the railing, facing the breeze. In the distance, across the choppy water of the bay, stood the skyscrapers of downtown Tampa and its police headquarters.

"My partner and I went to a dirty apartment building, a little rat hole, where this guy was selling drugs. It was a domestic dispute call, and everybody

in the place looked like they were starving to death except this big guy. He's on meth or something, but the kids haven't been showered in weeks. The girlfriend is full of bruises. So I'm talking to this guy, and he just let loose. He smacks his daughter, right in front of me. The kid's about four or five, and she was crying because she was hungry, and he backhands her and tells her to shut up. Sends her flying." He peered at Lanaya. "I had a bad temper. A quick temper. So I laid the guy out. I let him know what it was like to be on the receiving end of violence, so he'd think twice about hitting somebody next time. And . . . I busted his jaw." DeShear sighed, looking over the water. "Turns out, his dad is a big shot attorney, and they sued me for everything under the sun. I lost my job, and the big lawyer took my house, my car, my bank account, everything. Now I do this. And try to work on my quick temper."

"You still got three commendations. Those go to heroes." She stepped closer to him and lowered her voice. "I believe I'd be proud to have you work on my case."

He nodded. "Thank you."

The wind picked up again, taking a few scattered leaves from the sidewalk and carrying them across the wide boulevard. They came to rest on the manicured lawns of the mansions on the other side.

"When the Propofol is confirmed," Lanaya clasped her hands in front of her, "the police will demand to know where the information came from. If you tell them it was me, then that will make me a suspect. If you don't, they'll hold you as a suspect. I am not the person who did any of this, but if my name comes to light—from being booked as a suspect or being named in a news story—then people who want me silenced will know where to find me. Meanwhile, there have been several associates of Dr. Braunheiser's who lived around the country and who have died under ordinary-looking circumstances. Upon deeper investigation, their deaths were quite suspicious. Whoever did that is involved here. There may be other things involved as well."

He leaned against the concrete railing. "Well, again—murder goes over into the Tampa PD basket, and if they are around the country, it goes to the FBI."

"Yes, and while they assemble a task force and jockey for jurisdiction and rent office space and try to piece together what we already know, others will die."

"That's . . . not really my problem. I just can't—"

"Of course it's your problem." She stared straight into his eyes. "There are ruthless murderers after me. They'll happily kill you to get me."

CHAPTER 4

DeShear gripped the steering wheel and frowned as he drove toward Tampa International Airport. Driving a client to the airport wasn't a big deal, but potentially putting his life at risk and still not getting the whole story, that didn't sit well. He valued his butt a lot more than five thousand dollars.

He also didn't feel he was in a position to argue. He needed the money, but people who can drop that kind of cash on an hour-long interview can probably hire people to get it back, too.

But a cruise to the Bahamas would be nice . .

.

Then there was the story itself. Plausible, but thin. But there wasn't any harm in getting paid—and paid well—to listen to somebody's far-fetched story. It was a part of the job he didn't like, but it was still part of the job.

As long as he wasn't getting played somehow.

Maybe poke the bear one more time. See if she'll spill something.

"Listen," he said, adjusting his sunglasses. "If you really think your life is in danger, you need to go to the police."

She sat with her hands in her lap, clutching a small purse and staring out the window. "You still don't believe me. Well, what if I already did go to the police? You were a cop. What can they do? How many stories have you heard where some girlfriend was being battered, or an ex-wife's life was being threatened, and the police can't do anything until the guy makes a move? Well in my case, the move will be my death—and that's not really a good option."

"But I mean—"

"This is much bigger than that, and the best solution is for me to stay on the move, which I am. And you are potentially linked to me now. I've wired money to your account and we've spoken on your cell phone. We've met in person. I took precautions by using a numbered bank account and disposable phones, but any number of things could have been noticed on your end."

He nodded. "Well, thanks for that."

She turned and stared at him, keeping her hands in her lap. "Pull over."

"Don't get in a huff. You asked for a ride to the airport and I said I'd take you. Delta, was it?"

"Pull the car over right now."

He sighed, slowing the vehicle to make a turn. "I'll stop over here. This road's too busy for theatrics." He pointed to the vast, mostly empty parking lot of International Mall. "How's that?"

"That will do fine. Thank you."

Pulling past the rows of regal palm trees and coiffed topiaries, he eased into a parking spot away from any other cars. After turning off the engine, he turned and rested his back against the driver's side door, studying his soon-to-be-former client.

She stared at the small purse in her lap. "I've been trying to do you a favor, Mr. DeShear. Five thousand dollars is a lot of money, but I'm desperate. You can walk away right now and keep the cash. You did your part. You met with me." The quiver in her voice returned. It hooked him over the phone, and it reset the hook again now. "I . . . can get a cab from here. That's what I did to get to Bayshore. And I can—"

"I'll take you to the airport." He spoke in a low, soothing tone, almost a whisper. It was like a husband who was making up with his wife after a tiff where the words had been flung too hard. "I'm not a jerk. Not that kind of a jerk, anyway."

She raised her head and swallowed hard. "I'm not crazy. I have proof that I'm in danger, and I have information about much more than that. But . . ." Turning to him, a tear ran down her cheek. "I don't want to die."

He pursed his lips, drawing a deep breath. Her fear was real. That mattered.

A tiny *pop* opened the little purse, revealing a thick wad of hundred-dollar bills and a driver's license. She pressed them to one side and took out a few folded pieces of paper, handing them to him. "This is what you've been wondering about."

He removed his sunglasses. The papers were photocopies of newspaper articles. One reported the accidental drowning of Emmet Kincaid, a winemaking consultant in northern California; the other was the accidental overdose of Nilla Cunde in Missouri, from painkillers. Both had died within the last thirty days.

She glanced at the papers. "At one time in their careers, they were geneticists. Like me."

"Okay." He handed the photocopies back to her. "But I can't shake the feeling there's something a lot bigger that you're not telling me."

"What if I told you both of these people had Propofol in their systems at the time of death, and that they both used to work together—at the same facility where Dr. Braunheiser once worked?

He sat back. "Is that true?"

"What if I told you that someone knew they worked together with the others, and now all the geneticists who worked there are being systematically killed, one at a time? I can show you a list. But not here." She stuffed the papers back into her purse. "I'll show you in Atlanta."

The hook was already set, and he was the fish. He had to learn the rest of her strange story.

"Why Atlanta?"

"Will another five thousand dollars get you to come with me?"

Another five thousand dollars!

He tried to remain calm. Money caused people to do stupid things, and his spider sense was pinging away at this woman.

But ten grand is ten grand.

"A smart guy would say no. I get the feeling you're a rich lady who needs a body buried, and I'm gonna end up doing the digging. I'd like to still be a PI when this is all over, and not be in jail or the morgue."

"I'm not rich."

He put on his sunglasses and reached for the ignition. "You have ten thousand dollars to hand over to me in cash. That doesn't make you poor."

"I have a limited budget I procured for this instance, and I hoped it would never arrive." She lowered her voice and sighed. "I have the other five thousand in cash, in a locker at the airport. Can I hire you to go with me to Atlanta or not?"

"Cash in a locker at the airport. Sounds ominous."

"Yes. People with bad intentions stash boodles of money in lockers at the airport. You've been watching too much TV. Innocent people who need to move in a hurry might do it, too. I am not a person with bad intentions." She sat upright and wiped her eyes. "Start the car. I'll explain more in Atlanta. You can see the cash when we get to the Delta terminal. I'll give you half the money when you buy your ticket. The rest, you get when I'm safely checked into my hotel."

He glared at her, his jaw hanging open. "You're not gonna take no for an answer, are you?"

"Not when 'no' might get me killed."

He started the car, smiling. "Well, I guess I'd better pack a bag for my trip to Atlanta."

"There's no time. And I don't want to risk going back to your apartment. We may have already been compromised."

"Compromised, huh? You working for the CIA now?" He put the car in gear. "My place is on the way."

* * * * *

They never got past the fire trucks.

Smoke was still billowing out of DeShear's apartment building when they drove up. The captain motioned residents of the Polo Club Apartments to the front parking lot, and DeShear walked the rest of the way with Lanaya following. Three engines had been called out, but they hadn't extinguished the fire before his apartment was incinerated—along with half of the building.

Residents and pedestrians gawked at the carnage, gasping and pointing at the black mess.

All DeShear could do was stare.

Lanaya viewed the charred damage from over his shoulder. "Now do you believe our lives are in danger, Mr. DeShear?"

"Yeah. Yeah, I sure do." He was a talking statue—and barely that. Through his sunglasses, he watched firefighters spray water at columns of smoke that jumped and danced in the wind. Some white, some black, but all stinking of charcoal and lost memories and pain. And under it all, the burned-out remnants of his life.

Lanaya tugged his arm. "Come on. Let's go."

"All my stuff . . . my files, clothes, my furniture. Business records."

"Mr. DeShear . . ."

"Pictures." He turned to her. "Files."

"You backed your computer up, right?"

"I—sometimes. On a hard drive. That was also in there." He turned back to the blackened apartment building. "Crap!"

"Mr. DeShear."

"And I did have some money stashed in the drawer of my desk. Not a lot, but—"

"Hank! Look at me." She took his arm and pulled him aside, toward the hedges of the next building and out of the view of the gawkers. "This was not an accident. The arsonist who did this probably wanted you to be in that fire, and he may be nearby waiting for you to show up so he can finish the job. Let's not make that task any easier. We must go. Now."

"Yeah." He backed away from the smoking mess of his home, letting her guide him. "Yeah, let's get to the airport."

CHAPTER 5

The Greyhound waited in the ER lobby for over an hour, a small canvas gym bag at his feet, pretending to read his cell phone. Right after the evening shift change, a very concerned Hispanic family entered the hospital. From what he could overhear, there had been an automobile accident involving the young parents and their small son. The father had arrived a few moments ago in an ambulance. The wife and little boy were apparently unharmed except for a good scare.

The grandmother arrived shortly after, and then the sister, with her husband and their young daughter; eventually the grandfather appeared as well, and an uncle. Within thirty minutes of their arrival, the young couple's entire extended family was gathered in the ER.

The Greyhound had been waiting for a group like this all night. He left his chair by the TV and newspapers, walking to the water fountain. When he returned, he sat near the family. None of them appeared visibly upset; the paperwork gave the wife the most concern, not the car wreck or her man's broken leg. A few minutes later, the wife had been called to come visit her husband somewhere down the hall. The grandfather and sister went with her, leaving the boy with his grandmother until they were certain Poppy's leg injury wouldn't be too much for little eyes to see.

But they were distracted. They wouldn't be checking for injuries that weren't obvious.

"Abuelita," he said in a low tone.

The family had been speaking English since they came in, with an occasional smattering of Spanish by the older woman, so the term of endearment—addressing her as "little grandmother" in Spanish—would get her attention without raising her concerns. She turned to face him.

"Ask the doctors to check the boy for internal injuries."

Judging from his height, The Greyhound estimated the little boy to be about three years old. He had been scampering around the ER with the girl, bouncing on chairs or hiding under them, until she wore out. Chattering away to anyone and no one, the boy had continued to race around the lobby until his mother shoved his iPad into his hands and instructed him to play a game with his cousin. After a few minutes, he tossed the tablet aside and was up again, searching for the few toys in the lobby and grabbing his grandmother's hand to find *My Little Pony* on the TV.

The old woman smiled at The Greyhound's question and waved her hand. "They say he's alright."

"I know, he seems fine. A little ball of fire. *Bola de fuego*." The Greyhound leaned toward her. "But in any car wreck with a small child, you must check for internal injuries. For safety."

The boy had been persistently grabbing at the crotch of his pants since coming into the emergency room.

"Chico," The Greyhound said as the little blur ran by. "Do you need to go to the bathroom?"

The boy stopped and looked at him. "No."

"He grabs himself like that all the time," the grandmother said. "He's just at that age."

The boy sprinted away to check the mulch of the large planters. His aunt and uncle were on the phone updating other family members, and his cousin sat mesmerized by whatever was on her iPad screen. But having put the idea in play, his grandmother stood and asked if the boy needed to use the restroom. Again, he declined. With a quiet grunt, she got up out of her chair and strolled toward him, holding out her hand. "Come on, we might be here a while. Let's try to go potty."

He plopped to the floor in protest. "But I don't have to go."

"Lorenzo! Up!" A sharp snap of Grandma's fingers ended the standoff, her scowl rousing the child to his feet. The pair walked hand in hand to the ladies' restrooms and disappeared inside.

The Greyhound returned to reading his phone, waiting for the next round of the grandmother's family members to be called back to visit the injured father. A moment later, the wife and Grandfather returned to the lobby, announcing that her husband's leg was badly broken and he was headed for surgery. He was going to need pins and would be wearing a large cast for a few months, but otherwise he wasn't hurt too badly.

The ladies restroom door flew open.

"Cristina!" The grandmother's face was white. "Call the doctor. He's peeing blood."

The ER sprung into calm but fast action. Nurses and aides in scrubs appeared, ushering the boy and his angry-faced mother toward the triage rooms, and a chunk of the family followed. The sister's husband and daughter stayed behind with the uncle, but most of the rest—from what The Greyhound could see—followed along.

The Greyhound stood up and went with them.

He shoved his phone under the mulch of one of the large planters, picked up his gym bag, and moved with the group. The internists would eventually shoo the overflow of family from the boy's room, but The Greyhound only needed to walk with them past security. Since the shift change, no one on staff would know how long he'd been there, and with him sitting next to the family, they'd assume he was with them.

At the first corner, he turned left when the family cluster turned right.

The hospital's cameras and watchful eyes were everywhere, but The Greyhound knew as long as someone acted like they were where they were supposed to be, no one on the staff really noticed if they weren't.

He only needed to find one small room, make a quick adjustment to their inventory, and he'd be on his way.

Entering an empty elevator, he peeled off his shirt and sweat pants to reveal the scrubs he'd purchased at the uniform supply store. He shoved his clothes into the gym bag and pulled out a long, heavy metal box. Thanks to the ever-increasing need for businesses to put everything about themselves online—including their floor plans—he knew exactly where on the third floor to locate the surgery center. Down the hall from pre-op was the main drug holding area, a small, heavily locked area that contained the anesthesia. Near the surgery center was the holding room vault.

The Greyhound smiled as the elevator doors opened. Crossing to the nearby vending area, he slipped the gym bag into the trash, opened the heavy metal box, and withdrew its contents.

The best part about technology is how complacent it made everyone. Companies that sold things to hospitals didn't make any money if the hospital wasn't constantly upgrading to the latest, greatest thing. Oxygen sensors needed to be more portable and super lightweight; x-ray machines need to take digital images and send them instantly to the laptop waiting a few feet away. A heart rate monitor needed to slip over a finger and be every bit as accurate as its earlier, bigger, heavier versions. Everything—simply everything—must be high tech.

Newer hospitals utilized biometrics now—a password, followed by a fingerprint. Certain older ones—like those targeted for acquisition by the Angelus Genetics group, for example—still only required passwords.

With a steel-cased, electrically-encoded lock, a digital keypad on the door, and an overhead security camera, the most restricted drugs in the hospital would be unwatched ninety-nine percent of the time. Even the best security guards couldn't stay focused on a door that only opened a few times a day.

Complacency. The Greyhound counted on it.

Most of the time, a well-placed, powerful electromagnet would zap an older system, defaulting to not holding the deadbolt in the locking position—and rendering the door temporarily unlocked.

After that, the drug vault itself needed to be accessed. The same magnet would open it, too.

The Greyhound held his heavy electromagnet close to his hip, walking straight to the meds vault like he was the head of the hospital. His heart pounded as he moved toward his target. Would it open? He never knew until he tried. Sometimes yes, sometimes no.

At a prior attempt at a different hospital, an intern had stepped ahead of him and opened the door to the vault. That made access easier, but it meant disabling the man with some close quarter punches before grabbing the goods. He fingered the bandage above his eye. The fight hadn't been quick enough. He wouldn't make that mistake again.

Holding his breath, he stood in front of the secured room and pressed the big magnet against the lock, to the side of the knob and keypad, where the circuit board and deadbolt engagement system were located. The keypad's blue LED screen went black, and a clunk came from the thick door's insides.

His heart thumped in his ears as he reached out and grabbed the handle. With a gentle tug, the door opened.

A rush of adrenaline surged through him as he crept inside. Now, to the meds vault.

He blinked a few times, realizing that he was panting hard. His pulse was throbbing and sweat gathered on his brow. The small room was uncomfortably warm, but he focused on the vault.

The thick, tempered glass door displayed rows of tiny bottles behind it, each with an important-looking label. Black ink with a blue square or a red dot made about the only discernible difference in the bottles, aside from the bold print identifying each drug.

He lifted the magnet onto the side of the vault, waiting for the readout to fail and the default spring to be released, causing the noticeable clunk the same way it had on the vault.

The LED screen stayed blue.

The Greyhound swallowed hard, his heart in his throat. He forced the magnet downward an inch, scraping the painted steel side of the vault. Its metallic screech was like nails on a chalk board.

Nothing.

A bead of sweat rolled down his forehead and off the tip of his nose. Huffing, he gritted his teeth and shoved the magnet back an inch. It was only a matter of time before someone from security barged into the vault. He had less than a minute, at best.

But how long have I been in here already?

He wiped his brow with his sleeve and put a hand on the vault. Gripping the big magnet, he forced it to move in a circular motion over the side panel.

Engage. Now.

Time. There wasn't much time.

Blinking sweat from his eyes, he worked the stubborn magnet around, searching for the locking hardware. The electronics had to be there. It was on all the diagrams. Opposite the vault's hinges and an inch or so from the front.

Where is it?

The one in LA had given him trouble. Several had, in fact. St. Paul, Baton Rouge . . .

He tried to force that out of his mind, heaving against the magnet to get it to budge.

Keep moving it. The lock is here. It's on all the diagrams.

With each thrust of his sweating hands, the magnet scraped along the side of the vault in fractions of an inch. Would this be another one he had to walk away from?

Seconds ticked by. The guards would have been notified by now, and they would be on the way. A whole-floor lockdown would ensue in a matter of moments, and then he'd be—

Clunk.

His heart leaped. He righted himself and yanked open the vault door, reaching past the red and green labels to the large teal bottle that said Propofol.

Grabbing it, a bolt of pain lurched through his stomach. He winced and doubled over, groaning as the air rushed out of him. The bottles nearly fell from his grasp. Making a fist, he pressed his other hand to his belly and squeezed his eyes shut, leaning on the countertop to keep from falling to the floor.

Not now.

A wave of nausea swept through him. The room grew warmer. He sunk to his knees and leaned against the wall, swiping his shoulder across his forehead again. Swallowing hard, he pushed down the urge to vomit and slapped a hand onto the countertop, forcing himself back to his feet. He stood there, gasping and dripping, as he slipped the Propofol bottles into his pocket.

He glanced at the door. It swayed back and forth.

Get it together.

Closing his eyes, he hoped the door would be standing still when he reopened them. It complied. With a deep breath, he tightened his gut and took a step forward.

His legs went out from under him and he crashed to the counter again.

Walk. Move it or go to prison.

With a groan, he pushed off the counter and grabbed for the door latch.

A few seconds of acting normal and you'll be home free. It's less than sixty seconds to the elevator. In three minutes, you'll be outside.

He eyed the door. "Suck it up," he whispered to himself. "You can manage for three minutes."

He knew the nausea and pain would pass soon, but the bouts had been getting stronger, and each round was knocking him down for longer and longer periods of time. The last one came on fast and took him down for a week. That couldn't happen now. This needed to be a wave; it needed to come and go, not be the start of another crash.

He didn't have time for a crash.

Breathe.

Sixty seconds to the elevator. Another hundred and eighty to the rear parking lot.

The rest of your life depends on the next four minutes.

Nodding, he straightened up and clenched his gut. He opened the door and stepped into the hallway. The air conditioning was cooler there, for some reason. Less stuffy than in the small vault.

The nausea subsided. He took a few steps.

Normal. Walk normal. And with confidence.

He quickened his pace, glancing down the corridor to the elevator.

Fifty feet, then forty.

As he neared the elevator, relief swept through his system. He was going to make it.

The light over the elevator came on and the bell pinged. As the doors opened, several dark uniforms came into view.

Security.

He peeked to his right. The vending area. He slipped inside and faced a big machine filled with potato chips and granola bars. In the machine's glass, the dark uniforms raced by behind him. He dropped the magnet into the trash can and waited, closing his eyes to catch the sound of the elevator doors closing.

When they did, he walked to them. He waved his hands between the doors, forcing them to open. Once inside, he could collapse.

"Long day?" The petite African-American woman in the corner wore a light gray suit and carried a clip board.

And a badge.

The security captain.

The elevator doors shut as he faced the panel of buttons. "Yeah, I pulled a double."

The indicator was lit for the next floor down. He pressed L for lobby, the ground floor, and kept his face to the front.

"I work doubles all the time. Seems like the hospital admins never work late, but us low level folks can't work enough hours for them. You look exhausted."

"I feel exhausted. Like I'm going to pass out if I don't get to bed soon." He mustered a smile and glanced in her direction, not long enough to be perceived as checking her out, but not so short as to be dismissive. He needed to act normal and engage the way a hospital staff member would with someone they might run into again—and to not draw undue attention to himself. "Sorry. Guess I shouldn't complain."

She was attractive, wearing her black hair pulled back in a tight bun, but with high cheek bones and big eyes. Her suit was just snug enough to show off her figure, but this wasn't the time for that. He had to fight to act normal until she got off the elevator.

The nausea crept back to him. He pressed his hand to his gut and swallowed reflexively to keep the queasiness at bay, but it wouldn't stay back for long. When it came, it'd stay for a few hours or stay for a week, depending on if it was a small wave or a tidal wave.

The elevator pinged. The woman stepped to the front. "Well, see you around."

"Cheers." His gaze lingered just beneath the hem of her short jacket as she walked away.

Then the knot in his stomach seized up on him again and he leaned against the wall as the elevator doors closed.

He reached his rental car without further incident and crawled inside. He managed to drive to a fast food place a block away before he threw up, then he slouched in his seat until the pain in his stomach subsided. Once he made it back to his hotel, he could rest until the wave passed. Some water and carbs would be a good idea, too, before he regrouped to pursue the real target of his trip—St. Anthony's hospital across town, and a rendezvous with its chief of medicine, Dr. Asher Fishel.

CHAPTER 6

They passed a few hours in the airport lounge—gate side—with DeShear bouncing his heels under the chair and staring at his newspaper, doing his best not to get up and wear out the airport carpet.

If they tracked her to Tampa and connected her to me, then they can follow us to Atlanta.

He studied every bulge in every passenger's suit jacket to be certain it was not a gun, and reassured himself that every fleeting look from a maintenance worker was not a covert enemy operative calling in a kill squad.

When their flight boarded, he was finally able to relax.

His client was another matter.

The locker contained a laptop and a few other essentials. While they flew, she typed furiously—and constantly checked over her shoulder and up and down the aisle to ensure no one was watching her.

He toyed with his complimentary miniature bag of pretzels. Lanaya needed to calm down a few notches. "You warned me about being tracked digitally," he said. "Do you think it's safe to use your computer on an airplane?"

"They don't collect Wi-Fi data from devices on airplanes. It's too expensive to record all the searches and tie them back to the end user."

"What are you checking?"

She didn't look up from the screen. "Googling former co-worker names."

"To see which ones are still alive?"

"Basically."

"Okay." He reached over and gently closed her laptop. "I don't know exactly what kind of trouble we're in, but that's not helping you."

"I—"

"You need a break. Check it later. Right now, let me buy you a drink." He pressed the overhead "call attendant" button. In the front of the plane, an electronic bell dinged.

Settling back into his chair, he smiled at the flight attendant when she appeared a moment later. "My lady friend and I would like a drink. Do you have any Mexican beer?"

The young lady scribbled on her pad. "Yes, sir."

"Perfect. I'll have one. And my friend will have . . ."

"Tequila," Lanaya blurted out. "A shot of Tequila."

DeShear raised his eyebrows. As the flight attendant went down the aisle, he faced Lanaya. "Tequila? I figured you for a chardonnay gal."

"Normally, yes. But I realized my life may be ending soon, and there's a lot of things I haven't tried."

DeShear opened his mouth to speak, but stopped. He opened the bag of pretzels instead, and popped one in his mouth.

Lanaya slipped the laptop into the seat pocket in front of her. "I've arranged for two business class suites at our hotel."

"Okay. Good." DeShear lowered his voice. "You know, I've been wondering how you book airline tickets and hotel rooms." He held the tiny foil bag to his lips and tapped a few more pretzels into his mouth. "After a while a fake ID can be tracked just like a real one. You must have several."

"I have a friend's prepaid debit card." Lanaya whispered, rearranging the copy of In Flight magazine and the safety card that rested in the seat pocket with her laptop. "I gave her ten thousand dollars and she got me the card. We are close enough in appearance that I'm able to travel using her driver's license."

"That works?"

"Most women change their hair style over time, Mr. DeShear. Longer, shorter, highlights—or they gain or lose weight. They take their glasses off for the photo but wear them in person. If a license is more than a few years old, the image will have faded. At my age, as long as the resemblance is close and no one's calling the credit card services, it's not a big deal."

The flight attendant returned with their drinks. DeShear picked up his plastic cup of beer. "Cheers."

Lanaya lifted her cup and raised it to her lips. It hung there, suspended in midair.

"Is there a problem?" DeShear asked.

"I've never had tequila before." Lanaya stared at the clear liquid in the cup. "It smells awful."

DeShear chuckled. "It tastes even worse."

She sniffed the cup. "Why do people drink it?"

"Most? To get drunk."

"Oh. Of course." She inched the tiny glass closer and stopped again.

DeShear sighed. "How about we share drinks? Take half your shot, and chase it with a big sip of my beer."

"That—thank you. That sounds like a good idea." She closed her eyes and put the cup to her mouth, allowing the tiniest of swallows to cross her lips. "Oh!" She stomped the floor, shaking her head. "Oh! Oh! Oh!"

DeShear flinched.

"Ew! Oh my!" Lanaya screwed up her face, waving her hands. "Oh, that is awful. Quick, give me the beer."

DeShear handed over his drink. Lanaya gulped hard—and kept gulping. The cup went horizontal, then three-quarters vertical, then straight up. She slammed it on the folding table, shaking her head again. The last bit of beer had been completely drained from it. "Bleh."

She took a few deep breaths as DeShear held out a miniature pretzel. "So—ready for another?"

* * * * *

During her second Mexican beer, Lanaya finally seemed relaxed. DeShear was a few drinks in, too, so he probed a little more about her strange associates.

She wasn't having any of it.

"At the hotel, and definitely not while drinking."

DeShear knew when he was beat. He sipped his beer and made small talk, keeping her mind off their troubles—to the extent that was possible.

"I misjudged you, Mr. DeShear." Lanaya slurred her words a little. "You're brave and smart, and you have the commendations to prove it."

"I did have them. They went up in flames with that picture of me and the mayor."

"Yes." She took another sip of beer. "I'm very sorry about that. Your pictures were the only personal thing you really mentioned at the fire. They must have been very special. Family?"

DeShear sat forward. "Why are we on a plane to Atlanta?"

She shrugged. "Because walking would take too long." She burst into laughter at her joke. Alcohol consumed at high altitudes was allegedly more potent than at sea level. DeShear hadn't factored that in when he ordered the second round. Or the third.

"No." DeShear smirked. "I mean, why Atlanta? Do you have something hidden at the gate for when we land?"

"Killers tend to be less effective in places that use metal detectors to find guns." She giggled, waving her cup at him. "That's a plus for us."

He watched her, not smiling and not frowning, just waiting.

"Because," she sighed. "It's a major hub for nearly everywhere else in the United States, and we need quick access to California, Montana, Ohio, Minnesota . . . Now, that's all I'm telling you until—"

"—until we are checked safely into our hotel," he said. "Okay. You win."

"Mr. DeShear—Hank DeShear—why do you go by 'Hank'? Hamilton is a perfectly good name. Hamilton DeShear. It's practically regal-sounding."

"It's a little long."

"What's your rush? Hamilton DeShear is far more memorable."

"I guess I hadn't thought about being memorable."

"You were certainly memorable to those girls you saved. And to those library workers." She took another sip of beer. "Tell me more about Hamilton DeShear, the man I'm entrusting my life to."

DeShear reached over and took her cup, placing it on the empty tray table on the other side of him. "What would you like to know?"

"Tell me a fishing story about you and your father."

"He was my foster father. My real parents died in a car wreck when I was a baby."

"That's terrible."

"Now, Curt DeShear, he was a good guy. I loved him a lot. Good dad. I went to a couple of foster homes and stuff before he and his wife adopted me. I only remember a little about her."

"What happened to her?"

"Cancer took her when I was about ten. She gave it a good fight. Lasted a couple of years, but she was constantly in the hospital, and back then they didn't really have the things they have now. She suffered a lot."

"I'm very sorry," Lanaya said. "I shouldn't have pried."

"It's okay, you didn't know." DeShear drained the last of the beer from the cup. "I made the best of the family I got."

"Hmm." Lanaya settled into the seat, pressing her cheek to the cushion and drawing her knees up. "Was there ever a Mrs. Hamilton DeShear? Or children?"

"I told you, my story was a sad one so far. Are you sure you wanna hear it?"

"Perhaps we can change it going forward. Besides, you can't give a reply like that and then not tell the story. Give."

"We met in graduate school, got married right after. I started teaching and she landed her dream job at a big accounting firm, so we waited to have kids. But after a couple of years, we stopped waiting—and then it was the babies who wanted to wait. We just couldn't get pregnant, and then we had miscarriage after miscarriage. I just . . . a guy can only watch his wife's heart break so many times. To be so excited and then have it all crash, then the crying—for weeks. I couldn't keep putting her through it. But then we found out we were pregnant again, so I didn't say anything. And this time we had a baby. A beautiful baby girl, who erased all our sadness just by showing up. When she was born, she was the biggest ray of sunshine in our lives. The sky was bluer, the grass was greener. Then . . . when she was three . . . she got sick. She just, faded. They said it was similar to Leukemia. No cure. We spent a year watching her go. Most marriages can't last through that. Ours didn't. Each time we saw each other, we saw our daughter not there, and we just couldn't do it."

They sat there in silence, the low hum of the engines filling the plane. When the flight attendant dimmed the lights, the last of the passenger conversations dimmed as well.

Lanaya snuggled into her cushion. "You've had a lot taken from you in your life."

"I told you, I'm down but I'm not out. Not by a long shot." He took off his tie and rolled it up, stuffing it into his pants pocket. "And after we check into our hotel, you're telling me your story. The one that put us on a last-minute flight to Atlanta."

"Okay," she said, her eyes half closed. "I promise."

CHAPTER 7

The Peachtree Plaza was a downtown skyscraper of a hotel, one much nicer than DeShear expected his client to provide. Low key seemed to be Lanaya's M. O., but he wasn't arguing. Room service and a hot bath sounded good.

They passed through the crowded lobby to the front desk, where she checked them in. Holly had been strung across the countertop, and a big Christmas tree adorned the area near the elevators.

Lanaya had procured adjacent rooms. "So we can go back and forth to talk without stepping into the hallway where we might be spotted."

Shaking his head, DeShear slid his plastic key through the slot on the hotel room door. "I think you can calm down a little here. We should be fine in a busy hotel."

Lanaya opened the door to the room next to his. "You're the one who's been bouncing your feet all day."

Once inside, she knocked on the interior door. DeShear flipped the deadbolt and opened the door. Two inches away, Lanaya had cracked hers open. "When we're asleep, you keep yours open. I'll keep mine locked. Otherwise," she stepped back and pushed her door open the rest of the way. "We can work in here and strategize."

"Sounds good. Let me wash my face to wake up, and I'll be right over."

He returned a few minutes later with a towel around his neck and a Coke in his hand. She waved for him to join her at the little desk by the window, opening her laptop. She glanced at his soda. "Would you mind grabbing one of those for me?"

"Not at all." He tossed the towel onto the bed and opened the panel on the console under the TV, accessing the mini fridge. "Coke? Or something else?"

"Coke's fine."

"Not tequila?"

"Never again." She shuddered.

He smiled and handed her the little bottle. Aside from being her semi-body guard, he still wasn't really sure why he was here. But as she said, the money was good, so he could afford to be patient. She'd tell him when she was ready.

"I think our killer or killers will head to Minneapolis next." She pointed to a map on the laptop screen. "The researchers in the group I worked in were recruited from all over the country. I think that was on purpose. They'd have less in common, but upon release they'd return home—and be far less likely to connect with former co-workers. Two from my group work together in Minneapolis."

"I think you're about two jumps ahead of me," DeShear said, glancing at the lights of the Atlanta skyline out the window. A few blocks away, a tall, thin crane dangled a wreath above a construction site. "Let's back up a bit. You said the murder victims worked together. When?"

She closed the map window and a black screen appeared with lines of code. She typed on the keyboard and closed the program. "The better question is where."

"Okay." He lowered himself onto the bed, reclining on one elbow. "Where and when?"

She spun in the chair to face him. He said nothing, just cradled the Coke in his hands.

Lanaya sighed and cracked open her soda bottle, staring at it. "People don't set out to do bad things. I don't think they do, anyway." She raised her eyes to meet his. "I was a good scientist, Hamilton. I won the Tewksbury award my final year in my doctorate program. My parents were so proud. I got recruited to Centaur Genomics, and life was good. My work was highly praised in numerous publications. Then I got a call from Angelus Genetics. They weren't as established, but they were very cutting edge. Marcus Hauser didn't talk about changing the world—he was doing it. And they had it all, at Angelus. A big raise, free day care, student loan forgiveness. They offered below market rate loans to employees for cars and houses because they wanted the very best people on their team. I was young and ambitious. I jumped at the chance."

He let her talk. He'd learned confessions take time.

She leaned back in the chair, holding the Coke in her lap, slowly turning the bottle. "Fast forward a few years and you realize they own you. You're not going to make that kind of money anywhere else, and if you leave, you'd have to drastically change lifestyles. No more private schools or semiannual vacations to Hawaii and Aspen." She shrugged, watching the little bubbles work their way up the side of the plastic bottle. "Then one day they announced they were downsizing. Some of us were offered positions at their subsidiary in Arizona—Onyx Research. This facility was very different. Specialized. Very compartmentalized, and extremely secretive. You barely knew the name of the person in the next cubicle, much less what they were working on. I was assigned to a project that was the cream of the crop. The one that was going to make Angelus Genetics famous. These people weren't just curing cancer, they were removing the possibility of anybody getting it to begin with. And not only cancer. Diabetes, MS, Heart disease—all the biggies.

"Some of the younger employees created an online black screen site, to do at home what we couldn't do at work—talk—but using symbols instead of names. One girl, Double Omega, said her project's success rates were inflated. A week later, she was gone. Rumors on the black screen site said it was suicide. I didn't know her, but it seemed possible. Positions at the Onyx facility were extremely high-pressure, and the lack of interaction was depressing for a lot of people."

She sighed, getting up and facing the window. Her reflection showed her lost in thought, reliving things she wanted to forget. "I got reassigned to a new project. That happened a lot. Segmentation. One person started a project, another finished it, and who knows how many worked on it in between? But that way, Onyx guaranteed employees couldn't take secrets to a competitor. I soon realized I'd taken over Double Omega's project. She had it backwards. They were not inflating the success rates, they were hiding the failures. If the classification group succeeded at all, the viables were segregated out and given a new group name. This would show something like 80 or 90% success in the new classification group, but they were only taking 10% of the entire pool. So the project actually had a 90% failure rate or worse. That's much closer to industry norms."

She shook her head, turning to him. Her eyes were red and brimming with tears. "I was a very good scientist, Hamilton. And now . . ." Her voice broke. "I'm probably going to be publicly discredited and murdered in a way that looks like an accident."

DeShear sat up on the bed. "So these killings, our case . . . somebody's committing murder over a bunch of faked reports?"

"It's big money, Hamilton. World-wide patents that might eradicate life-threatening afflictions are worth billions of dollars, possibly trillions. People shoot each other in a neighborhood poker game. They can certainly be killed over billions of dollars. But no, our murders didn't take place because of Onyx's DNA sequencing successes. They're happening because—"

There was a knock at the door. "Room service."

DeShear slid off the bed. "I'll get it."

"Don't!" Lanaya hissed. He stopped and looked at her, opening his mouth. Her eyes were wide. "I didn't order any room service."

The knock on the door came again. "Room service."

DeShear put a finger to his lips and rushed to the door. Through the peep hole, he could make out the top half of a large man in a white culinary service jacket. He went back to Lanaya, whispering in her ear. "Get up. Tell him to leave it outside, then go into the bathroom."

She rose, her hand to her mouth. DeShear quietly placed his drink in the trash can by the desk, then put his hands on Lanaya's shoulders and leaned in close. "Thank him first. I've got this."

"Thank you," she said, inching across the room. "Please leave it outside."

"Good job," DeShear whispered. "You're doing fine."

"Yes, ma'am. I need you to sign for the bill."

DeShear moved in front of her, holding a hand out and moving the other one back and forth under it.

She nodded. "Can you slide it under?"

Giving her a thumbs up, DeShear looked around the room for a makeshift weapon.

The man in the hallway thumped the door bottom a few times. "No, I'm sorry, it doesn't fit. This new carpet's too thick."

"One minute." She faced DeShear, mouthing, "What do we do?"

He guided her into the bathroom and pulled the door halfway closed. "Stay here. Don't say or do anything."

He went to the door and stared at the handle, drawing a deep breath. Glancing to the bathroom to make sure Lanaya wasn't visible, he leaned close and held his hand above the latch.

Could be an honest mistake by the hotel.
Could be an execution.

Jerking the handle downward, he flung open the door. The waiter stood next to a room service cart. Two flat metal plate covers rested on top of the cart's long, white tablecloth.

The waiter launched himself into the doorway. Jumping backwards, DeShear grabbed the man's collar and heaved him face-first into the heavy door. He held the intruder by the back of the neck, pinning him. The man grunted and flailed, reaching for the waistline bulge at the small of his back. DeShear rammed a shoulder into him, slamming the man into the door again. Grabbing the intruder's hand, DeShear forced it skyward. The assailant howled in pain.

DeShear dropped the man's hand and yanked up the jacket, revealing a holster and a large gun. He pulled the weapon free and gripped it tightly, then slammed the butt of the heavy gun into the side of the man's head.

The intruder slumped and fell to the floor.

DeShear stood over him, panting. Grabbing his assailant under the arms, DeShear dragged him toward the bed, then went back to retrieve the room service cart.

He called to the bathroom. "You can come out now."

Lanaya peeked past the bathroom door.

DeShear rolled the cart toward the bed. "It's okay. This guy's done for the night."

As his client crept out of the bathroom, Deshear lifted the metal plate covers from the room service cart. There was nothing underneath. He tossed them onto the bed and flipped up the tablecloth, exposing a sawed off, pump action shotgun. He grabbed it and took it to Lanaya. "Do you know how to use one of these?"

She recoiled. "I'm a scientist, not a cowboy!"

"Okay." He tucked the pistol into his belt and went into his room, ratcheting the shotgun barrel repeatedly until all the shells were ejected onto the mattress. After sliding the shotgun under the bed, he gathered the expended shells and carried them to his bathroom, where he deposited them into the toilet tank.

He pulled the pistol from his belt and sprung the magazine, checking its ammunition.

Full load.

Motioning to Lanaya, he stepped toward the door and pressed himself to the wall. She followed.

"Keep quiet," he whispered. "If our friend has somebody waiting in the hall, we don't want them to know it's us coming out."

He eased the handle downward and inched the door open. At the end of the hallway stood a man in plain clothes, doing nothing.

That's unusual for a hotel.

DeShear opened the door the rest of the way. "Keep calm. We're a husband and wife going to dinner." She went through, then he joined her, walking side by side with the gun behind her lower back.

They moved down the hallway toward the man.

"Honestly, darling," DeShear said. "It's very late. I'd just as soon skip dinner and grab a drink at the bar."

Lanaya said nothing. She swallowed hard and trembled.

DeShear carried on the act, solo. "Hmm? Well, if you insist, my love."

The man stared at them as they approached.

DeShear smiled at him when they got close. "Excuse me, friend, but do you have the time?"

The man looked past him.

"No?" DeShear pulled out his gun and shoved it into the man's face. "Well, then, can you turn around and grab the wall? Feet spread."

The man hesitated.

"Your buddy's dead," DeShear scowled. "Don't join him."

Lanaya gasped. "You killed him?"

DeShear winced. "Shh!"

He patted the man down and relieved him of a .45 caliber revolver.

"Walk with me to the elevator," DeShear said to the stranger. "You're going to get in and go straight to the top floor."

When the elevator arrived, DeShear shoved the man into the back and leaned inside to press the top button. "Don't get cute and exit early. If I see you downstairs in the next hour, it's not gonna be pleasant for you."

As soon as the elevator doors closed, DeShear stepped back and watched the floor indicator light show the man was going up.

"Now," DeShear said. "We take the service elevator to the laundry room and get out of here."

He grabbed Lanaya's hand and they raced down the hallway.

CHAPTER 8

Dr. Asher Fishel blew a long stream of smoke at the computer screen, scowling at the spread sheet displayed there.

"Don't you ever go home, Ash?" Dr. Kuntara leaned in the doorway of her friend's office, fanning the haze of smoke away from her nose. "And open a window, would you?"

Fishel coughed a few times, pulling the cigarette from his mouth as he lumbered to heft his massive frame up from his desk. A half-eaten cheeseburger rested on a cafeteria tray, next to an overflowing ash tray and a can of Diet Coke. "I have work to do. Marcus is up my rear about the merger."

"Maybe another cigarette will help you with that cough."

He walked past his dusty treadmill to the window, sliding it open. The blinds swayed in the night's chilly breeze. "We can't all be smoothie drinking marathoners like you, Tahvia." Fishel held his cigarette out the window. "Between the merger, the board review, my high blood pressure, my high cholesterol, the new regulations . . . there's so many things that are trying to kill me, I'm lucky I'm still standing."

"It's possible we board members have concerns about the long-term health of our key man. But suit yourself, boss. See you tomorrow. And don't let Dr. Hauser work you too late." Kuntara grabbed the door knob and pulled the door shut behind her.

"When do I ever?" Fishel grunted. He went back to his cluttered work space and swigged his soda. A computer screen full of spread sheets stared at him. He took a swig of his drink, sucked on the cigarette, and hunched over the keyboard.

A knock came from the door. Fishel glanced at his watch. According to his Rolex Presidential, it was almost eight-thirty. "Housekeeping," he muttered. "As if I didn't have enough distractions." He called out in the direction of the door. "Come back in an hour."

The man on the other side mumbled something, then knocked again.

Fishel didn't look up from the computer. "I said come back later!"

The door opened and a tall man in blue coveralls backed into the room, pulling a large cleaning cart. Rags and spray bottles hung over the sides, and a big trash can rose from the center.

"Are you new? Or deaf? I'm busy. You'll need to clean later." The doctor glared at the cleaner and took another drag on his cigarette. "*Habla* English, you moron? Later. Come back later."

With his back to Fishel, the cleaner pulled something from his pocket and raised it to his head. When he turned around, his face was covered by a black ski mask.

* * * * *

The Greyhound shoved the office door closed and leveled a gun at the frightened chief of medicine. "Do you *habla* .38 caliber, Doctor Fishel?"

The blood drained out of the doctor's face. "I—I . . ." His hands slid from the keyboard and disappeared under the desk.

Keeping the gun aimed at the doctor's head, The Greyhound held up a smart phone with a video image playing. "You have a silent alarm button under your top drawer. Before you answer the phone and give the security answer for an emergency rescue, you need to look at this."

His mouth hanging open, Dr. Fishel peered at the screen. The Greyhound came closer, holding the phone in front of him. "This is live streaming video of your wife at the bookstore where she is attending her book club. As long as you do exactly what I say, when I say it, your wife will not be hurt. If you do *not* do exactly as I say, she will be murdered in the parking lot on the way to her Volvo. Nod if you understand."

The doctor stared at the screen, white faced. "Shanna . . ."

The Greyhound slammed a hand down onto the desk. "Nod if you understand, Dr. Fischel."

He nodded.

His heart pounding, The Greyhound swallowed hard and set the streaming phone next to the doctor's keyboard. "Do not touch the phone. My man on the other end needs to hear me every thirty seconds or he kills your wife. Nod if you understand."

As his office phone rang, the doctor glanced at it, then back to The Greyhound. He nodded again.

Stepping around to the chair, The Greyhound put his gun to the doctor's head. The phone rang a second time.

A sharp pain ignited in The Greyhound's stomach, throbbing and sending stabs in all directions. He winced and re-gripped the gun with his sweaty fingers, forcing himself to remain upright. He balled up his other hand and pressed it to his abdomen.

The pain flared again.

The Greyhound sucked in his breath and leaned on the credenza. "When I tell you, answer the phone and give security the 'all clear' password. If you do not, your wife dies. If security comes in and tries to apprehend me, my man at the bookstore opens fire. Nod if you understand."

The doctor nodded. The phone rang a third time.

"Answer it," The Greyhound said. His lungs ached and his head throbbed. Pulses of green and red flashed over his vision. The gun stayed pointed at the trembling doctor.

Fishel lifted the black receiver from its cradle. He held it to his head and closed his eyes, swallowing hard. "This is Dr. Fishel. Nightingale. I repeat, Nightingale."

The Greyhound breathed hard, sweat running down his neck. He raised his other hand to steady the first, the gun staying pointed at the chief of medicine.

"No, everything's fine. The cleaner came in and I mashed the panic button trying to get up. Getting too plump for my chair, I guess."

Eyeing the doctor and then the video playing on the phone, The Greyhound shifted his weight. So far, so good.

"Thank you. Happy holidays to you, too. Goodnight." Fishel hung up the phone. "I did it. They aren't coming. Now . . . what do you want?"

"We'll get to that." The Greyhound panted. "First, I need you to take this." He tossed a white cotton cloth onto the desk, then pulled a small bottle from his pocket. "Put one drop of ether onto the handkerchief, hold it to your face, and inhale it deeply."

The doctor's shaking fingers stretched in the direction of the cloth. The Greyhound reached past him and placed the bottle on a stack of papers. He dug into his pocket again and withdrew a syringe.

"One drop only, Doctor."

The knot in his stomach erupted, sending The Greyhound to his knees. He grabbed a corner of the desk to keep from crashing to the floor, coughing uncontrollably as his lungs burned like they were on fire. The room swayed.

"You're ill," the doctor said. "You—you're white as a sheet. You need help."

The Greyhound shook his head, staggering to his feet. "Not from you!" He pointed the gun back at the doctor. "First, do no harm." Steadying himself, he wiped the spit from the side of his mouth. "Or were you absent the day they went over the Hippocratic oath at medical school?"

"Son…" the doctor spoke in low, calm tones, his voice wavering. "Whatever's bothering you, we can talk about it. Let me get you some help first."

"Put a drop of ether on the cloth." He grimaced and cocked the gun. "Shanna's keeper will lose patience soon."

Fishel lowered his gaze to the bottle. He picked it up and unscrewed the cap, then held the vial over the cloth. The bottle shook in his grip. A drop of liquid fell onto the small white cloth. He set the bottle down, quivering so much he almost knocked it over. The wet tiny dot spread across the handkerchief.

"Put it over your nose and mouth, and inhale. One big breath. If you try to cheat, I'll know." The Greyhound pointed the gun at the video. "Think of your wife."

The doctor nodded. "I'll do as you say. Don't hurt my family."

Blinking the colors from his eyes, The Greyhound glared at his victim. "Don't talk to me about hurting people. Let's go. One big breath. Do it."

Lifting the cloth near his face, a whimper escaped the doctor's lips. He raised his eyes to the man in the black ski mask. "Why are you doing this?"

"Angelus Genetics and Onyx Research. You remember them. You were a big deal over there before you bought your way into respectability."

The doctor's jaw dropped. "We-we did legitimate research there."

"You," The Greyhound narrowed his eyes, "are a despicable human being for what you did."

"I—I didn't. I . . . in the Arizona facility, they—I had no idea until—"

"You had every idea. Nilla Cunde said it was your goal from the outset. Emmet Kincaid said the same thing. They're both dead now. So is Dr. Braunheiser. And Dr. Contiglio. Bendina Tasson, Theo Waldrop, Mina Farris—all gone. But not before they gave me things."

"Oh, no. No . . ."

"I have notes from meetings you attended, where you and Hauser rolled out your grand plans. How you'd get the financing. I have it all, doctor."

"We . . . shut it down. We stopped!"

"You moved it to Indonesia, you lying piece of garbage. U. S. laws couldn't touch you there. Do you want to try to explain the deal you did with Cambodia? What you allowed to happen there?"

"Please." The doctor swallowed hard. "Science. We . . . our ideas were for the benefit of mankind."

"Stop lying! Ideas are one thing. What you put into practice—deciding right and wrong, life and death. You made up the rules, like the megalomaniacs you are. I'd shoot you right now, but I need to fly under the radar until—" His lungs exploded. He coughed, backing away and gasping for air. When he recovered, he wiped his mouth with the back of his hand. Blood stained his sleeve.

He pointed the gun to the handkerchief. "Let's go."

The doctor lifted the cloth and pressed it to his face, closing his eyes. His chest swelled and relaxed as he inhaled, then he looked at The Greyhound.

"Put it down."

When he did, The Greyhound went to him and held out the syringe. "Inject yourself with this." He handed it to the doctor. "If you do not, my man will kill your wife."

The old man lurched forward, grabbing at a letter opener. The Greyhound shoved him back into his chair. "Your wife is alive, doctor. Do you want her to stay that way?"

"Help!" Fishel yelled, his words slurring. "Help me!"

The Greyhound curled back his fingers and rammed the butt of his hand into the doctor's ear. The old man crashed to the desk, grabbing his head and wailing. "Don't kill me!"

"Administer the syringe! Now! I have people watching your son in Malibu and your daughter working at the Cleveland Clinic."

"You're sick," the doctor cried. "You're enjoying this."

"I hate every minute of this, believe me. But I will see your wife die if you don't plunge that needle into your arm right now."

The doctor sniffled. "Okay." He picked up the syringe and stared at it.

"Do it."

Dr. Fishel placed the wavering tip of the needle near the crease of his forearm, sliding it along a raised blue vein. The skin depressed for a moment until the needle penetrated the skin, then he pressed the plunger.

He winced as the fluids entered his system.

The Greyhound took the syringe and slipped it into the pocket of his coveralls. "Now, up. To the treadmill, doctor."

Perplexed, the old man rose and slowly went to the treadmill.

The Greyhound followed, his pain and nausea subsiding. He reached over to switch on the machine and pressed a button on the keypad. The console beeped, and the dark gray vinyl tread rolled backwards.

"Get on."

The doctor's trembling hands grasped the rails. He climbed on the exercise machine and eased one foot onto the moving tread. As it went backwards, he stepped forward with his other foot and started walking.

"Now, I need you to take this respirator gage and put it into your mouth." The Greyhound held an opaque hose and mouthpiece up. They were standard equipment in stress tests, as the doctor well knew. The Greyhound held out a heart rate finger monitor to the doctor, keeping the readout in his hand.

As he put the equipment on, the old man shivered violently. The Greyhound retrieved the cell phone and placed it on the treadmill's console, shoving aside a yellowed magazine. The streaming video continued to display his wife.

Brandishing the gun, The Greyhound gestured to the screen. "Here's where we are. Your wife is alive and well. All you have to do is stay on this treadmill and keep moving until I say stop. This won't take long." He reached across the doctor and pressed the "up" arrow. The treadmill increased its speed. "If you stop, she dies. If I stop talking, or if I don't get what I want quickly, my friend on the other end does his job."

The doctor wheezed into the respiratory gage, his brow brimming with sweat and his hands shaking.

The heart rate monitor read 120.

"Keep going."

Fishel gasped, rubbing his chest.

"That's the Synthroid you injected. Keep going."

Sweat formed on the fat old man's face. The synthetic metabolism hormone was overloading his system. But at his age, a dead guy on a treadmill wouldn't even get an autopsy.

Moisture stains appeared on the doctor's shirt collar and under his arm pits. His abductor kept his eyes on the readout. "It hurts, I know."

The doctor groaned, grabbing his chest.

"Keep that hose in your mouth, doctor." The Greyhound raised the gun. "And stay on that treadmill." He pushed the "up" button again.

The doctors' eyes grew wide. His pace became unsteady, wobbling as he walked. He hunched forward, clutching the rails of the exercise machine.

The Greyhound pulled a stun gun from his coveralls pocket. Lifting it in front of the doctor's face, he pressed the button that sent a two-inch lightning flash across the electrodes on the tip. "Faster, doctor." He reached over and pressed the "up" button again.

The old man wobbled and bounced on the treadmill, wheezing and moaning through the tube as the video of his wife's meeting ended and the camera holder followed her into the parking lot.

The Greyhound viewed the heart rate monitor. It spiked to over 200. The doctor wheezed and gasped, leaning on the railings of the treadmill. His eyes widened. The hose fell out of his mouth. A long string of saliva dropped onto his shirt. "You—you're . . . an animal."

Gritting his teeth, The Greyhound scowled at the old man. "Would you have ever stopped if I didn't do this? If that makes me an animal in your eyes, I wear the label proudly. This has to be done, and not to gain the respect of someone like you." He jabbed his chest with a finger. "I didn't decide my ambitions were more important than other peoples' lives. Not like you. I'd never do that. Not for all the money in the world."

Fishel leaned on the rail, his feet moving but his face gray. The readout jumped to over 200 again.

"Keep going." The Greyhound picked up the streaming phone and gathered the rest of his things. "It's almost over."

The old man gagged and fell sideways into the railing, his arms flailing. He threw his head back and clutched his chest, sliding down onto the treadmill and collapsing. The tread pushed him backwards until his body came to a rest on the office floor, only his head remaining on the dark gray vinyl. His jaw hung open and his eyes stared outward at nothing, the tread churning against his cheek. Blood tricked from his nostrils, but otherwise he was still.

The monitor read zero.

Sagging into the wall, The Greyhound lifted the phone to his mouth and blinked tears from his eyes. His voice fell to a whisper. "It's done."

CHAPTER 9

Centennial Park brimmed with giant, twinkling Christmas trees and hordes of holiday revelers. Ice skaters glided over the temporary rink, and vendors plied everything from hot chocolate to snow globes. Holiday music filled the air. With Lanaya at his side, DeShear eyed the wide spans of grass beyond the paved pavilions. He raced toward the park, each breath throwing a puff of white in front of them.

"I can't run anymore." Lanaya gasped. "Where are we going?"

DeShear slowed to a walk. "I'm sorry. I'm a runner. I forget other people can't keep up sometimes."

She shivered and rubbed her arms, glancing over her shoulder. "I don't see anyone."

"Good. Let's hope it stays that way." DeShear slipped out of his suit jacket and put it around her shoulders. "We might be able to get a souvenir sweatshirt over there." He pointed to the little vendor kiosks clustered near the ice rink. "But we can probably find a café that's open down the street, and get you out of the cold. Either way, it's best for us to be somewhere public right now."

They walked past a police officer on horseback near the park entrance. Inside, several teenagers with hockey sticks sent an old sneaker back and forth over the ice. Several extra sticks rested against the wall.

A "hot coffee" sign flashed from the vendor on the other side of the rink.

"That sounds good," Lanaya said. "Buy you a cup?"

"Sure." DeShear tucked his hands under his arms and followed her to the kiosk.

She pulled the jacket close around her. "Why don't we take a cab out to the suburbs? I'm not crazy about downtown Atlanta right now, and I'm sure we can find a Starbucks or coffee shop there."

"I bet there's a MARTA hub near here." He glanced up and down the adjacent street. "Train stations have security cameras, so our friends from the hotel won't try anything if they spot us. Plus, it'll be warm."

Lanaya ordered two coffees from the man in the wooden window and handed him a twenty-dollar bill.

"Can we grab the train around here?" DeShear asked the vendor.

"About two blocks that way." The man pointed toward a big intersection, then handed Lanaya her change.

They stepped to the side to wait for their order. Two picnic tables and an overflowing trash can stood behind the kiosk, under some pine trees.

"Okay," DeShear said. "Now we have to figure out our next move."

"I have that already. Minnesota."

"But our little chat got interrupted." DeShear cupped his hands to his face and blew warm air through his fingers. "You know why these doctors and scientists are being murdered, and by who. You seem to know who's next. What am I missing?"

She shivered. "Let's talk about this at the train station."

"No, let's talk here. Things have gotten awful dicey since I met you. I might be able to help us both stay alive if I know what you know."

"But it's freezing out here."

"Then talk fast."

Lanaya rubbed her hands together, then shoved them into the suit coat pockets. Over the speakers, *Silent Night* played. She stared at one of the sparkling Christmas trees. "If I tell you everything— what I know and what I think—you'll say I'm crazy. Where do I start?"

"Start with the dead bodies we already know about."

"Well," she said. "The first several murders happened over a few years. The next six took place over six months. Now he's killed three in three weeks—that I know of. It could be more. I don't have all the names."

"Why's the pace getting faster?"

"I believe he's running out of time. He's from the third group, the Gamma caste. He's taken out a lot of the top players from Angelus Genetics and Onyx Research—partners, senior management, project leaders. It's becoming more and more difficult to get information off the black screen site. People always posted rumors and speculation about their projects, but now threads are being deleted out of rampant paranoia, and new posts aren't appearing anymore. I get bits and pieces at best. Innuendo. Guesses. But occasionally someone posts a legit tip for a while. Like the newspaper clippings I showed you."

"Or the employee roster."

"Correct."

"And no one, no authorities are looking for a connection between so many prominent scientists dying in a short time period?"

"They were spread out. It's hard for people to see beyond what's in plain sight. An old man's traffic accident this week in Tampa doesn't tie neatly to a forty-five year old woman's accidental drowning last month in Missouri, especially when her resume doesn't mention she worked at Onyx Research a dozen years ago. These jobs were kept quiet. When people left, they were threatened with nondisclosure lawsuits. Most don't put it on their resume at all."

"Ma'am, your order's up," the vendor called out. "Two coffees."

DeShear went to retrieve them. "Well, your guy's not running out of time based on anything I've done. I just found out about him. And it looks like he's got help now."

At the painted wooden board that served as the coffee kiosk's condiment table, Lanaya poured cream and sugar into her steaming coffee. DeShear left his black, cradling it with both hands to warm his fingers.

"If they're all Gammas, then they all have the same problem." Lanaya picked up a soda straw and stirred her coffee. "There's no assurance of that, but they'd all be driven by the same motive. The top brass at Onyx may not even be aware of what's happening, or they concluded they could wait them out. I suppose if you're wealthy enough, when a problem comes to your attention but you know it will go away in a few years, you might try that option. And it worked until the problem tracked them down." She blew on her coffee, sending a little steam cloud into the air.

"But why would the killer—or killers—be limited on time?" DeShear frowned. "What keeps them from tracking down folks from Angelus and Onyx over the ten years or however long it takes?"

"The subgroup I worked on had an eighty-percent fail rate at the peak median point, once the Gamma sequence had commenced. The corporate high-ups are playing the odds."

"Okay, now say it in English."

"I worked in genetic sciences, Hamilton. DNA selection. People denigrate my field with phrases like designer babies, but this is more than pre-selecting a child to have blue eyes or an athletic build. We were developing ways to find and advance genes that were completely devoid of the most common-occurring natural fatalities in human life.

And it was applied science. But . . . there are down sides."

She shuffled to the picnic table and stared into the shadows of the trees. "For every successful group of embryos whose DNA we altered to grow up and never get cancer, we had groups that failed. Rumor had it that the vast majority were terminus pre-utero, but not all. That was okay, we told ourselves. We could terminate any errant viables." She turned to look into his eyes. "It was a gray area, but most of us felt we could rationalize taking that step with an embryo that couldn't function without a host. Those who didn't agree, left. But I think once a decision like that gets made, it's easier for the top brass to make the next one. We heard that a huge opportunity opened up with organ harvesting. We had viables that weren't cancer resistant, but we could grow their stem cells into whatever was needed. Again, tricky choice, but you could see how some scientists . . . the results could help a lot of people. Then, we heard some new ideas came in." She circled the table, waving her hand. "You see, you'd work on the middle of a project that didn't seem to make sense, but as long as the results were there, it moved forward. You didn't know what its goal was, but from your end it looked like testing. That's where the people on the black screen site could connect the dots. We weren't compartmentalized there. We thought we could figure out what was happening."

"Which was what?" DeShear set down his coffee on the picnic table and leaned on the side of the wooden kiosk.

Lanaya looked down, lowering her voice. "We heard someone at the top of Angelus Genetics realized it was far cheaper to allow the errant viables to continue than it was to attempt to grow mass volumes of healthy organ tissue from stem cells. Makes sense, from a numbers standpoint. The stem cell curation process alone would cost billions. They already had the embryos, so it would be easy enough for someone to take the next step. What did it matter if a viable was terminus at stage nine or stage nineteen, or stage three hundred and fifty four, it was always going to be selected for terminus."

She swallowed hard. These were difficult confessions.

"So, we think they did it." She shrugged. "That's the rumor. They allowed the errant viables to develop—to grow up. Many of the resulting children would have severe deformities, or nonfunctioning higher brain functions—it's much easier to choose a good gene to move forward with than to find the dozens of bad genes you want to leave behind—but if the children's organs worked perfectly fine, then . . . I mean, if that's true—if they used my research to . . ." She wiped a tear from her cheek, staring at the sky. "The world can be a cruel place. There were black screen rumors that errant viables were being sold. Some went to black market orphanages. Others, to the drug trade to serve as slaves, or to human traffickers. Media in other countries isn't like what we have here in the States. With the facility in Indonesia, the news was more controlled, so negative information couldn't get out. The politicians were in on it. We heard Onyx connected with a Cambodian human trafficking ring. The money poured in, all washed through a subsidiary of a subsidiary of a subsidiary, so the people at the top could claim they didn't know—but they'd have to know." She narrowed her eyes. "No executive makes that kind of revenue without knowing the source of every dollar."

DeShear folded his arms. "You were involved in that?"

"I most certainly was not. They used information from employees like me to advance the programs, but we were kept in the dark. But if it's true, it has to be stopped. Enough odd things have already happened to think this is possible. Double Omega's death seemed far more nefarious based on what I'd learned, and I certainly didn't think it was a mere suicide anymore. When I got the information about the other murders, I was scared. I decided to leave the company quietly, and not raise any eyebrows while I got my ducks in a row. Possibly, find others to help, or who knew more. If anyone caught wind of what was happening before we pieced it all together . . ."

"If you can stay alive long enough." He nodded. "Yeah, that's a little more than a missing persons case."

"Dying became a real possibility, but if the rumors are true, Angelus Genetics must be stopped. I'm sorry I deceived you, but I have to be careful about what I divulge. Many have already gone underground, which makes it difficult to know who's still alive. Some have changed their names, or acquired different identities."

"Like Lanaya Kim? Her name wasn't on your airplane ticket. Or the hotel bill. Akina Cho flew on Delta Airlines and Dara Han checked into the Peachtree Plaza hotel."

She held her hands out. "Does it matter? Would you divulge your name to a stranger in this circumstance?"

DeShear took a deep breath and let it out slowly. "No. And the killer we're after, he got screwed by the company—so now he's a psycho bent on revenge?"

"No, no. He didn't get screwed by the company—he was born there. He's an illegally produced, genetically altered human embryo. He's part of a gene selection process that was made illegal decades ago in this country and in many others. And at the median age of fifty-five, over 80% of the viables that didn't die post-vitro, die from overwhelming organ failure within ten months of detecting the start of the sequence. Just as we grow our organs in nine months as babies, the Gammas have a life curve that causes organ depletion. If normal humans lived to be two hundred years old, at some point the brain would naturally fall to dementia, the kidneys would suffer renal failure—all human organs wear out if the host lives long enough. With Gammas, that's at a median age of fifty-five. If they'd have left his genes alone, he'd live to be a median age of eighty-five or older, like any normal person."

"I can see how somebody might have a problem with that."

"That and the other horrendous things the company may be engaged in. He obviously is taking measures to see that it stops. But he may have a limited time if the Gamma sequence has already commenced. Simply put, I believe the killer is dying, and he intends to kill the people responsible before he does."

DeShear studied her face. "From what you've said about Angelus Genetics, I'm not sure he should be stopped."

She set down her coffee and tucked her hands under her arms. "For the most part, he's going right down the list I copied, with few deviations—probably people he can't find. But the list doesn't distinguish between people who were in a position to know what was going on, and people who weren't. The executives and board members had to know about the horrendous activities, but the list has project managers on it—people who were compartmentalized, and who had no idea what the data was used for. People like me." She lifted her head to bring her gaze to his. Her eyes brimmed with tears. "I don't know how to contact them without potentially exposing myself, and what if some of them are working with him? It's just—he doesn't realize there are innocent people on that list."

"Or he doesn't care."

She sniffled. "Oh, I think plenty of people would view him as highly righteous. He merely doesn't have all the facts—and he doesn't have the time left to get them."

"Dara!" A man's voice broke through the still, frosty air. "Dara Han!"

92

Lanaya glanced at the stranger. He stood next to a woman in a red leather jacket, just past the mounted police officer near the park entrance. The man waved a hand and ran toward them, putting his hands in his pockets.

DeShear bolted upright. "Does anyone know you're here?"

"No, I—"

"Get down!"

The man pulled a gun from his pocket and fired. The bullet whizzed past DeShear's head and *piffed* through the pine tree branches, sending a cascade of twigs down on him. He grabbed Lanaya and pulled her behind the coffee kiosk. Screams went up from the tourists gathered around the park. People ran in all directions.

The assassin ran toward the kiosk, firing his gun repeatedly. A tree branch exploded behind DeShear. In front of him, a woman running with a shopping bag whipped her head backwards and dropped to the ground. The next shot pinged off the condiment table. The next hit a man who ran in front of DeShear.

The mounted police officer turned his horse and galloped after the crazed stranger. The woman in the red leather jacket grabbed a hockey stick and swung it at the officer as he came by. It broke over his chest, sending him backwards off the horse.

She chased it down and grabbed the pommel, flinging her leg over the saddle. Righting herself, she grabbed the reins. With a thrust from her heels, the horse drew up and raced forward toward Lanaya and DeShear.

The woman pulled a gun from her pocket, pointing it in Lanaya's direction.

"We're trapped!" Lanaya shouted.

"Stay behind me." DeShear peeked out from behind the kiosk and took the gun from his belt. He held the gun with both hands, lifting it near his face. The wooden corner of the coffee hut burst into splinters as another shot went past. Flinching, DeShear ducked back behind the corner and dropped to one knee, taking a deep breath.

Bullets ricocheted around them. Tourists screamed as they ran from the gunman.

Sliding his finger onto the trigger, DeShear swung himself around the corner and scanned his field of view. He leveled the weapon at the coming stranger, waiting for a clean shot. Running shadows crossed before his eyes.

As the man waded through the scattering crowd, DeShear squeezed the trigger. The shot caught the man's shoulder and pulled him backwards. He shook it off and raised his gun again.

DeShear stood and advanced. "Everyone, down, down, down!" The gun firmly between his hands, he stared down the barrel at the attacker and fired three quick shots. Three red puffs burst from the assassin's torso. The man sagged and fell face first into the ground.

Pivoting to the horse, DeShear fired again. The first shot missed the racing rider.

She aimed her gun at him. Flash after flash came from the muzzle. She was thirty feet away, then twenty. Her shots soared past him.

As the galloping horse drew near, DeShear ran forward into its path and dived into the grass. The horse leaped over him, unbalancing its rider. DeShear rolled onto his back and pointed his gun at her, firing.

She slumped forward and slid from the saddle. Tipping sideways, her body went limp and hit the ground, one foot still caught in the stirrup. The horse kicked and bucked, turning in a circle as it dragged her.

A pedestrian raced forward and grabbed the reins, calming the horse. DeShear sprinted back to the coffee kiosk. Lanaya stood there, her knees shaking and her mouth hanging open.

He put his arms on her shoulders and pulled her to his chest. "You did good."

She nodded. Her mouth moved but no words came out.

Taking her by the hand, he moved toward the shadows of the trees. "You can thank me later. It's time to go."

CHAPTER 10

Mark Harriman resisted the strong urge to shove the mountain of paperwork off the desk and into the trash can next to it. His eyes were red and sore from staring at a computer screen, and his back ached from slouching over its keyboard.

As the assistant duty officer approached, he leaned back in the chair and groaned. "Jayda, no."

She shrugged, placing another set of reports on top of the pile. "Sorry, friend. You told the lieutenant you'd do them all. This is 'them all'."

He shook his head and reached for the new stack of reports. "Next time, tell me to keep my mouth shut."

"Next time, ask me first." Jayda strolled back to the elevator.

He groaned, flipping through the papers. "This would go a lot faster if these guys learned to spell."

The phone console beeped. "Mark, are you still at Detective Sanderson's desk?"

"Yep," he replied to the speaker phone. "Whatcha got?"

"The fire inspector is on line eleven."

"Thank you." He waited for the speaker to cut off and lifted the phone from its cradle, pressing the flashing button. "Officer Harriman speaking."

"Hey, Mark. It's Dyson Spinks. We're filing our PFR and you said you wanted what we had so far on the DeShear fire."

"Yeah, thanks, Dyson. I appreciate it. How's it look?"

"It's definitely arson. We found accelerant everywhere. Gasoline, looks like, but we'll know for sure tomorrow. And the swimming pool camera caught some images of a suspicious character lurking around the building right before it went up."

Harriman rocked back in the chair. "Wow, that's good work. Your gang is rocking it. I'll let Hank know to keep his eyes open."

"Well, that's the thing. A neighbor of his was home sick with the flu all week. Said she saw our person of interest go into the apartment, alone, right before the place went up in flames."

"The flu?" Harriman frowned. "What, was she spying on him from the toilet?"

"There's different kinds of influenza. There's the diarrhea kind and the upper respiratory kind. She had the cough. It's going around. I had it a while back, and—"

"Anyway . . ."

"Uh, anyway, she knew DeShear from saying hi at the mailbox and the pool, so she noticed when it wasn't him going into the place that day. She didn't think anything of it at the time, except that normally no one would be going up there alone without DeShear. After the place went up in smoke, she thought it was suspicious. She gave a statement to our investigator, but it's not much more than that."

"Can you send me the images from the pool camera?"

"Yep. And Mark, there's one more thing. The boss doesn't like it—DeShear's place burning and him suddenly out of town and not returning calls."

Shaking his head, Harriman leaned forward in the chair. "Hank's no arsonist."

"Hey, stranger things have happened. The manager said he'd been slow with the rent a few times lately. He hasn't paid for December yet, and it's a week until Christmas. His credit report said his insurance on the place lapsed, so we called the insurance company to verify. Guess what? The premium got paid the morning of the fire."

Harriman winced. "Okay, the guy was having a bad stretch. Every time he makes a buck, that butt wad Tullenstein hauls him back into court and takes it. That doesn't mean he torched his apartment."

"All I'm saying is, lots of people get in a tough spot and want a clean slate. They figure an insurance check will buy them a new life. It'd be nice if DeShear would talk to us. A guy going away the same day his home burns to the ground, and then not returning calls—that doesn't look good."

Harriman sighed. "Yeah, okay."

"He's your friend. Give him a call."

"I'm on it." Grabbing a pen from the desk, Harriman scribbled a note on the pad. "Can you send me the video from the pool camera?"

"Sure. The hedges hide most of it, but we separated a few still images that look pretty clean. We'll use those in the morning to get the neighbor to verify it's who she saw. I'll email them."

"Thanks, buddy." He tossed the pen onto the desk and rubbed his eyes.

"And Mark . . ."

"Yeah?"

"Have DeShear call us. Like yesterday. The longer this stays unresolved, the worse it looks."

* * * * *

The nearly-empty vending machines at the MARTA station provided their last bag of stale Fritos and some questionable-looking cupcakes to DeShear and his companion. He handed her the bag of chips and viewed the lobby. "At least it's warm in here."

Lanaya opened the Fritos and sniffed, scrunching up her nose.

DeShear took a bite of a cupcake, stopping midway through. "These are no better." He tossed the package into a trash can.

With a huff, Lanaya sat down on a bench, shoving her hands into the suitcoat pockets.

DeShear paced back and forth across the unswept lobby. "If they'd shoot at us there, in a public place—with a cop present—they're . . . well, they . . . I don't know." He put a foot on the bench and leaned forward, folding his arms over his knee.

"What I wonder is, are these guys two steps ahead of us or are they tracking us somehow?"

Lanaya withdrew her hand from the suitcoat pocket. She held up a cell phone.

"Oh, crap," DeShear said. "I thought I left that in the hotel room." He took it and mashed the home button. "I put it on airplane mode for the flight, and didn't remember to take it off."

"They may have been able to track us using that." Lanaya hunched her shoulders. "It won't receive signals in airplane mode, but it'll still ping cell phone towers and give your location."

"Great. Sorry, I didn't know. So I can't use my phone, and we left all your stuff back at the hotel, your computer and—"

She shook her head. "Don't worry about that. My computer is encrypted and set up to not keep histories. The phone was a new disposable. They won't get anything."

"Good. What about the keys to your many secret airport lockers and the fake IDs? Those might be in the hands of our gun-happy friends now."

"I doubt it. I tossed my purse and the keys in the hotel room safe when we got there. Until they get a hold of a daytime manager, they won't be able to get into that safe—and even then they're probably going to need the person registered to the room to do it." She looked at him, raising her eyebrows. "Unless they're law enforcement."

"Nah. Not these guys." He stood up and paced again. "The way they were shooting, they had zero clue how to handle a gun. There's no—hey, that's something." He stopped and rubbed his chin.

"Yeah, they're amateurs. Even rookie cops wouldn't fire into a crowd like that—there's no chance of hitting your target. These clowns shot like they were in an arcade. That means they aren't law enforcement or former military. They're, like . . . well, like you. They've seen guns on TV, but they don't know how to use them."

"And that's a benefit how?" Lanaya threw her hands up. "You said we'd be safe in the open, then the OK Corral happened!"

"It means they won't use coordinated attacks or ambush planning. We can outsmart them. Plus, after that crazy melee in the park, there'll be Atlanta police all over the place." He frowned. "Which means the cops will be after us, since we were shooting, too."

"It was self-defense," Lanaya said. "They shot at us first."

"Yeah, and that will all get sorted out eventually." DeShear rubbed his chin again. "But not before we're sitting in a holding cell—and *then* if they have any law enforcement help, we'll be sitting ducks." He looked at one of the substation security cameras. "We need to get on the move. Now." He headed for the exit.

"Yes," Lanaya said, jumping up. "To Minnesota."

Stopping at the exit, he turned and waited. "Minnesota will require an airport. Airports have cops. Besides, we're linked now. Booking me an airline ticket is almost the same as booking you one, so they'd be able to track us. You don't have an ID anyway now—do you?"

She reached into her back pocket and pulled out a driver's license. "Lanaya can still fly. And I have some money stashed in a locker at the American Airlines terminal. One with a keypad. There's enough for two tickets to Minnesota."

"You are something else." DeShear grinned, pushing open the door. "Well, anywhere but here is a good idea right now. But no trains and no buses until we're at the airport—and then we get the first flight to anywhere. We can't afford to get picked up in the airport while we're sitting around waiting for a flight."

She pointed to his cell phone as she breezed past him to step into the cold night air. "Call a cab. They don't have security cameras, and we can hire one to take us a hundred miles if we need to."

* * * * *

During the wait for the cab, DeShear checked his voicemail messages. One was from Mark Harriman. The toxicology report had come back positive for Propofol in Dr. Braunheiser.

There were standard, post-accident messages from his insurance company; he skipped over those to see what else was pressing. The fire inspector had called several times. Not surprising after an arson, but since DeShear was on the run, the folks at TFD could work things out for themselves for a while.

The last message was another from Harriman. The fire investigators had pictures of a person of interest, seen outside DeShear's place right before the fire. Harriman would email it. And without directly saying so, apparently TFD as much as implied DeShear may have been working with the person to burn the place down.

Fair enough. I'd have thought the same thing.

He opened his email and waited as dozens of messages tried to load, but didn't. The signal wasn't strong enough outside the substation. He tucked his free hand under his other arm and shuddered against the cold.

A cab approached from the other side of the street, slowing to make a U-turn. DeShear walked to the curb and waved.

The driver didn't speak much English, but that was an advantage for the moment.

DeShear's phone might divulge that he'd called for a ride—if anyone was tracking him online—and maybe even where they were headed, but he figured powering down his phone would stop them from keeping on his trail through the use of cell towers. Then online trackers wouldn't know if he'd changed destinations or taken a detour after boarding the vehicle.

He opened the rear passenger door for Lanaya.

The wind whipped her hair into her face. "Are you sitting in front?"

"No, I thought we might both sit in back. So we can strategize."

"Oh. Very good." She climbed in. DeShear followed. The burst of air from the car's heater was a welcome relief. He rubbed his hands together and leaned back into the soft, warm seat cushions.

The driver had been instructed to take them to the airport, but Lanaya's earlier comment had some merit. Driving a hundred miles would deliver them halfway to the Florida-Georgia border, far away from the current troubles in Centennial Park and the Greater Atlanta police.

The cab driver could call in a change of plans and take us to a rest stop, and we could hire a second cab to take us into Florida. From there . . . well, who knows, but at least we wouldn't be on anybody's radar screen, and that might keep people looking for us in Atlanta while we got to, say, Jacksonville—and took a plane to Minnesota . . .

Except he didn't have a fake ID. If he used his real one, they'd be tracking him again.

Crap.

He sat back, sighing, and closed his eyes. The heat in the cab was nice on his feet and hands.

Opening one eye, he glanced at Lanaya-Dara. "What's in Minnesota?"

"Don't you mean who? I told you, there were two people from Onyx who now worked together in Minnesota."

"You and your husband?"

The headlights from an approaching vehicle illuminated her face. She was tired, but held her chin high. The car passed, sending the cab back into darkness. The only light was the green glow of the dashboard gages.

DeShear's voice was soft. "It's the only place I've really seen you get excited about, so it had to be."

"Very good, Hamilton. My daughter and two sons are there, too. At a safe location. Not our house."

"Good."

It was a big admission, saying the kids were there. It showed trust, but it showed there was more at stake than just her own well-being.

DeShear rolled his shoulders and stretched his back, easing into the seat cushion. "I gotta admit, I feel a little silly about calling you the wrong name this whole time."

She shrugged. "Couldn't be helped. My sister Tinara went by different names. To our mother, she was 'Yeon-in'—Sweetie, in American English—but always Tinara to my father. My brothers and sisters and I called her Tia, as did her grade school classmates. High school friends called her Tina, and in college, she was Tinara again. When someone walked up and said hi to her, the name they used told us where they knew her from. That's where I got the idea of using different names on each missing persons case."

"How many people are you involved with?"

"No, I'm the missing person in each case. Dara Han might be looking for Lanaya Kim. In a different city, Akina Cho has hired a law firm to look into the wrongful death of Kiri Jiang."

"Sounds like a CIA operation." DeShear chuckled. "Let me guess. Lanaya flies to Tampa, but Akina checks into the hotel room and pays cash. Then Kiri flies to Atlanta. I like it. The killers can't figure out where you are very quickly."

"And different people would know me under different names, so . . ."

"So you'd know who to trust." DeShear nodded. "I get it. Okay, then. You can still be Lanaya."

She smiled. "How very generous of you."

"You know," he turned to her. "I was thinking. We can change cabs and get to a different airport, then head back to Tampa. Apparently I have some things to clear up there, but I might be able to call in a favor, too. If you think your family is safe—"

"They're as safe as I could get them, but who knows for how long? My husband and I are on a short list that keeps getting shorter. If time is tight for the killer, two targets in one place would be very appealing. That's where you come in. As a private detective and former police officer, you know how to set up stakeouts. We could even set up a ruse with the police—a break in or domestic dispute of some sort, possibly a stalker—anything that would get them involved and watching, so as soon as he showed, we'd have him. He might even know if any of the big rumors about Angelus are true, too."

"It's a good plan, but it could take a while," DeShear said. "What if we crank it up a few levels?"

"What do you mean?"

"Our guy originally kept the murders quiet because publicity would cause people to eventually link the murders and take the fight to him. He couldn't have that because he wanted to keep eliminating the people on the list. But after what happened in the park, that's probably done. And if he only has a short while to live, that strategy doesn't work anymore, anyway. But if he knew there was a gathering of all the high-level muckety mucks from the company that gave him an early death sentence, I would think that would prove too tempting to resist."

"But I told you, they live all over the place. What would cause such a thing to happen?"

He leaned forward, tapping the seat with a finger. "You indicated that most of the top executives were motivated by money."

"Most, but not all."

"And Angelus Genetics is an American company?"

"Yes, but the work now takes place in subsidiaries located all over the world."

Folding his arms, he sat back. "Doesn't matter. Nothing will get an American company's entire executive staff on a plane faster than the stock price falling, and nothing will make a stock fall faster than classifying its major investments and subsidiaries. You raise a stink with the IRS and cry for an audit, and the big wigs will come running to defend their numbers and keep everything quiet. They'll all be in the same place at the same time, guaranteed."

"Classifying?"

"It's an accounting term. It means declaring the investments as crap. I learned it from my ex-wife, Camilla. She worked her way up at one of the big accounting firms. Now she's a bureau chief with the IRS." DeShear grinned. "Trust me, between your inside information and what happened in Centennial Park, the IRS will be conducting a severe rectal probe on Angelus Genetics in twenty-four hours. And as a bureau chief, Cammy can get us on the audit team."

"Sounds intriguing." She smiled. "I think Lanaya should rent a car at the airport so we can drive to Tampa tonight."

CHAPTER 11

The man stood across the street from Centennial Park. Christmas trees lined the grassy perimeter; police cars and ambulances lined the street. Victims covered by blood-stained sheets lay silent through the park while holiday music serenaded them from the public address system.

Frowning, the man pulled a phone from his pocket. He tapped the screen and held it to his ear. "This is your bird dog. Just letting you know, I'm out."

"What! Why?"

He moved away from the gathering crowds and news van lights. "You said this was an eyes-on operation to follow a scientist. Well, she's got a friend. After the two of them put your room service clown into a coma and sent me on an elevator ride, they went a few blocks down the street and took out your operatives in the park."

"I told you, things can change on the fly."

"And I told you, I've already seen the inside of a federal penitentiary. I don't care to see another one. It's amateur hour out here, and I'm done."

"I can get you more money," the man on the other end of the line growled. "How much? Name your price."

"Lose my number." The man ended the call and put the phone in his pocket, walking away from the park entrance and heading back toward the Peachtree Plaza hotel.

* * * * *

"But you say airport!" The cab driver pulled his car into the Dunkin Donuts parking lot. "This, *not* airport."

"Sorry. Change of plans," DeShear said, leaning forward. "You can let us out right here." He turned to Lanaya and lowered his voice. "Do we have enough for a tip?"

She counted out some cash. "Our funds will be nearly depleted after we pay for this little detour, but as long as we get to my locker at the American Airlines terminal, we can do whatever we want." She handed the cash to the cab driver.

"Okay," DeShear said. "Let's go."

They went inside as the cab drove off. DeShear chose a quiet booth in the back, away from the counter and employees. When Lanaya was seated, he leaned across the table and placed his phone in front of her. "Call another cab," he whispered. "Take it to the American terminal, get your traveling money, and rent a car. Then come pick me up here."

He glanced around. An eighteen-wheeler pulled into the massive parking lot of the Flying J gas station next door. "Better yet, pick me up there, at the truck stop."

She nodded, staring at the phone. "What if . . ."

"If people have seen us together, splitting up makes the job of tracking us harder for them. But I'm a big liability to you right now." He sat back, tugging at his shirt collar. "I'm wearing the same clothes I had on in the park when I was shooting the place up. If they put my image on TV and I step into a busy airport, it's game over. My hands are still covered in gunshot residue."

Lanaya pursed her lips.

"Hey." He reached across the table and took her hand. "I'm not abandoning you. I kept watch to see if we were being followed on the ride over. We weren't. In all the video footage anyone might have, you're wearing my suitcoat. Leave it here. I'll throw it in the dumpster outside. Pull back your hair while you're in the cab. With what you have on, you'll look different enough to get in and out of the airport without raising eyebrows, so you'll be fine—right now. In a few hours, probably not."

He gave her hand a gentle squeeze. "It'll work."

"Okay." She forced a smile.

"There we go," he said. "How much cash do we have left?"

"Eighty-three dollars."

"Okay. Give me twenty. I'll wait with you here until the cab comes, then I'll go next door and buy some kind of different shirt. Pick me up there. Between the ride to the airport and back, it shouldn't take you more than an hour." He pressed the home button on the phone to check the time. "One more thing. Don't act nervous. The TSA folks watch for that. They'll stick you in an interview room to make sure you're not a terrorist, and you'll end up creating more questions than you can answer."

"I know. I *have* been in an airport before."

DeShear shifted on his seat. "Oh, I didn't mean to—"

"It's just—it's all suddenly gotten a lot more real."

"Yeah. Bullets flying at you will do that."

Lanaya's hands were shaking again. She stared at the Flying J parking lot. "What if I come back and you're not here?"

He took a deep breath and let it out slowly. "Then they got me—and you head to Minnesota. From there, you call Mark Harriman and you tell him everything. All of it. Don't hold anything back."

She swallowed hard, her voice wavering. "And if I'm not back in an hour?"

He picked up the phone and put it in her hand. "Then I will come find you. And whoever's in my way will pay a steep price."

* * * * *

DeShear waited at the booth while Lanaya climbed into her cab. As they pulled away, she saw him get up and head for the restaurant exit. They drove past the Flying J, its extra-long parking spots accommodating the many tractor trailer trucks of its clientele. Many would gas up and continue on; others would spend the night.

Sleep. What a nice luxury.

Remembering what DeShear told her, she gathered up her hair. "Do you have a rubber band?" she asked the cab driver.

He held up a plastic box of miscellaneous items—pens and paper clips, a butane lighter. Digging through it, she found a hair tie with two big beads on it. She held it up to the light. The platinum-haired super hero Storm adorned one bead; her alter ego, Ororo Munroe, smiled from the other.

Lanaya smiled back. "Warm it up a little around here, would you?"

The cab driver glimpsed Lanaya in the rearview mirror. "What, ma'am?"

"Nothing. Sorry." She slipped the tie around her ponytail.

At the airport, she had the cab stop near the end of the departures area. Traffic was light, but there were still plenty of cars coming in and out. She put her hand on the car door latch. The cab suddenly felt very secure.

TSA watches for nervous people in the airport. Act calm.

She wiped her sweaty hand on her leg, then put it back on the latch.

Here goes nothing.

She opened the car door. A gust of icy wind rushed over her cheeks and hands, making her flinch. She exited the vehicle and walked toward the nearest entrance, hunching her shoulders against the cold. Her steps were awkward and stiff, like she'd forgotten how to walk and was trying to remember. Keeping her face to the ground, she entered the building.

She tried to walk fast without appearing to do so, but the trek to the American terminal seemed endless. She only peeked up to maintain her bearings, convinced that doing otherwise would bring forth swarms of gun-toting assailants. Her stomach was a knot, barely even taking notice when she passed the ever-aromatic Cinnabon.

As she approached the lockers, she slowed her pace and peered over her shoulder. If the killers had tracked her to DeShear in Tampa and then to Centennial Park, they could be anywhere. Sweat dotted her upper lip. Nobody seemed particularly interested in her activities, though. A maintenance woman pushed a trash cart through the quiet lobby. In a far corner, a man in coveralls guided a spinning floor polisher over the shiny surfaces between the acres of carpets. The distant PA system announced an arriving flight.

Lanaya stared at the rows of lockers and swallowed hard. She crept toward the one she'd rented, stretching a shaking finger out to the keypad.

Beep, beep, beep.

With her code entered, the latch released. Holding her breath, she opened the little door.

Inside, her belongings were just as she'd left them. She let out a sigh of relief, her heart settling back into her chest.

She leafed through the backpack holding her money. She'd managed to stash more than enough for a trip to Tampa, but how long would she be gone now? A few days? A week? She glanced around the area. No one was watching her, but there were a lot of variables at play. Take it all? Leave some in case she needed it later?

Half. Take half.

With trembling fingers, she pulled several stacks of hundred dollar bills out, tore off the paper band, and jammed the bundles into her pockets. With a shove, the backpack went into the locker and she closed the door.

The blue screen blinked at her.

Her stomach jolted. Money. She needed quarters to get the door locked again. Heat came to her cheeks. She closed her eyes and leaned her forehead against the wall of lockers. *Stupid, stupid, stupid.*

She scanned the lobby. A news stand-gift shop was still open. She could leave her belongings in the unsecured locker get to the store and back before anyone noticed. The thought made her stomach churn again. The locker held too much money to leave unattended. But the thought of getting identified halfway across the airport lobby with so much cash on her was equally unsettling.

Her heart throbbed. *Be calm. There's hardly anyone here. Go over, get some gum, and come right back.*

And what if the locker's empty when you return? Then what? Years of saving, gone—and possibly your life with it. These lockers had bailed her out of a jam more than once.

But she'd brought it in increments, never wanting too much cash on her at one time, and never fearing someone was on her tail. This was different.

She'd have to risk it. She had to take it all with her to get change.

She reached into the locker and stuffed everything into the backpack, then straightened up and smoothed out her clothes.

"You'll look different enough to get in and out of the airport without raising eyebrows. It'll work."

She tucked the backpack under her arm.

The maintenance woman and floor cleaner both remained next to the trash cart, glancing at her as she passed. The radio on the woman's hip crackled with indistinguishable chatter.

It's nothing. They aren't watching you.

Her pulse thumping in her ears, she stared at the floor and hurried across the carpet to the news stand.

She entered the shop, trying to control her nerves. Outside, the maintenance woman and the floor cleaner spoke for a moment, then parted ways.

Focus. The shop has change. Get it and get back to the locker.

She grabbed a pack of Juicy Fruit and placed it on the counter.

The cashier set down her phone. "Will that be all?"

"Yes. And three dollars in quarters, too, please. Thank you." Lanaya looked around as the cashier scanned the gum. No one else was in the store.

"Ma'am?"

She looked at the cashier.

"I said, it's a dollar seventy-three, please. Would you like your receipt?"

"No. Thank you." Lanaya watched the lobby as she reached into her pocket, handing the woman a bill.

The cashier held it up to the light. Lanaya's heart skipped a beat. A one-hundred-dollar bill! *What did you do with the twenties?*

The cashier picked up a yellow-colored marker and drew a line on the bill. She frowned, drawing another line. Then another. "Excuse me one moment," she said, heading to the back of the shop.

"I have another. A smaller—" Lanaya rifled through the backpack, her pulse pounding. Nothing but hundreds.

Panic surged through her system. Lanaya patted her pockets. One was empty. Jamming her hand into the other, she found the money she'd been carrying. She yanked it out. "Here. I have—a twenty." She slapped it on the counter.

The cashier disappeared through a door at the back of the shop. "It's no problem. One moment."

Lanaya's heart raced again. What was the woman up to? She checked the lobby, holding back the urge to run from the news stand. The maintenance lady was standing in front of the shop now, near the corner of the front display window. Lanaya clutched the backpack to her chest. On the other side of the doorway, the floor cleaner moved his machine back and forth, watching her. She was trapped.

I can't run for it. I'll never get off the airport property, it's too big. It's too far. I'll need a car, but I have to . . .

Her mind was a blank. A drop of sweat ran down the side of her face.

. . . do what? What should I do?

The maintenance woman peered into the shop. Her eyes met Lanaya's.

Another jolt went through her. *That's it. They're coming for me.* She backed away from the counter. *They're coming.*

Her eyes darted around the shop. *Where does that back door go? Was someone with the cashier, getting ready to pounce?*

Lanaya rubbed the side of her face, panting. *Think. Focus. How can you escape?*

The door opened and the cashier entered the shop again. Lanaya stared at her, trembling, but saying nothing. The woman walked toward the front of the store.

This is it. She drops the security gate. Run. Run now.

The woman went to the cash register. "All set." She held up a pen. "My testing marker was out of ink. I'll have your change for you in a second."

Lanaya inched toward the counter. She peeked at the rear door, then to the display window. The maintenance woman wasn't there.

With trembling fingers, she took her change and the red and white plastic shopping bag containing her gum, stepping away from the counter to scan the lobby again.

Get to the locker, then get to the rental car desk. Fast.

She hurried across the carpet, looking everywhere she could without raising her head.

Act natural, act natural, act natural.

The lockers were only a few feet away. When she reached them, she yanked open the backpack and grabbed several thick wads of bills. She shoved them into the shopping bag, pushed the backpack into the locker and slammed the little door shut, jamming coin after coin into the slot as fast as the machine could take them. She wiped her upper lip with the back of her hand, staring at the machine until the keypad read "Secure."

Turning, she ran a hand across her forehead. The car rental counter next, and out of here. Her ears hummed, a slight headache coming to her.

She moved quickly, her heart racing, walking to the rental counter. The young man there smiled. "Hello. Do you have a reservation?"

"No," Lanaya said, her voice wavering. "I don't have a reservation, but I do need a car."

"Thank you." He typed on the keyboard. "May I get your name and home address?"

As the young man registered her fake ID, Lanaya drummed the countertop.

"Nervous flier?"

"Excuse me?" Lanaya asked.

He pointed to her tapping fingertips.

"Oh." She dropped her hand to her side, shifting her feet. "Very sorry."

He slid a form onto the counter. "Sign here, please. Your car is in spot three-thirty-one. Through the doors and to the right."

"Ma'am." The woman from the shop called out to her.

Lanaya turned, heat rising in her cheeks. The maintenance lady was with the news shop cashier. They came toward her.

Her stomach churned. She grabbed the car key from the counter and headed to the doors.

"Ma'am." The cashier moved faster. "Ma'am!"

"No!" Lanaya screamed. She broke into a run. "No! Get away from me!"

The doors opened and a man in a dark suit came through, pulling a suitcase behind him. Lanaya slammed into him. He broke her fall, dropping his bag and backing up. They both managed to stay on their feet.

She pushed herself away, her heart racing and her ears humming.

"You left this." The cashier handed her a twenty-dollar bill. "I'm sorry I scared you."

"Oh, uh . . ." Lanaya swallowed hard, taking the bill. "The mistake was all mine. I'm very sorry." She turned to the man in the suit. "Please forgive me." She gestured to the clerk at the car rental counter. "I'm a nervous flier. I need to calm down."

The maintenance woman shook her head and reached for her radio.

"You'd better wait a few minutes before you try to drive," the man said, bending over to pick up his suitcase.

"I will. Thank you. Sorry for the trouble." Lanaya backed away. "Thank you."

With the four of them staring at her, Lanaya disappeared through the doors.

CHAPTER 12

Wearing a black University of Georgia "Bulldogs" sweatshirt and a gray pair of sweatpants he bought at the Flying J, DeShear drove the rental car onto I-75 and headed south. Lanaya had said she was too nervous to drive, and he didn't question it. She looked frazzled when she finally came to pick him up.

It would be a long drive to Tampa—about 450 miles—but it was critical to get on the road before the inevitable Centennial Park investigation had a chance to review videos from witnesses and security cameras. The authorities would eventually see him on the MARTA substation videos with Lanaya, and then getting the cab, so they'd call the cab company and learn the car was hired to go to the airport.

The airport cameras wouldn't show him at all, and if Lanaya had gotten in and out of the airport without drawing too much attention to herself, they'd have a decent head start on avoiding a holding cell and doing a lot of explaining.

DeShear checked his speed and set the cruise control at seventy miles per hour. The dashboard GPS said it would still take about eight more hours to get to Tampa. He preferred to drive about ten miles over the speed limit on long drives, to shave a little off the clock, but on this trip, he'd stick to the speed limit. Not getting pulled over was more important than saving a few minutes.

In the passenger seat, Lanaya knitted her hands as she stared out the window.

"What are you thinking about?" DeShear asked.

"Just . . . everything."

"It's all a lot to take in," he said. "So don't try. Not right now. Let the fog of war pass."

"I can't believe how many mistakes I've made. I can't—I can't focus. It's very unlike me. Everything since Bayshore Boulevard has been a complete blur."

"That's adrenaline. It's normal. In the army, after a firefight, you'd see soldiers rocket along for a while, almost numb to the intense loss of life happening all around them. Then after they're safe for a bit, they crash like a ton of bricks. But all sorts of things can happen. Some get nervous and forgetful after the fact. It's common."

Her expression stayed the same. *Time to change subjects.*

"We'll stop in a bit and get something to eat and a change of clothes." DeShear rubbed the stubble growing on his chin. "A hotel would be nice, but it's more important to get to Tampa fast, don't you think?"

Lanaya didn't seem to hear him. He tried again.

"You said the people who killed Dr. Braunheiser might be running out of time. But the disease—"

"The Gamma sequence."

"Right, the sequence." He didn't necessarily want to make her have this discussion, but she seemed to need to unwind, and talking often did that for people. The subject might not even matter. "Do the killers know what's involved?"

"Yes, I believe they know." She folded her hands in front of her and looked at him. There were bags under her eyes. "Angelus intended for them not to interact, but I think the company kept tabs on them somehow. That was the thinking on the black screen site, because we'd see hospital data. Where else could it have come from? They had to be tracking the Gammas. No one else knew. But in doing so, the company may have inadvertently tipped off some of them that they were being observed. In any case, the ones doing the killings certainly seem to know, and they are understandably concerned. It's an extremely harsh way to die, and for Gammas, there's no avoiding it."

DeShear shook his head. "They're acting like it's worse than death."

"In many ways, it is. It comes on with a harsh, persistent cough. Most people think they're getting the flu or pneumonia, but after a week or so, the symptoms clear up. But this isn't a virus, Hamilton.

It resurfaces after about a month, accompanied by migraines and extreme fatigue. Kidney and abdominal pain follow. One by one, all the vital organs of the afflicted shut down. Lungs, liver. There is constant nausea, and symptoms associated with dementia. Some get massive skin sores that won't heal. Everything goes at once."

He placed his elbow on top of the car door while he drove. "There has to be something the doctors can do."

"Most of the people go into the hospital, but about one third don't. The result is the same either way." She sighed. "No team of physicians can rectify every organ failing at once. In an average case, once the sequence has started, the subject spends the next ten months in severe, debilitating pain. And somewhere along the line, they get overwhelmed and can't keep fighting. Only about one in five survive."

"No wonder they're killing the people involved. Can't be fun, knowing that's waiting for you. What is a person supposed to do when they discover they only have a few weeks or months to live? I mean, before the bad stuff starts." He glanced at her. "Have you thought about it?"

"Not recently. I've been pretty focused on trying to stay alive. I suppose I'd get my affairs in order, say my goodbyes. Prepare my children for a future without me." She turned to face DeShear. "What about you?"

"I don't know." He shrugged as he stared at the road. "I don't have any family. No real affairs to get in order. I'd try to enjoy what time I had left, I guess. Go on a cruise."

"Some do that. Many of the afflicted choose to not endure the eight months of pain at all. That's another indication they've found out about the sequence."

"I can understand that, staring at eight months of pain with death waiting at the end." DeShear held the steering wheel and sat up straighter. "There was a cop in my precinct a few years back—got diagnosed with cancer. Young guy, headstrong. He rubbed a lot of people the wrong way. Anyway, the cancer was already bad when they found it, so they told him to start planning. You know, like you said—get your affairs in order." DeShear stared at the highway. "Watching what he went through, week after week, it was hard. We'd visit him in the hospital, me and the guys. Most days he wasn't himself. He was a frail old man all of a sudden, and then he was in a lot of pain. Just nonstop. He was that way for a year, almost. I . . . it was a long year." He glanced at Lanaya. "A lot of people would have found a way to end it and get out of that nonstop pain, you know?"

Lanaya lowered her voice. "Did he pass away?"

"No, the kid was a fighter. He battled back. I'd get off work, I'd be tired or whatever, but I always went to go see him, at least a few times a week, usually more. I had to go. I felt like, if I didn't, he might not be there the next time, and I wanted to be sure he knew . . ." DeShear's voice wavered. "That somebody was still pulling for him. I went to that hospital for almost a whole year, and I never saw that kid give up. And he made it. He's been cancer free for almost ten years now." DeShear sniffled. "Whenever I'm in a tough jam, I think about him fighting death from that hospital bed all alone, with those tubes hanging off of him and all those machines . . . and I know that whatever challenge I'm facing, I can beat it if I just don't quit."

Lanaya reached over and patted his leg. "I'm sure your visits were a great comfort and inspiration to him, Hamilton. Do you still see him since you left the force?"

"Yeah. Harriman and I go to hockey games together when we can."

"Mark Harriman? No wonder he spoke so highly of you." She sighed again. "That's a nice story. I like a story with a happy ending." She clutched the red and white shopping bag as she stared out the window. "I hope mine has one."

CHAPTER 13

The hotel suite at the Fairmont *Le Château Frontenac* was littered with tissues stained with blood. The gold-colored trash can in the ornate bedroom overflowed with them, as did the one in the massive bathroom, where a large man stood vomiting in the steamy shower. Just beyond the rumpled bed, a cell phone rang on the nightstand. It vibrated against a box of prescription migraine medicine and an empty bottle of Pepto Bismol.

Coughing, the man wrapped a towel around his wet, muscular torso and grabbed the phone. "Hello?"

"I'm checking in," the woman on the other end said. "You weren't answering. I got nervous. Is Maya with you? Or Britt?"

"Not this trip. It's only me." He wiped his mouth as he sat on the bed. Blood smeared across the back of his hand. "What do you want?"

"I thought we all agreed you wouldn't be traveling alone now."

"I got new information, and it should be a fast trip. I'll be back in New York tonight. Now—what do you want?"

"Like I said, I'm checking in—like you asked me to."

"Right." He rubbed his eyes. "Sorry. I . . . I had a rough night."

"Aren't the new drugs from Maya working?"

He glanced at the desk by the window. The top was filled with bottles and syringes. "It's hard to tell. Transfusions have worked best so far."

"You'll have to wait. I don't know anybody at the hospitals in Quebec, and I can't just call and ask them to offer the blood and equipment. Transfusions cost a lot of money and they take time."

"Money, I have. Time is a different matter. Speaking of which." He lifted the Patek Philippe wristwatch off the night table. "I need to get on the road if I'm going to get all the way up to Saguenay before our target wakes up and gets moving. She'll be much harder to get once she's at the lab." He held the cell phone to his ear with his shoulder as he strapped on the watch.

"Tristan, listen to yourself. You're pushing too hard. You should rest up."

"Can't." He stood, leaving the towel on the bed and going into the bathroom. "I'm getting weaker every time. The steroids and HGH can only do so much. I have big spans of strength—days and days where I feel great—but they're getting more spread out, and the crashes are getting worse." He reached into his shaving bag and picked up a stick of deodorant, swiping it under his arm. "If I can keep mustering a few days here and there for transfusions . . ."

"Do that. Rest up. We got this."

"You got this?" He frowned. "You completely blew the last assignment. It was a mess."

"We—"

"I'm not blaming you." He stared at his reflection, running a hand through his damp hair. "It was a bad idea—my *bad* idea. From here out, I'll handle it." Setting the phone on the marble counter, he pressed the speaker button and ran the deodorant under his other arm. "I have an easy target here, then another in Maryland. Then I can get two in Minnesota. That's four in a week, and I might start letting the word out that they're connected."

"How? It's too risky going to the press. If we expose the others, they'll be hunted down."

"I'm not going to the press."

"Well what, then?"

He peeked at the large gun inside the shaving bag. "Let me worry about that."

"Yeah," she huffed. "You'll handle it—if you don't pass out in the middle of the next one. You were running on fumes an hour after Tampa."

"I'll be fine. The transfusions help a lot." He picked up the brown plastic medicine bottle from the counter and shook a few pills into his hand, swallowing them without water.

"But it doesn't have to be *only* you. We can help. I know the last one went wrong, but—"

"You've been helping, and I'm grateful. But less blood on the hands of others is better."

"That's not realistic."

"That's how I want it. Now, I really have to go. I'll see you in New York."

She sighed. "Do you ever think we're wrong about all this? Not in what we're doing, but how we're doing it?"

"Every day. And every night before I go to sleep. I wonder if what I'm doing makes me worse than they are." He crossed the room to the window and stared out from the majestic Fairmont *Le Château Frontenac*, gazing over the lights of the Quebec City skyline. The castle-like hotel towered over the old city. In the distance, the big river rippled and flowed, casting shimmering reflections out from its dark, curving swath.

He swallowed hard, a knot forming in his throat. "But I think about innocent kids suffering and I remember how this started. Then I don't worry anymore. It has to be done, and this is the only way. And now I know I'm the only one who can do the job."

"Other greyhounds would probably step up if they were asked. Or if they knew."

"But I'm not just any greyhound." He squared his shoulders and stared at his reflection in the glass. "I'm *the* Greyhound. And as long as I'm breathing, the job stays with me."

CHAPTER 14

DeShear's eyelids had been getting heavy as he passed by the odorous paper mills and swampy roadside ponds of southern Georgia, but the blue flashing lights in his rearview mirror took any sleepiness out of him. He gripped the steering wheel and glanced at the speedometer. Seventy-one. No way any cop—not even a Georgia highway patrol trooper with a quota—was going to pull someone over in the middle of the night for a measly one mile an hour over the limit.

Lanaya sat with her eyes closed and her head resting against the door, her red and white shopping bag in her hands.

She finally gets some sleep, and now a state trooper's going to wake her up.

But why is he pulling us over?

It seemed too quick for the Atlanta police to connect all the dots and track them down, but it still wasn't good. If the officer started looking around the inside of the car, he'd find a big bag of cash, a few unregistered guns—who knows how many felonies those were involved in—and he'd haul them in on suspicion. Then, while they were sitting in a holding tank, the authorities would eventually link them to the park shooting and the hotel assault. Sitting in lockup would also make things pretty easy for anybody who wanted to put some bullets in them— just wait for the arraignment, follow them outside to the car, and pop, pop, pop.

It was simply a can of worms DeShear didn't want opened right now. None of that helped protect Lanaya's family or stop the killers.

DeShear flipped on the rental car's emergency flashers and eased the car toward the side of the road. He drummed the wheel as options raced through his mind.

It can't be about Centennial Park. There hasn't been enough time. The hotel incident wouldn't get attention this far away. It's not feasible that it was related to the killers, and if the killers were connected to the police, they'd have used the cops earlier in the game.

But it didn't matter. He'd find out soon enough.

"Lanaya, wake up."

She didn't budge.

"Lanaya." He tapped her on the leg. "Hey. We're getting pulled over by the police. Wake up."

That did the trick. She gasped and sat upright, clutching her bag to her chest. "What's going on? And what's that smell?"

"The old paper mill, the Georgia swamps . . . Georgia in general. We have a state trooper pulling us over. Try to act calm, like you did when you went to the airport."

She swallowed hard, nodding.

He eyed the shopping bag. "See if you can— without bending over—see if you can slide your big bag of money under your seat."

"Why? It's my money. We didn't steal it."

DeShear held his hands out. "Look at us. Do you know what a Georgia cop thinks when he finds a couple of sleepless people, dressed like they're practically homeless, driving a car in the middle of the night with thousands of dollars in cash—ten minutes from the Florida border?"

"Drugs?"

"And they don't take kindly to that. Now, shove it under the seat without bending over. He'd see that from his patrol unit, and it would give him probable cause to search our car, and then he'll find our guns. Try to slide the bag, and then kick it the rest of the way with your foot. If we don't give him a reason to search the car, we'll probably be fine."

"Probably?"

"We don't know why he's pulling us over yet. Maybe the rental agency caught the fake ID. Did everything go okay at the airport when you went to get the car?"

She stared straight ahead. "Yes. Why? Of course it did. Why wouldn't it? Take the ticket. Or talk your way out of it. You were a cop."

"I don't think that's our best plan of action." He pulled the car to a stop, glancing at the GPS. A blue car icon pointed down a purple highway, bordered on the right by the big green patch of a swamp. The Florida border wasn't on screen yet, but it was close. "These southern Georgia boys like to write their tickets. Just sit tight and act like a sleepy wife on a long, boring road trip. We went to Gatlinburg for the week."

The silhouette of the officer approached, one hand shining a flashlight into the rental car, the other resting on his gun. DeShear peeked at the side of the road. The narrow emergency lane had a short span of grass next to it that disappeared down a hill, no guard rails.

The officer was shorter and rounder than most state troopers. DeShear continued to hold the wheel with both hands, forcing himself not to drum his fingers. After the officer had come a few steps closer, DeShear slid a hand onto the armrest and pressed the button to lower the window. The sharp, cold wind bit his cheeks.

The beam of the flashlight bounced off DeShear's face, then moved around the car's interior.

"Evening, sir," the officer said, his breath making white puffs with every word.

The accent was thick. Pure southern Georgia. And his uniform wasn't the gray and light blue of a state trooper uniform and a Stratton hat. Some kind of county deputy, maybe.

Why is he on the highway stopping us?

"Evening officer," Deshear said, squinting in the bright light.

"License and registration, please."

"Sure. Why did you pull me over?" DeShear rubbed his eyes. "I had the cruise control set at seventy."

"Welcome to Chipley. It's fifty-five through here, right on to the Florida border."

He pronounced "here" as "hyah," with two syllables.

"Well, I'm sorry, I used the cruise control because I wanted to be sure not to speed." DeShear reached for his wallet.

"And you didn't pay attention when it went to fifty-five."

DeShear winced. The whole situation that was now putting them in potential jeopardy could have been easily avoided. "No. Guess I missed the slower speed limit sign."

"You and everybody else in a rush to get to sunny Florida."

Over the officer's shoulder radio, the dispatcher calmly gave instructions to another unit.

"Do y'all have the registration for this car, sir?"

"Suh" was another one, said southern style. In Atlanta, there wasn't a discernible accent at all.

"Uh, it—it's a rental." DeShear shrugged. "Let me look for it."

Stepping back from the vehicle, the officer shined his light on Lanaya. "Take your time."

She held completely still, more likely from fear than DeShear's earlier instructions, until the light passed from her face.

DeShear dug his wallet out of his pocket and withdrew the license, contemplating his next move.

He couldn't risk the officer running his ID. The computer might not have the car flagged, but it might have him. He glanced in the rearview mirror at the flashing blue lights behind him.

"Here you go." He held the license up, but didn't extend his hand outside the window. "I'll check the glove box for the registration." He leaned a little toward the glove box, inching his hand further into the car.

"That's fine, sir." The officer reached for the license.

The dispatcher came on again. "Unit 454, we have a make on your tag." Static interference garbled the last part. It sounded to DeShear like she said, "TSA reports 10-29-F. Proceed with caution."

DeShear recognized the code. The vehicle was wanted in connection with a crime, and by TSA. His heart pounded. They couldn't get picked up.

This guy's not highway patrol or a county deputy sheriff. He might not have dashboard cameras.

The officer frowned, leaning forward for the license with one hand as he pressed the mic with the other. "Say again, Dispatch."

DeShear dropped the license and grabbed the officer's wrist with both hands. He pulled forward and grabbed the shoulder mic. As the officer scrambled for his sidearm, DeShear yanked the hip radio off his belt.

The officer jumped back, drawing his service weapon and pointing it at DeShear. "Stop! Get out of the vehicle!"

DeShear dropped the car into reverse. "Hold on!" he shouted to Lanaya. Stomping the gas pedal, he launched the car backwards. The wheels squealed as DeShear threw an arm behind Lanaya's seat so he could keep his eyes looking out the back. The squad car grew in the window.

The officer chased after them.

"He's coming!" Lanaya shouted.

DeShear steered the car wildly as it raced backwards. "I have to slow down to make sure the air bags don't deploy on impact, but you're still gonna feel a bump."

Lanaya put a hand on the dashboard. "What about the cop?"

"He shouldn't shoot at us. We're not engaging him."

"Shouldn't?"

Aiming the car at the cruiser looming in the back window, DeShear hit the brakes. Lanaya bounced backward into her seat. The cars touched bumpers with a metallic crunch. Mashing the gas pedal, the tires squealed again as the vehicle strained to put the police cruiser in motion.

DeShear gritted his teeth. "Come on. Come on!"

Smoke poured off his tires.

DeShear forced all his weight onto the pedal as the officer closed in on them. The cruiser inched backwards.

"He's right on top of us!" Lanaya screamed, sliding down in her seat.

"There we go." The cruiser moved slowly, grinding over the asphalt, its locked wheels not turning as it slid. "Come on, baby."

The grill of the squad car groaned as the sedan forced it to move. DeShear jerked the steering wheel to the left. The rear of his car went toward the highway, but the rear of the police cruiser went toward the side of the road.

The green swamp glistened in the night.

"There we go, baby! Come on!"

The cruiser picked up speed as it headed toward the embankment.

"Hang on!"

"I'm hanging on!"

He swerved, sending a jolt through the car as they sped off the asphalt and over the grass. DeShear and Lanaya bounced upwards into the ceiling.

The cruiser teetered on the edge of the short precipice, its tail pointing down toward the swamp.

The grill raised slowly, then the squad car slid down the hill. It gathered speed and bumped along over the wet, uneven ground until the angle got too steep, then it rolled over onto its side. A second later, it fell onto its roof with a muffled crunch. The patrol car slid sideways for a few more yards before coming to rest upside down, a few feet into the muck of the murky green swamp.

DeShear jammed his vehicle into drive and punched the gas again, sending dirt and gravel upwards as he sped forward. The officer took a position near the side of the road, pointing his gun and shouting. DeShear swerved wide to the left, nearly into the median, so the deputy wouldn't think they planned to run him down. As DeShear passed, the officer kept his gun on them, but no shots were fired. Their vehicle sped down the highway and away from the scene.

DeShear squeezed the steering wheel, smiling and bouncing up and down as they raced past an exit. "Yeah! Whew, baby, we did it." He looked at Lanaya. "You okay?"

"Barely." She maintained her grip on the dashboard. "Slow down."

He eased his foot off the gas and let their speed drop to fifty-five, his heart pounding. "Yeah, good call." There might be more than one deputy on this span of I-75. No sense in getting pulled over again. They wouldn't be so lucky a second time. He peered at Lanaya. "You did well back there."

As they went around a wide bend in the road, a gravel swath appeared up ahead in the median.

"Okay," DeShear said. "One more time. Hang on." He swerved the car over the gravel and onto the northbound lanes.

"What are you doing?" Lanaya said. "The cop is this way and Tampa's the other way."

"There's an exit before we get to him. We have a very short window of time before we're right back where we started, getting pulled over." DeShear checked the GPS, then picked up the officer's radio from the floor boards and tossed it in the back seat. "When Officer Friendly doesn't report in a few minutes, they'll go looking for him—and then all of cop world is gonna break loose. They're going to look at the last stop he called in. He would've given the make, model, and license number of this car. If there's video in that squad car, they'll download it and have the color of the car and the number of occupants. They already know it was headed southbound. So we're going to go north for a minute, back to that little town we just passed. We need to be in a different car."

"Where are we going to rent another car at this time of night in the middle of nowhere?"

DeShear took the first exit off the highway. "Who said anything about renting?"

* * * * *

The first truck stop they came to was brightly lit, with a lot of eighteen wheelers parked all around it, but no regular cars. At the 7-11 next door, however, several cars out back appeared to be where an employee might park. The dingy bar next to 7-11 had even more selections.

DeShear circled back to the truck stop and pulled in. "Stay here. Keep your head down, but you're not hiding. You're just not drawing attention to yourself. If somebody sees you, don't act like you're asleep, act like your husband's inside going to the bathroom."

"What does that expression look like?"

"Annoyed. I'll try to find a vehicle at the bar. If I'm lucky, the ones by the back exit belong to employees, so nobody's going to need them too soon and come looking for them. But I don't want to have the bouncer catch me borrowing his car when he comes out for his smoke break." DeShear opened the door. A blast of cold wind shot through the rental car. "Stay put. I'll be back in less than ten minutes."

She frowned. "But then you'll be driving a stolen car."

"You will, once I procure one, and only for a few minutes. I'll drive the rental—the car the cops are looking for—and we'll find a pond and roll the rental into it. Then I'll hop in the stolen car with you and we'll head south. First chance we get, we swap plates to a Florida tag. It'll buy us a few hours, and by then we'll be in Gainesville, and our Georgia deputy and the big bad Georgia Highway Patrol won't be looking for us there. Neither will TSA, for whatever's chafing their butt. We snag another car from the university in Gainesville, and keep on trucking until we're in Tampa. Depending on if we make good time or not, we might get there before daylight. And whatever personality you used at the rental agency, she probably needs to disappear, too."

Lanaya sat back, nodding. "You're quite resourceful, Hamilton."

"That's what you're paying me for, but let's not start high-fiving yet. We're not in Tampa, and we'll have a bunch of killers looking for us when we get there."

CHAPTER 15

When the garage door opened and Danielle Tremblay's white Audi SUV backed out, The Greyhound was ready.

Arriving before sunrise, he had parked three blocks away from the quiet *Rue De Lampe* number nine, then braced the icy Canadian morning to wait outside the Tremblay residence. Wearing two thin jackets—to discard the outer layer after it got covered with blood splatter—he squatted behind the neatly trimmed hedge on the side of the house, trying to think about anything except what he was about to do. When the garage door rumbled, his stomach lurched with adrenaline and nervousness, his thoughts crashing back to the reality of his mission. He reached past the two layers, his gloved hand sliding to the shoulder holster that held his .22 caliber Smith & Wesson handgun.

The car's engine turned over and hummed. He exhaled slowly and slinked around to the driveway.

The weapon was scary-looking, with its long silencer. He confirmed that thought when he approached the car and held the gun to the window. Danielle Tremblay's jaw dropped and her eyes went wide as she leaned away from the stranger wearing a ski mask and holding a big gun.

His stomach jolted again. She had children; what if they were the ones to find her? There was a husband. Neighbors who thought they lived in a safe, quiet neighborhood.

Wincing, he forced all that from his mind. There was a job to do.

He squeezed the trigger.

The first muted blast put a dime-sized hole in the glass, coating the inside with red spray. The driver slumped over the center console of the Audi, her face to the ceiling, a red cavern in her forehead. The car rolled a few inches toward the street as The Greyhound tugged the door latch. Opening the door, he walked alongside and he pumped five more muffled shots into his victim's torso. When the car hit the stone mailbox, it came to a stop.

He stepped back, shaking the adrenaline out of his hands. Tucking the gun into its holster, he shut the car door and walked up the street to his vehicle, but not before leaving a message behind.

Stuffed in the victim's mouth, police would find a business card that read *Angelus Genetics*.

* * * * *

Harriman's phone rang as he drove to the station. He lifted it from the cup holder and read the screen. The fire marshal was up early. It wasn't even seven yet. That meant it probably wasn't good news.

He pressed the button and held the phone to his ear. "Mark Harriman."

"Officer, this is Harmon Crenny." The man spoke in a slow, deliberate cadence, giving his words a nearly pleasant delivery—if there hadn't been iron in every word.

"Yes, sir. What can I do for you?"

"I understand you are friends with a certain fella by the name of Hamilton *Dee-shear*, and he doesn't seem to like returning calls from my field investigators."

"Well, sir. It's just that . . . I believe Mr. DeShear is on a case, and apparently—"

"Apparently he's dodging us. This here is what's known as a courtesy call, officer, and it's the only one you gonna get, 'cause I'm telling you, this kinda stuff don't fly. Tampa Fire don't mess around when it comes to arson, y'hear? Now, I've been patient so far—your department and mine, needin' to play nice in the sand box with each other and all—but that time is over, so listen up."

"Yes, sir."

"I understand friendship, son, but this here is a serious matter. So I don't care if y'all are friends or cousins or if your momma knew his family way back when. If I don't hear from Hamilton DeShear in the next eight hours, I'm putting a warrant out for his arrest. And once I do, it might be a while before he sees the sky again. Am I making myself clear?"

"Yes, sir. I know you don't have any choice. I appreciate the call."

"Good. You're very welcome. You have a nice day now, officer." The fire marshal hung up.

Harriman sat at a red light and pounded his steering wheel. "Dammit, Hank, where are you?"

* * * * *

As the sun peeked over the privacy fence and through the trees behind it, Lanaya sipped her coffee and stared at a large, two story house. "Are you nervous to talk to her, Hamilton?"

He shook his head. "No. It's . . . this is just not the kind of story you want to show up with after not speaking for a while." He moved his eyes over his odd assortment of clothing. Sweatshirt, sweat pants, dress shoes. Unshowered, unshaven, bad breath. "Especially not looking like this."

"Forgive me for prying. Are you two not on good terms?"

"We are. We just . . . People drift apart." DeShear toyed with the coffee cup, turning it slowly in the cup holder. "My work and hers don't intersect much. We don't run in the same social circles anymore. She remarried, so . . ."

"I see," Lanaya whispered.

The home was impressive. The lawn looked freshly mowed—almost a formality this time of year in Florida—but most homeowners had their service continue mowing through the holidays to keep the weeds down. Not that this house had any weeds.

A corner of the swing set was visible from the street, and it needed a new coat of stain. That may have been the only thing on the property that wasn't in showcase condition.

DeShear ran his fingers back and forth over his lips and along the beard stubble on his chin, staring at the house.

"I think you misjudge your wife," Lanaya said. "She knows you and trusts you. I think she'll understand your current appearance."

"Yeah." DeShear pursed his lips. He sat forward and put his hand on the door latch. "Guess it's time to find out."

He opened his door and stepped out into the frosty morning air. The thought of explaining—what to say, what to not say—worried him. The story had a lot of moving parts, none terribly believable until the part where the shooting starts, and then Camilla would refer it over to the police.

Lanaya followed him up the driveway. He thought about asking her to wait in the car, but Camilla would see her eventually and he'd have to explain anyway.

On the porch, he pressed the cold, glowing doorbell with his thumb and leaned back, drumming his fingers on his thigh. Three muffled tones came from inside the house, melodic and regal, like distant church bells, or a deep, well-trained wind chime. DeShear looked down and smoothed his Georgia Bulldogs sweatshirt.

The entry wreath swung backwards as the big door opened.

Camilla was a pretty woman, and she was dressed well. Her charcoal gray suit hugged her curves without being unbusinesslike, and her hair and earrings were both a radiant shade of gold.

Her eyebrows furrowed. "Dash?" A half smile came to her face as she opened the door wider, cocking her head. "What are you doing he—"

Dash. DeShear's enjoyment at hearing her old nickname for him vanished when her gaze dropped to his attire.

"Oh, my goodness. Dash, what's happened? Have you been in some sort of wreck?"

He opened his mouth, shrugging. "It's a long story, very involved, but it's one that I need to discuss with you. I'm sorry for showing up like this. If there had been any other way—"

"It's nearly seven." She adjusted an earring. "I have to get to the office."

"I know. It's important, though. I'm in the middle of a complicated case and the IRS is going to want to be directly involved."

A man's voice came from behind her. "Darling, who's at the door?" Harper Madison III, assistant U. S. Attorney, appeared. Tall, thin, and just the right amount of gray at the temples to seem distinguished without simultaneously appearing elderly. He worked on the last adjustment of his necktie as he approached, then slid the silk knot neatly into place at the front of his starched white shirt collar.

Camilla stepped back. "Honey, you remember Dash."

"Yes." Madison's face was rigid. "I'm sorry, Hamilton, but it's a bit early for a social visit, isn't it?"

DeShear nodded. "It is. But this information involves your department, too. And the FBI. If I could just come in for a minute, I can explain."

"You know," Madison said. "The fire marshal's office called us. They were asking if we'd seen you. Something about arson on your apartment. So we're required to call them and tell them that you're here."

"Honey, that's not—"

"Mom, where is my language arts folder?" A girl came down the stairs. She wore a plaid skirt and a stiff burgundy Polo shirt embroidered with the crest of the exclusive Tampa Day School.

"Cassidy." Madison swept his hand toward the door. "Say hello to Mr. DeShear."

"Good morning, sir. I mean, good morning, *Hamilton*." She stood by her father and stared at DeShear's ill-fitting sweat pants. "Ew, what happened to you?"

Despite the awkwardness of the entire situation, her comment made DeShear laugh. "I got into some trouble, and you noticed." Putting his hands on his knees, he leaned forward and faced the young girl. "You're smart, like your mother. How old are you now? Eight?"

"Ten," she said.

"Ten? Wow. Almost all grown up."

Mr. Madison cleared his throat. "Again, Hamilton, it's a bit early . . ."

"I know, I know. I think I have some information that you need to hear, and the reason for my appearance is because we've been on the run from—" he glanced at the girl "—we've been *working on* some things that will interest both of you. But time is critical."

"Fine," the attorney said. "I'll call the fire marshal and you can discuss it with them. If there's anything they need me to hear, they can tell me."

"Actually, it's primarily an IRS matter." His eyes went to Camilla. "A multinational corporation with illegal funds. It'll fall under a RICO statute violation, but that's just for starters. There's intent to defraud shareholders, and probably a ton of undeclared income. But it'll require federal marshals and FBI."

Mr. Madison frowned, putting his hand on his wife's shoulder. "Darling, I'm due in court at eight-thirty."

Her eyes stayed on DeShear. "Let me listen to what they have to say." Camilla turned to her husband. "Then I'll take them to my office. You come by after your hearing."

Harper turned his chin up. "You sure?"

She patted his shoulder. "Drop off Cassidy on your way."

He grumbled, heading down the hallway.

Camilla stepped back from the door, sweeping her arm toward the living room. "Please, come in. And where are my manners?" She held her hand out to Lanaya. "I'm Dash's—Hamilton's—ex-wife, Camilla Madison."

DeShear let Lanaya pass him to enter the house. "This is my client, Lanaya Kim," he said.

The ladies shook hands. With her arm still holding the edge of the big door, Camilla looked at her ex-husband. The half-smile came back. "It's good to see you, Dash."

"Thanks, Cammy."

He ignored the butterflies in his stomach and stepped inside, the door easing shut behind him.

CHAPTER 16

Camilla got up from her living room sofa. "I don't know, Dash. It's pretty thin." Glancing at her watch, she walked to the hallway and plucked a set of keys from a large, baroque armoire. "Look, why don't you visit the fire marshal and get that situation cleared up, then we'll sit down again in a few days and see where everything is."

DeShear shook his head, rising. "Can't. That won't work. People shot at us in Atlanta. Her family's in hiding, for Pete's sake. The others on the list are in danger. Why won't you act on this?"

"It's not IRS jurisdiction. It's mostly overseas, and what isn't in Indonesia is a matter for the FBI and the police. I'll act on it. I'll refer it to the right agencies, and they'll move on it. But it's not really an IRS thing."

"But IRS is the key. Cammy, these guys did a lot of illegal stuff, but they did it to make money. It's not feasible to think none of that cash came back here. And when it did, they sure didn't declare it to the IRS and pay taxes on it. Even Al Capone didn't do that. All we have to do is show one dollar from that activity making its way back to the States, and we have the thread that unravels the sweater. Now, Lanaya has solid evidence of what activities occurred at the Arizona facility—"

"Ten years ago," Camilla said. "Or longer."

DeShear paced back and forth. "They're still doing it, and they're washing the money. So it's tax evasion or it's money laundering, or both, but that's IRS all the way. If you declare an emergency audit on a publicly traded company, they have to comply. Demand to see all assets, leak it to the press, and they'll have no choice. They'll have to take you to Indonesia to inspect—or watch their stock price plummet."

She folded her arms. "It's not that easy. It requires coordination with a lot of federal agencies."

"Which is what that Fast Fly team used to do, right? Storm into financial institutions without any warning and seize everything in a surprise raid? I seem to remember you going on a lot of those back when we were newlyweds. And when you leak the news about the audit, the killers will come out to take down the board members they haven't already gotten. You stuff a plane full of FBI agents and federal marshals dressed like auditors, and take them down to arm the Indonesian facility like it's Fort Knox. If the killers set one foot in the airport and buy a ticket to Indonesia, we have them on conspiracy. Lanaya doesn't think there are more than a dozen of them, so a platoon of federal marshals will have no trouble bagging the thugs the second they make their move. IRS will look like a hero and FBI will get a bunch of arrests. Everybody wins."

"Yeah, we could utilize the RICO statutes to get the ball rolling." Camilla twirled her keys, her gaze focused on a distant wall, but not really looking at it. "Between the potential IRS violations, the racketeering, and the conspiracy to commit murder, it makes a compelling case. The political arm will like it, and Fast Fly is good at making headlines."

DeShear leaned forward. "And who puts Fast Fly in motion?"

"IRS."

"Yeah, but who, specifically?"

"Bureau chiefs. I can ring the alarm and engage a Fast Fly team."

"Yes, you can." He grinned. "Cammy, please. I'm not going to embarrass you. I didn't burn my apartment down, and I'm not wrong about this. Do it, and put us on the audit team. Get me on site. I'll find out what they're up to."

She checked her watch again. "I'm not doing anything until I get some more details."

DeShear stepped back, chewing his lip.

She sighed. "Ride with me to my office and we'll talk on the way. I need to clear my schedule."

* * * * *

"Good morning." Camilla's assistant stood and handed her a stack of messages.

Camilla took a glimpse at the papers as she crossed the outer office area. She turned to Lanaya. "Ms. Kim, would you wait out here for a moment please? Tonia, would you get Ms. Kim some coffee?"

"Of course, Camilla." The assistant stood and walked down the hallway.

"Dash, would you join me in my office?"

DeShear nodded. "Sure."

The door shut behind him as his ex-wife went to her desk and sat. She placed her car keys on a folder on her desk, leafed through the messages, then picked up a pen and pointed it at him. "What kind of trouble are you really in?"

"None, really," DeShear said, shifting his weight on his feet. "Not the police kind, anyway. My client has shooters after her, and they burned down my place and shot at us in Atlanta. I fired back."

"Using what?"

"A gun I took off a guy who attacked us in the hotel. Then we—well, I—assaulted a cop and stole a car . . ."

She winced. "Who did you hit?"

"I didn't hit him. I grabbed the deputy's arm to take his radio, but that's technically assault. On the video it will look bad, and he'll say I assaulted him. Then . . . I disabled his patrol car and put it in a swamp. Oh, and the guns are probably stolen. I don't think the guys we took them from were really the above-board type."

Camilla closed her eyes and rubbed her temples. "Anything else?"

"That's about it."

"Well, it's good you aren't in any trouble." She tossed the pen to the desk. "What about the fire at your apartment?"

DeShear raised his hands. "I had nothing to do with that. I went to the gym and then had breakfast at Ihop, then I was with my client. That's all verifiable."

She leaned back and put her elbow on the arm of the chair, resting her chin in her hand. "Okay."

"So what I need is for you to arrest me."

"What?"

"Us. Arrest us." DeShear took a seat in one of the chairs in front of Camilla's desk. "Call a federal marshal from downstairs and arrest us, to be remanded into your custody. Then we'll be able to take care of business with you. The local jurisdictions don't supersede federal authority, so the Tampa fire marshal and the Tampa police, the Georgia deputy—none of them will be able to interfere with Lanaya and me unless you give the green light. Which you won't because I'm bringing this giant, promotion-getting case to you."

"Yeah, it's all for me. Thanks for making it so easy, too. The fire marshal and Tampa PD won't mind at all. Here's an idea. I think I'll get them over here and let them express their happiness to you in person before I take you out of their reach."

"That's a different way to go, but okay. They've all been leaving messages, anyway. But I was a little busy not getting killed to return their calls."

She sighed. "What about clothes?" Camilla pointed to his sweatshirt. "You can't help run a task force meeting looking like that. I'd say you look like you slept in that gear, except you don't look like you've slept."

DeShear rubbed the beard stubble on his chin. "No, it's been a while. But my place burned, so . . . we have some cash, though. We can buy some clothes. If we make a list, can somebody run to the mall for us? I mean, since it's not really safe for us to be on the street."

"I guess so. We've done stranger things. I'll send an agent."

He eyed the keys on her desk. "Would a federal marshal object to escorting us to your place so we can grab a shower?"

She frowned, sliding the keys to him. "Anything else? Want a pizza?"

DeShear stood. "We should contact the owner of the stolen car in front of your house. The license tag on the vehicle isn't his, but they can track him down from the VIN number. And there are two stolen guns under the front seat. I think that's it. Oh, no, there's another stolen car in Gainesville."

She glared at him.

"Yeah, that's it. Have I told you how pretty your eyes are?"

She spun around in the chair to face the wall and a stack of folders piled high in front of a mirror. "Go. Get coffee, food, a shower. Then get back here. We have a big meeting to put together."

He nodded. "Thanks, Cammy."

As he moved to the door, he glanced back. Camilla had leaned forward to the mirror and lifted her chin, gazing at her reflection's eyes.

DeShear smiled. "See?"

She looked at him in the mirror. "Go!"

CHAPTER 17

The Greyhound held a brochure in his hand as he stared out the penthouse window. Clouds of morning mist lifted and floated over the churning waters of Niagara Falls, the rocks around the basin white with a thick coat of ice. The railings of the observation deck were white with ice, too, like an artists' sketch that had run out of colors. Only a few people ventured out into the cold and past the wire Christmas trees to enjoy the view.

According to the brochure, the falls were to be bathed in colorful lights each night, and on New Year's Eve there'd be fireworks as well.

"The view from anywhere in this hotel should be beautiful." He tossed the pamphlet to the desk. "It'd be nice to use that to make a statement, somehow. Maybe throw Dr. Graff over the falls at the stroke of midnight. Maybe throw a few other board members from Angelus Genetics over, too. Really make a splash, so to speak."

As Maya readied her equipment, Dominique tied a length of rubber band to his arm.

"Why do you hate them so much?" Maya asked.

"I don't hate them." He tossed the brochure into the trash can and pushed himself back on the large bed. "I'm fine."

Dominique leaned in, lowering her voice. "You're not fine."

"Okay, have it your way. I'm not fine. I'll never be fine again, and I don't want to be. I hate what these people have done." He yanked the tourniquet off his arm and stormed to the window. "I had everything. A great job as a hedge fund manager, flying all over the world trading equities. Boats, cars, houses. A beautiful young family."

Britt and Maya stopped what they were doing, watching.

"I'd like to think I'm not motivated by hate, though, Maya. Some people might even say I'm being generous by not dragging this out somehow and hurting the people from Angelus the way they hurt others." His eyes narrowed. "They bred us like cattle or dogs, selecting the attributes they wanted to advance without worrying about what other latent characteristics might tag along. And the poor pups that didn't fit the bill? Oh, they were discarded like trash. Snuffed out, without a thought. Did you know, they even referred to us as dogs? It's in the records I discovered. Dogs! That's what we were to them."

Dominique stood in silence next to the transfusion equipment that awaited its patient.

"They called the alpha group Airedales. The betas were Bassets." He stared out the window. "And my group, the Gammas, we were Greyhounds." His voice softened, his thoughts elsewhere. "I think referring to us as something other than human made the byproducts of their research more palatable for them. The Nazis did the same thing. Ironic, for a company named Angelus—'Angel'—don't you think?"

The Greyhound turned to face his confederates, scowling. "But if people hate them, it's deserved. They earned it. Genetic changes don't just affect the subject. It's passed on. I watched so many die a slow, painful death because of what these monsters did. Then one day, my own children—one after the other, they'd fade and start their decline. As soon as we buried one, the next would get sick, like the Grim Reaper was taking turns as part of a sick game, to torture us."

His gaze fell to the floor. "After our youngest passed away, Megan was overwhelmed with grief and depression. Just overwhelmed. There's no word for that kind of pain. We tried to work through it. We saw counsellors. You eventually try to live life again, but you never really do. During my next business trip, she called me in tears. She said she couldn't stand the pain, that all she could feel was darkness inside, and that each breath hurt to take." He lifted his eyes to Dominique. They were brimming with tears. "I understood. I felt it, too." The Greyhound swallowed hard, his voice a whisper. "Then she hung up and cut her arms open from the elbow to the wrist."

He closed his eyes and leaned against the window frame, the palatial suite in front of him and the massive waterfall churning behind him. "Angelus took everything from me. From me and a lot of others. I was able to build a new life for myself, but a lot of others—innocent people, children—they suffered and died for no reason other than for Angelus Genetics' bottom line." He clenched his teeth. "If evil has a face, it smiles from the board room of Angelus Genetics, in the body of Dr. Marcus Hauser. And as long as there's breath in my body, I'll keep fighting to stop them."

He stood, stepping to the bed, but stumbled.

"Doctor Carerra!" Britt ran forward, grabbing The Greyhound's arm as he slumped to the floor.

Dominique went to him, cradling his head in her hands. "Tristan?" He didn't respond. She glanced at Maya. "Help us get him to the bed."

"Yes, Doctor," Maya said. She grabbed one arm as Dominique held the other. Britt took hold of the legs, and they hoisted their unconscious patient onto the mattress.

Dominique leaned over him, gently lifting his eyelid and shining her pen light into his eye. "We need to start the transfusion, stat." After checking the other eye, she went to the centrifuge and turned it on. "Maya, get your meds ready. Britt, bring more units of whole blood up from the van."

He jumped up. "Yes, Doctor."

Dominique pulled another rubber swatch from the box and slipped it over Tristan's arm. "We have to act fast or we could lose him."

CHAPTER 18

DeShear strolled past Camilla's Christmas tree and into the kitchen. A large, muscular man with a square jaw and a crew cut followed him, wearing a khaki t-shirt that read "Federal Marshal" across the front. His camouflage fatigue pants appeared to have been recently ironed, and his face was unwavering and stern.

DeShear pulled the coffee maker forward on the counter. "Officer, would you like some coffee?"

"I would not." He spit the words out like they tasted bad in his mouth.

"What about your fellow marshal?"

The officer straightened up and flexed his shoulders. "I'm sure neither I nor officer Vulpes wish to have any coffee with you or the other asset currently in our custody. Let's not dawdle. Ms. Madison wants us back at her office asap."

"Can't go anywhere without clothes, my friend. When they get here, we'll shower and dress as quickly as possible." DeShear opened the coffee. "But I can't get over feeling I must have wronged you somehow."

"Let's just say I don't appreciate escorting a felon around, and that I'd prefer our other hard-working officers take care of the proper business of the federal marshal's agency rather than be sent on a shopping trip to the mall."

It was too much to unscramble to someone who didn't seem to have an interest in the truth, so DeShear let it slide with an "I see." Hopefully, within an hour they'd part ways, never to see each other again.

"I'll have a cup." A large, muscular, female federal marshal walked into the kitchen. "Thank you."

DeShear looked at the officer with the crew cut, then called out to the living room. "Lanaya, coffee?"

"Are you making some, Hamilton? Are you sure that's allowed?"

He gathered cups from the cabinet. "I think Cammy will understand the intrusion. We can only watch so much TV while we wait."

"Then, yes, I'd like some very much."

DeShear pressed a button on the front of the machine. With a beep, it came to life. "There we go."

In the hallway, the doorbell rang with its elegant chimes. DeShear wagged his finger and grinned at the crew cut marshal. "Did you order a pizza?"

Frowning, the marshal headed to the door. He returned a moment later, following a third marshal holding several colorful paper shopping bags and a long plastic dress bag. "Merry Christmas," she said. "Your clothes are here."

Lanaya took the dress bag from her. "Thank goodness."

Taking the remaining bags, DeShear moved past the other marshal. "Let's do this again soon."

Following Lanaya down the hall to the master bedroom, DeShear emptied a bag onto the bed. "Pretty sure whatever's in that dress bag is for you. These men's pants are probably for me." He sifted through the garment packages. The next bag contained ladies' underwear. "Oops. This bag is probably yours. In fact," he glanced at the door. "I'm going to . . . if you want to go through the bags and pull out the men's clothes, I'll wait outside."

"Oh, nonsense," Lanaya said, dumping a bag onto the bed. "You were married. I'm sure there's nothing in here you haven't seen before."

"No, but it's rare to know my clients' underwear choices."

"I see. Rare, but not completely unknown, then."

"I, um. I . . ."

"Why, Hamilton, I believe I've made you blush." She leaned over the bed and rummaged through the bags, handing him items. "These would be yours. Here are socks and a belt. Here's another, a shirt. That looks to be about it." She stood up straight. "If you'll use the bedroom upstairs to dress, I'll see you in the living room in ten."

"Sounds good." He stepped into the hallway, then stopped. "Lanaya, there's one more thing."He turned to face her, putting his hand on the door frame. "I'll ask you this once, and whatever you say, goes—I won't bother you with it again. You've gotten your family to a safe place. I don't need to know where it is, but from what I've seen, you're pretty good at that. If we're successful in drawing the killers to Indonesia, that takes them away from your family, but it puts them in proximity to you. It's very brave, but it's also very dangerous. It puts you at risk, and I don't want you to get hurt." He shrugged, smiling. "I've kind of grown fond of you."

A smile crept across Lanaya's lips as well. "Possibly, you've merely grown fond of my money."

"You said you didn't have a lot of money."

"I don't."

"Guess that's not it, then." DeShear locked onto her eyes, his face serious. "I'm just saying, you don't have to do this. The people we've involved now, they're professionals. They can handle everything from here. If you don't like the odds, say the word and you can be out—no questions asked. You can watch it all from the sidelines and no one will think less of you. Tricking killers to come after us, that's a risky game, and there are no do-overs."

She folded her hands in front of her, looking down. "Hamilton, people are fond of saying that humans and dolphins share ninety-seven percent of the same DNA. Some say dolphins and humans are closely related—even though our most recent common ancestor died ninety-five million years ago. Humans and chimps share ninety-eight percent of the same DNA, but we can talk and they can climb trees with their feet." She lifted her gaze and stared out the window. "The science of genetics is a journey into an amazing, powerful world, and it has fascinated me since I was a child, because it's the little things in genetics that make *all* the difference." Her eyes met his. "We share a high percentage of DNA with fuzzy animals and cute sea creatures, but we share 100% of the same DNA as mass murderers like Jeffrey Dahmer, the Son of Sam, and Adolph Hitler. That's reality. When we bring a gene forward, who knows what things are brought with it? Given another roll of the dice, with the wrong environment and a little neglect, those things could create a group of Charles Mansons instead of Mother Theresas. I took part in what happened at Angelus. It may have been an unknowing role, but that doesn't change the end result. A long time ago, I decided I wouldn't sit by and let others do what I considered to be my responsibility. I need to try to correct what I am responsible for."

"Can't talk you out of it, huh?"

"I called you, remember? If I was able to be talked out of it, I'd have never started into any of this. Besides, we may be headed to Indonesia, but the destination is a genetics lab. That's *my* turf."

* * * * *

"Thank you for coming." Camilla shook the hand of fire marshal Harmon Crenny and a lieutenant from the Tampa police force; then she greeted Mark Harriman. "Please, sit down. We'll be starting soon."

Harriman took a seat, leaning forward to whisper to his host. "Is Hank here, Cammy? I'd like to see him as soon as possible."

"So would I," grumbled the fire marshal.

"I know you all have business with Mr. DeShear, and you'll speak with him soon." Camilla sat, looking at the small group assembled in front of her. "But he is a principal source in an IRS matter that we are exploring, and it is of the utmost urgency. I'll ask that you respect federal-state-county hierarchy and let us maintain him as our resource until the matter is closed. That said, I will let him speak with you, and he should be here any—well, speak of the devil." She stood. "Here he is now."

DeShear strutted forth, in clean clothes and a necktie, leading a little parade of federal marshals, an IRS agent, and his client. He smiled as he approached Camilla's group. "Remain seated, everyone."

Harriman jumped to his feet, frowning. "Why haven't you returned my phone calls?"

"Sorry, buddy." DeShear clapped him on the shoulder. "Had to power my phone down to keep some killers from, well, killing us."

The federal marshal with the crew cut approached Camilla. "Ms. Madison, will you have any further need of us?"

She nodded. "Stay close. It's a secure building, but we'll be assembling the task force and possibly leaving quickly. Coordinate with your sergeant, and be ready."

"Yes, ma'am."

The fire marshal growled at Deshear. "Don't think some fancy footwork by your ex-wife will save your butt from arson charges, son. They're on my desk, signed and ready to go."

DeShear swallowed and looked at Camilla. "Not while I'm working for the feds, right?"

"Maybe not." Crenny scowled. "But the minute they're done with you, I take you away—in handcuffs. And that'll be sooner than you think."

Camilla raised her hands like a traffic cop. "I'm sure there's no need for—"

"What the . . ." Harriman stared at Lanaya, his jaw hanging open. "It's you."

Lanaya backed away, her face a puzzle.

"You okay, there, Mark?" DeShear said.

Harriman whipped around to him. "What are you up to?" he hissed.

"I guess our pictures finally got around from the park shooting and the other stuff. It's all—"

"Other stuff?"

"It's nothing." DeShear shrugged. "Well, it's not nothing, but it's a self-defense shooting. We were completely in the right, we just didn't have time to stay and clear it up. But we will. Promise. That's all gonna go away."

"But . . ." Harriman glanced at Camilla, then back to DeShear. "We need to talk. Now. In private."

"Can it wait until after the meeting?" Camilla asked, taking a glimpse at a wall clock.

Harriman grabbed DeShear by the arm. "I don't think so, Cammy. Can I use your office for a minute?"

"We're waiting for a link up to Washington. I'd prefer we don't keep the vice president waiting."

"The vice president?" DeShear said. "Holy cow."

"Yeah, you said some of the right buzz words." Camilla stood, pointing to the clock. "Genetics and money laundering had the director's eyes glazing over, but when I said human trafficking, that lit him on fire. That's a hot button for the vice president, and that got us a big green light for our official inquiry."

Official inquiry was a coded term for what the IRS asked for right before one of its raids. The board of directors of the company in question would turn their noses up at an official inquiry, getting some blustering lawyer to request a postponement, then the Fast Fly team would kick down the doors, having already been staged. The IRS investigators seized everything, in every location, while the executives at the home office peed down their legs. Camilla had delivered.

"Money laundering? Human trafficking?" Fire marshal Crenny narrowed his eyes. "DeShear, what kinds of seedy crap y'all involved in, son?"

"Not him, sir," Camilla said. "The people he's been reporting to us about."

"Reporting?" Crenny echoed, pounding the arm of his chair. *"Reporting?"*

"Yes," Camilla nodded. "We're using Mr. DeShear and his client as informants."

"How long has that—"

"Would everyone like to join me in the conference area?" She walked away from the fire marshal and pointed to a large glass room with a long table centered in it. "The vice president will be on the video call with the director."

"We'll be right there." Red-faced, Harriman dragged DeShear into Camilla's office and shut the door.

"What's up with you?" DeShear said, shaking his arm from his friend's grip. "I know I didn't call the fire investigators back, and that was wrong of me. But like I said, the bad guys were shooting in my direction at the time."

"Did you open the emails I sent you?" Harriman put his hands on his hips, shaking his head and staring at the floor. His face remained red. "On your phone or anywhere?"

"No. I powered down, and we've been on the run."

"I sent you an image of the arsonist." Harriman put his hand to his temple. "You didn't check it?"

"Not yet. Why?"

"I've got some bad news for you, then." Harriman stared at Camilla's group as they crossed the lobby and filed into the conference room. He pointed to Lanaya. "The arsonist in the picture is your client."

CHAPTER 19

The motel door burst open, its wooden frame splintering as its door knob shot across the floor. Jim Clayman leaped off the bed, racing for the gun laying on the tiny desk.

"Don't try it." Two men and a woman charged through the broken door. The closest intruder, sporting a shaved head and a dark brown goatee, spoke first. "There are more of us than there are of you, and we're better armed."

Clayman stared at the intruders. They stood side by side, each pointing a large gun at him. Two said nothing, just kept their guns aimed at his head.

He slowly sat back down onto the bed.

"You called your employer and said you were out," the man with the goatee said. "He says you're not."

"What?" Clayman said.

"You said the situation in Centennial Park was amateur hour. Well, now he's hired some professionals, and we say you're not out until the boss says the job is done. Is that understood?"

Staring at the three large guns pointed at him, Clayman nodded.

"You didn't do your job, little bird dog. You were supposed to keep eyes on the targets, and you ran away instead. That's amateur. So now you're going to come with us and make things right."

Clayman swallowed hard. "How?"

"We'll explain in the car. Let's go."

"Who are you?"

"Oh, you think you're in a position to ask us questions, huh? Okay. I'm Elvis Presley." He pointed to the others. "That's Janet Jackson on the left, and the other one is George Michael." Elvis raised his gun and smashed it into Clayman cheek, sending the hostage's head back. "Any other stupid questions?"

Clayman gasped, putting a hand to his face. Blood covered his fingers.

Elvis leaned in close, raising his voice. "I asked you a question. I expect you to answer me. Do you have any more questions of any kind, at this time, for myself or my associates?"

Clayman flinched. "No."

"Then let's go." Elvis stepped back and gave him a big grin. "We have a car in the parking lot. Walk to it quickly and quietly. Don't say a word. If you try anything funny—or anything at all—we'll shoot you to death right there in the parking lot. Don't think we won't." Elvis waved his gun at the door. "You'll disappear like your targets did, but you won't be on your feet."

He grabbed Clayman by the collar and hoisted him up. "When the big boss pays you to do a job, you do the job. You don't call him and say you quit. The big boss decides when you're done working for him. Understand?"

"Yeah."

Elvis drew back and cracked Clayman with the gun again. "You say 'yes sir' when you're talking to me."

Clayman howled in pain, blood dripping from his mouth and other cheek. "Yes, sir!"

Gritting his teeth, Elvis put his nose to Clayman's, whispering. "I'm about three seconds from putting a couple of rounds into your chest and two in the back of your head. So smarten up, little bird dog." He spaced his next words for emphasis. "You're . . . not . . . calling . . . the shots."

With Janet Jackson holding one arm and George Michael holding the other, they crossed the parking lot toward a gray sedan. As they neared it, Elvis dug in his pocket and pulled out a key fob. The car lights flickered and the trunk popped open.

"No!" Clayman kicked and twisted. "No! No!"

Elvis stopped and turned to face the hostage, shaking his head. "Some people just don't listen." He gripped his gun and brought the butt down on the back of Clayman's skull. The hostage sagged in the arms of his escorts.

* * * * *

DeShear stormed into the conference room, with Harriman following him. Camilla and her assistant were tinkering with the A/V projector.

Around the large conference table sat the police lieutenant, the fire marshal, several IRS agents, and representatives from the FBI and the federal marshal service.

"I need to borrow my client for a minute," DeShear said, walking up to Lanaya and pulling back her chair. She stood, her jaw hanging open.

"Will you quit screwing around?" Camilla said. "The meeting's about to start!"

A blue image appeared on the left half of the wall screen, displaying the seal of the Vice President of the United States. The right side flashed the words, "connecting," and then went to an image of several people sitting around a small table, the IRS Directors logo on the wall behind them. A woman's voice came over the monitor. "Bureau Chief Madison, we now have you connected with Director Fleming. Please hold for the Vice President."

DeShear and Lanaya headed into the lobby.

"Dash! What are you doing?" Camilla called after them.

The conference door swung shut. DeShear walked briskly, his hand at the middle of Lanaya's back.

"Hamilton, I do not appreciate being manhandled." She took his hand and pushed it away. "Please."

He kept walking. "Stay quiet and get in here."

Entering Camilla's office, he pushed the door closed and turned to his client. "I'm going to ask you one time, and then I turn you over to the fire marshal and Harriman. What did you do?"

"What? What do you mean?"

"You know what I mean! My apartment. The fire. No more lies. Out with it."

"I do not appreciate—"

"Enough!" He pressed his hands against the sides of his head, pacing back and forth in the office. "They have pictures, Lanaya. Images of you walking around my apartment building ten minutes before the whole place went up in flames. The neighbor in the next building identified you. She knows me. She saw you go into my unit right before the fire."

Lanaya stood rigid. "Whatever the authorities have, I assure you, they do not have pictures of me."

"What, it's your evil twin sister? It's you! You're wearing the same running shoes."

"If you check, you will see those are a very popular brand and style. Over three hundred pairs were sold in the greater Tampa Bay area this year."

"Stop!" His cheeks grew hot. "Just tell me why. They wanna hang this on me. They think I conspired with you. And in a few minutes, when Camilla's meeting is over, those two guys—the fire marshall and the police lieutenant—they're gonna talk to Harriman, who will mention the uncanny resemblance you have to their suspect. Then one of us is going to jail. Well, it's not going to be me, sister. I didn't burn my place and I sure didn't conspire to have it burned. Everything I had was in there. But you—you probably waited for me to leave, and then—"

"Arson is a very serious matter." Lanaya's tone was calm and even. "Frankly, I'm offended you think I'm capable of such a thing. I'm certain they ensured everyone was out of the building first—whoever the arsonist was."

DeShear shook his head. "You did it, didn't you?"

"As I said previously, no, I didn't do it."

"Okay, so some random woman who just happens to be your height and build and hair color, and with the same facial features and the same running shoes, comes by my place when you just happen to be in town, and she—she just wanders by, and—"

Lanaya looked directly into his eyes. "Would you have believed me?"

"What? Believed what?"

She kept her eyes locked on his, her voice falling to a whisper. "My case. The links between the deaths, the Propofol. Would you have believed me if you hadn't seen for yourself what these people were capable of?"

"I—I already said yes to meeting you when—"

"You wanted to turn it over to the police, as I recall. You said so several times in our meeting. You humored me for the large fee I offered, but it wasn't until you saw your own self in danger that you really signed on."

He shook his head. "That's not true, and don't try to turn this around."

"Turn what? Those were real bullets they shot at us in Atlanta. Did I stage that, too?"

"Atlanta was real, but . . ."

"And the murders. Those were real. Or did I kill Dr. Braunheiser and Emmet Kincaid and Nilla

Cunde and a dozen other people? Wake up. This is all real. People are dying. And whoever burned your place, they saved your life."

"How in the world do you figure that?"

She proceeded to the window that looked into the lobby, toying with the cord that controlled the blinds. "Were they only shooting at me in Atlanta? They shot at you, too. I said we were linked, and we are. Atlanta proved that. If someone burned your place to get you away from it, they did you a favor—whoever it was. And any conscientious person would ensure there were no people remaining in the building first."

"It's—Lanaya, this is a big deal. This—that fire marshal is gonna string you up, and me right along with you. They play for keeps."

"Then let them!" She turned to him. "The killers play for keeps, too. We learned that in Atlanta, when they killed several innocent people simply to get to us. I play for keeps as well. I'm in this thing, and I'm staying in. If someone who looks like me burned down your apartment, let the police and fire marshal do their jobs. They'll see Lanaya Kim was nowhere near Tampa until her flight came in an hour before our meeting. There wasn't enough time to get there, do what they propose, and still get to the meeting."

"Lanaya . . ."

"Hamilton, I will not keep repeating myself. It's decision time. The cards are dealt." She pointed to the glass conference room. "Your ex-wife has the Vice President on the phone to send a squad of auditors and armed personnel overseas to deal with a situation that twenty-four hours ago they didn't even know existed."

"I'm sorry." He looked down. "I think this might change things."

"Does it?" She went to him. "The fire marshal and police are ready to arrest the woman in the picture, and yet they've subordinated their interests for the bigger cause—a cause that needs your help. I certainly can't do this without you. But I'll respect your decision. You must be true to your own sense of what's right."

He stared at her, chewing his lip.

"Hamilton, you might be a private investigator right now, but you weren't always, and it's not your true calling. A blind man could see it, but somehow you can't. You're destined to be a hero and save lives—through whatever format fate chooses to manifest it—but make no mistake, that is your true calling. It's your nature to stand up to the bad in the world, and that will always drive you, no matter what your job title is. And that's who I need with me for this."

She looked to the window. Camilla's assistant walked across the lobby toward them. "Now, unless I miss my guess, that nice young woman is coming over here to tell us to return to the conference room. What are you going to do?"

* * * * *

Arriving at the site they'd settled on earlier—a small clearing at the end of a long dirt road—Elvis and his associates went about the second part of their interrogation. Janet Jackson opened the trunk and snapped a tube of smelling salts in half, holding it under the nose of their hostage. Clayman's head jerked, then jerked again as he struggled to avoid inhaling the pungent fumes that brought him back to consciousness.

"Told you," Janet Jackson said, leaning on the side of the car. "We should have clipped this goofball in the hotel room."

"When you're right, you're right." Elvis nodded, sighing. "Okay, let's get to it. We have a conversation to finish."

Janet and George grabbed Clayman by the arms and hauled him from the trunk. Dragging him around to the front of the car, the headlights would allow for additional illumination until the rising sun cut fully through the thick trees overhead. Clayman's eyes rolled around for a moment, then he gagged and vomited down the front of his shirt.

Beyond the car, a lone cricket chirped in the chilly swamp.

Elvis grabbed Clayman by the hair and held his face up. "Time to come clean, little bird doggy. Your targets got away. You had a gun. Did you use your weapon?"

"I, uh . . ."

Elvis raised his gun and fired a shot into Clayman's shoulder. The burst splattered red onto Clayman's face and neck as he screamed in pain. He grabbed his shoulder and doubled over, pulling free of the grip of the men who held him. He rolled on the swampy ground, wet leaves sticking to his back and face.

"Pay attention," Elvis said, grabbing his victim and setting him upright. "Are you awake now, bird dog? This is not the time for stalling. It's a simple question, so you should be able to answer fast and without deliberation. What happened to your weapon?"

"The guy took it from me!" Clayman whimpered, blood spilling from his hand as he gripped his shoulder. "The guy with the scientist."

"He hit you?"

"He, he . . ."

The second shot went past Clayman's ear, clipping the lobe. A patch of dirt splattered a few feet behind him when the bullet hit it. Clayman shrieked, slapping a hand over his ear.

"Gotta work on your aim, Elvis." George chuckled.

Elvis glared at George. "Shut up." Turning his focus back to Clayman, Elvis grabbed his victim's hair again and wrenched his head back. "Again, did he hit you?"

"No!"

"How did he get your gun?"

Clayman groaned, blood dropping through his fingers. "He surprised me and took it."

Cocking the gun, Elvis put it to Clayman's head. "I'm not hearing the 'how' part. How did you, a guy with a gun who was hired to watch the hallway, end up getting disarmed and letting the targets get away—but no shots were fired and there ain't a mark on you?"

"He—he sucker punched me. Hit me in the gut!"

"Nope." Elvis shook his head and stepped back, firing a round into Clayman's thigh. "Wrong answer."

Clayman rolled over onto the muddy ground again, holding his bleeding leg and crying in agony.

"I think you're smart enough to know, this night only gets worse for you, little bird dog. See, you let your partner get attacked, but he got a concussion, so I can see why they got his gun. The waiter routine was lame, but whatever. It could have worked if there'd been competent people involved, but it's done now. The gunman in the hallway, though, that scene doesn't add up to me. Did the targets pay you off?"

"No."

"Did they threaten your family?"

"No. I don't have a family."

"Good thing. I'd hate to have to break the bad news to them that their stupid, screw up, cowardly son and-or father and-or brother died in a swamp after disgracing himself." He raised the gun again.

"No!" Clayman raised his hands to stop the bullets, turning his face away. "No! No!"

The two blasts from Elvis' gun lit up the darkness in the swamp, like flash photography at a wedding reception. Chunks of red and tufts of hair splattered onto the wet oak leaves. Clayman splashed face-first onto the muddy edge of the swamp.

"Toss him in deeper." Elvis tucked the gun into his belt. "So the gators will find him."

"There's no gators eating in weather this cold," George said.

"Just get him in the water, George," Elvis growled. "Or they'll find two bodies."

George hustled over to the body and dragged it through the muck.

Janet pulled the tarp from the trunk of the car, balling it up and tossing it into the murky swamp. "What now?"

"Now," Elvis glanced at his watch. "We go tell the big boss at Angelus that we tied up his second loose end from the Peachtree Plaza hotel, discuss a fee to eliminate this scientist lady and her friend, and then get rid of this Greyhound joker."

George waded out of the swamp, slapping mud from his hands. "By now the scientist is long gone from Georgia. They're either in Florida or Minnesota."

"And The Greyhound will be coming after them soon, if he's not already." Janet turned to Elvis. "It's awful cold in Minnesota this time of year."

"Yeah, it is." Elvis spun the key ring on his finger as he walked to the car. "So I guess we'll start in Florida."

CHAPTER 20

Camilla's assistant was cordial but firm. "I'm sorry to interrupt, but Ms. Madison requests your presence in the conference room."

"Okay." DeShear sat on the edge of the desk, rubbing his chin. "We'll be there in a second."

"She'd like you to report now." A smile tugged at the young lady's lips. "I believe her exact words were, 'If he resists, I'll have the federal marshals shoot him and drag him to my meeting.'"

"Okay, let's go." DeShear stood. "That crew cut guy would probably do it."

Most of the meeting went faster than DeShear expected. The Vice President was on and off in less than five minutes, asking to be kept up on the situation as things unfolded. The FBI and CIA asked very few questions, as did the federal marshal service. The Director of the IRS seemed to take it all in stride, as though this sort of thing happened every day.

The one person sweating bullets was Camilla—or she would have, if she were the type to sweat. Her poker face was *par excellence,* but keeping her hands under the table while she capped and uncapped her pen, that had been her "tell" going back more than two dozen years.

DeShear was glad he still knew her well enough to catch it. No doubt his pre-meeting antics had caused some of that stress, but it was now a lose-lose proposition to say anything about Lanaya's arsonist activities to anyone.

He studied his client.

Do I believe her?

He was still tossing around his options when the person next to him stood and pushed in her chair. Others did the same. The wall screen went dark, and people filed out of the conference room. Cammy stood and gathered her notes.

Only Lanaya and DeShear remained seated, each staring silently across the table at the other. Her gaze appeared hopeful. His, he knew, did not.

"Seems like you two have some unfinished business," Camilla said as she headed toward the door. "You can have the room for a few minutes, but we'll be moving quickly now. Be ready to get in one of our vehicles and head to the airport on my signal."

"Gotcha." DeShear kept his eyes on his client. "I'll be ready."

Lanaya thanked Camilla for the clothing and the hospitality, then turned back to DeShear. She said nothing. The door clicked closed behind Camilla.

DeShear cleared his throat. "I'm not sure what happened at my place . . ."

"You know," Lanaya said. "When I said I had a friend who looked similar enough to me that I could travel using her ID, you didn't question it. Is it not much more likely that the people who are chasing us—who were only chasing me until I came to Tampa—that they found a similar-looking woman to be seen lurking around your apartment?"

"Why not kill me when I was inside, asleep?"

"You weren't the target then," Lanaya said. "I was. But they could definitely send a message once you agreed to meet me. To scare you away from the case. As it happens, you're the type who doesn't back down in the face of a bully. They misjudged you in that. And me."

DeShear shook his head. "I don't know . . ."

"Maybe there were too many people around that night, and the arsonist feared being spotted. Or they couldn't get their lookalike to your apartment until the next morning. Does it matter? We still end up here, with the IRS getting ready to raid a genetics facility in Indonesia." She lowered her voice. "And me, wondering what you're going to do."

He folded his arms. Across the lobby, Camilla exited her office, shoving an earpiece under her hair and crossing the lobby toward the conference room.

Lanaya leaned forward. "Hamilton—"

"I don't think you're the arson type." He got up from his chair. "You're too nervous. You'd have been a wreck if you burned my place and then went back with me. And even if I didn't believe you, if the fire marshal and police can subjugate their concerns for the greater good, who am I to question it?"

Lanaya smiled. "Thank you, Hamilton."

The conference room door banged open. "They will serve demand letters on Angelus Genetics tonight at 4:55 P. M." Camilla raised her sleeve to her face, cupping a small microphone in her palm. "Ready all units, we are go. We need to be rolling in ten minutes. Reply with your affirmative and meet me downstairs in the parking lot. The transports are assembling now."

* * * * *

When the police cruiser turned south onto Bayshore Boulevard and the convoy of Chevy Suburbans followed, DeShear spoke up. "This isn't the way to Tampa International Airport."

"That's because we are headed to the MacDill Air Force Base airport," Camilla replied from the front passenger seat. "We're going to hop on a couple of Cessna Citation X's, and get our butts to the rally point before anyone even knows we're gone."

"We're flying in Cessnas? Aren't those a little . . ." He frowned, holding his hands close together.

"Don't think single engine prop plane." She held her hands far apart. "Think private jets of the rich and famous—and drug runners. Those babies can reach speeds close to Mach one, and have been refitted to carry twenty passengers."

The Suburban swerved to pass a slower vehicle, the flashing blue lights of the squad car in front of them leading the way. Cars eased to the right lane as the convoy passed. DeShear grabbed the handle over the window to steady himself when the big vehicle bounced around. "What are the planes refitted from?"

Camilla waved a hand. "We just add seats. Drug dealers like to travel in comfort and style. We can confiscate any asset used in a drug deal, including a forty-million-dollar private jet."

"And you get to keep them?"

"Yeah." She adjusted her sunglasses. "The IRS gets to do all kinds of stuff nobody knows about. Flying from MacDill allows fewer eyeballs on us as we depart, too. Hold on." She lifted the hand mic to her face. "All units, this is Bureau Chief Madison. We have approval to enter the base through the Bayshore Gate. Our escort will meet us there and take us to the airfield. We are cleared for immediate departure."

"It's over ten thousand miles to the Indonesia facility," Lanaya said.

"On these planes, it'll go by in about ten hours," Camilla said. "Including pit stops in San Diego and Hawaii. The bulk of the agents and marshals are following in a KC-135, but we'll have the recon team with us."

DeShear nodded. "How many people are we bringing?"

"I can't discuss operational details, but let's say it's enough to get the job done. Twice, probably. But it's a coordinated raid. Everybody storms the Bastille at zero hour, eastern standard time." Camilla rubbed her hands together. "Those executives will be having heart attacks when they start getting phone calls about IRS agents busting into every facility they own all over the world." She reached into the black canvas bag at her feet and pulled out a holstered gun, placing it in her lap. "Man, I love my job."

CHAPTER 21

The relatively small size of the jet, as compared to normal airline jets, belied its prowess. The Cessna Citation X had a sleek exterior and a luxurious interior. Premium leather was in abundance, and the row of bench seats the IRS installed allowed for nearly double the number of passengers the plane originally held.

"I don't know if it's worth forty million dollars," DeShear said as he moved to the rear of the cabin and took a seat. "But it's impressing the heck out of me right now."

Lanaya made her way down the aisle, sitting next to DeShear. She spoke loud enough for the other passengers to hear. "I hate to ask, but may I borrow a computer—and does anyone know if this plane gets wifi? It's been a while since I checked in."

At the front of the plane, Camilla greeted the FBI and IRS agents as they boarded, handing each an "Indonesian cheat sheet"—simple, common phrases and their translations. "We have secure wifi access," she said to DeShear, "and I can lend you an IRS laptop. The next meal opportunity is North Island Naval Air Station in San Diego."

The agents passed back some protein bars. DeShear held up one of the slender green packages. "You guys really come prepared."

"It's a ten-hour flight." Camilla said. "It pays to not have people getting stir crazy in such a small space. Try to learn some Indonesian phrases."

Sliding down in his seat, DeShear reviewed the cheat sheet. "Is napping allowed?"

"It's encouraged." She patted the last agent on the back as he entered the plane, then took a step onto the stairs at the door. "Everybody, strap in. We'll be wheels up as soon as I go thank the General for the use of his runway."

DeShear peered through the tiny window. A gray, military-style ATV approached, carrying one large passenger and one skinny driver, both in khaki green uniforms. Camilla shook hands with the large man. After they chatted for a moment, the ATV drove off as quickly as it had appeared. Her business finished, Camilla climbed back on board the little jet.

She clapped the pilot on the back. "Steggy, let's rock and roll."

"Roger that, boss." He flipped a few switches, and the monstrous egg-shaped engine outside DeShear's window commenced its high-pitched whine.

* * * * *

Misty white cloud slivers zipped past DeShear's window, barely visible at the jet's cruising speed.

Good acoustics and awesome speed. Drug dealers know a good plane when they see one.

Lanaya typed on the laptop. A metal asset tag reading "Property of Internal Revenue Service" was glued near the left side of the keyboard.

"Paco," Camilla called from the front of the plane. "Trade seats with me for a sec."

The agent in front of DeShear got up and moved forward. Camilla took the seat and faced DeShear. "When we get to the facility, we'll have anywhere from an eight-hour to twenty-hour advantage over anyone not already there. Executives in New York will hop on their corporate jet and hot foot it to wherever the action is, trying to keep us from finding their dirty little secrets. If what Lanaya says is true, we'll be in the cat bird seat. If she's wrong, or they moved the facility, we'll still be less than ten hours away from anywhere it could be in the world."

"It's there," Lanaya said. "I checked a few days ago. Even Angelus can't move a genetics lab that fast. Not with what they're doing."

"Okay." Camilla nodded. "When we land, you two will be front and center with me. We'll be moving fast, looking for the stuff that's out of place."

DeShear sat up. "Like what?"

"According to your client, the operation is too big to be easily hidden. They have a large group of people, and that means food, water, beds . . .

showers and bathrooms, hopefully. The higher the head count, the harder it'll be to hide."

"My reports indicate they disguised it as a grade school," Lanaya said.

"Makes sense. Nobody would question that." Camilla leaned closer. "The real key is in the element of surprise. You start having IRS and FBI agents ask questions to a bunch of scared low-level employees, it's a gold mine."

"What if they request an attorney?" DeShear asked.

"Doesn't matter. Lying to an FBI or IRS agent is a federal crime, and anyone who tries to hold out for an attorney runs the risk of not immediately complying with the demand letter—also a crime. Bottom line, if they don't grant us full access to everything we want, somebody goes to jail."

"Even though we're not on U. S. soil?" Lanaya asked.

"Any American employees that lie or impede the audit will be tossed in the clink the second they set foot back in the good ol' USA. That would include the board of directors, the executives, and any key project managers."

"Wow."

"Don't mess with the IRS." Camilla smiled. "We have FBI agents with us that are experts in human trafficking, and DEA agents who'll dig up the money laundering links. You two will stick by my side and guide the investigators. Not everything will be on site, and Lanaya, you'll know what's missing. All I need is one on-site person in authority to open their mouth about the process, and we're all set."

"Pfft," Lanaya huffed. "Ask them."

Camilla cocked her head. "What?"

"Simply ask them," Lanaya said. "Most of these geneticists are former or future professors. They love to brag about their work, especially to people who don't seem to understand it. With a few of the right questions, they'll kick into condescending lecture mode and tell you all about the place."

DeShear nodded. "Then the right person can ask a few key follow up questions . . ."

"Which," Lanaya said, "having already engaged, they'll be remiss not to answer."

"Not answering will be considered an impediment to the audit." Camilla rubbed her hands together. "A fact that I'll be only too happy to explain. Answering will tip their hand."

"Wow," Lanaya said. "And while they're hesitating, trying to think of what they ought to do or not do, the noose will tighten. Answer, lose your job. Don't answer, go to jail. I like it."

"We'll have this whole place bagged and tagged before the board gets here," Camilla said. "Then we interview the executive committee, and anything that doesn't match what we've already been told, somebody's going to jail. These witnesses will flip to our side and rat on each other like you've never seen."

Lanaya looked out the window. "It's hard to believe we're so close to shutting this whole sordid mess down."

"We're close. Real close." Camilla stood, returning to the front of the plane. "Keep it together, though, because things never go exactly as planned."

Lanaya sat back and re-opened the laptop, entering the three, twelve-digit passwords to access the black screen site.

"Back to work, huh?" DeShear said. "Good for you. I think I'm going to catch a little slee—"

Lanaya gasped.

"What is it?" DeShear sat up. "What's wrong?"

Her face white, Lanaya turned the computer to him, displaying the only message.

Your life is in danger. The Greyhound is heading to Indonesia. DO NOT GO to the Angelus site there.

-Double Omega

CHAPTER 22

The tail lights of Dr. Hauser's Rolls Royce shut off with the engine, and the heavy driver's door swung open. A foot, clad in an Italian leather loafer, stretched out to the concrete floor of the parking garage, followed by a dark, wooden cane. Eventually the other foot appeared, and the tiny, stoop-shouldered old man himself.

Dr. Hauser's knobby fingers gripped the car door until he was certain his feet would keep him upright, then he let go and shoved his hand into his suitcoat pocket. He took a half step—and abruptly stopped. In the spot next to the one marked "Reserved for the Chairman of the Board, Angelus Genetics," the van door slid open. Two men and a woman stepped out.

The closest man to the doctor had a dark goatee. He glanced at the old man's cane. "Arthritis?"

Hauser narrowed his eyes, a white puff escaping his lips as he spoke. "Excuse me?"

"The cane," the man said. "Is it because you have arthritis? Your knees give you problems in cold weather?"

"I'm old." Dr. Hauser frowned, looking over his expensive but ill-fitting suit. "Everything gives me pain in cold weather. Warm weather, too."

"I'm sorry to hear that. Maybe my news will take some of the sting out of this frosty December morning."

"So you're not here to rob me, then."

"No."

"Good." The doctor pulled his hand out of his suit coat pocket, holding a .38. "I'd have hated to put a bullet hole through the pocket of this jacket. It's a Brunello Cucinelli. Cashmere and silk."

The man smiled. "You know, I wondered why a man who drives a Rolls Royce would walk around alone in a parking garage. People who drive a Rolls have things other people want to take from them."

"I park here because it's my parking spot and I'm a creature of habit. This has been my parking spot at Angelus Genetics for over a decade. But I'm not stupid, either." He slid the gun back into his pocket. "We live in dangerous times, and they keep getting more dangerous." Pointing to his car, the doctor sighed. "Did you know the Silver Cloud comes with bulletproof glass and run-flat tires, as standard equipment? No world should need cars like that."

He raised his chin and peered down his nose at his three companions, his words echoing off the concrete walls of the parking garage. "Well, then, I suppose you've come to talk business. You are recently from Atlanta, I take it?"

"We are, sir." The man lowered his voice. "And we are here to report a successful set of conclusions regarding the unfortunate incidents that took place in Centennial Park."

"They're dead, are they? Both of them?"

The man nodded.

"Good. Can't say I'm unhappy about that. I did the best I could to find competent people the first time, but one doesn't simply Google 'assassins' and get ten good killers from Angie's List."

"Angie's Hit List, maybe."

"So why are you here?" The doctor's voice was gravelly and low, almost a mumble. "I thought payment had been arranged through my attorney."

"Mr. Jennings saw to it that me and my associates were paid very well. We feel our relationship has advanced to a point where you'd want to retain our services for some additional challenges the company seems to be facing at the moment."

"The IRS?" The doctor growled, hoisting his cane at his car. "That's where I've just come from, meeting with the lawyers about the *Infernal* Revenue Service. They slapped a demand letter on us and now I have to catch a plane to keep their big noses out of our business in Indonesia. Still, not a good idea to start shooting government types. There are a lot of them, and some carry big rifles and drive tanks."

"Sir, we have come to believe the geneticist and her friend are on the way to Indonesia."

"And how," the doctor cocked his head, "did you come to believe that?"

"We get paid well for our services, and in turn we pay our sources well. Those government types with the big guns? Notoriously underpaid, as are cops and IRS agents. We simply network enough to let people know we can assist them with their financial burdens, and information magically flows to us." He looked around the garage. "It's amazing what a teller at a police or military credit union can tell you about folks with top secret clearances who are struggling to make ends meet."

The doctor nodded. "I'm impressed with your candor—and it takes a lot to impress me. Go on."

"We've also recently learned that a small group of people have been quietly making key employees of Angelus and its subsidiaries disappear. With you and the other board members all rushing to get together to protect your Indonesian asset—the largest asset on the Angelus balance sheet—I think it's very unlikely these assassins would waste such an opportunity."

"I don't like the idea of guns, mister . . ."

"Presley. But please—call me Elvis. And these are my associates, Janet Jackson and George Michael."

"Hmm. As I say, I don't care for guns—unless they're mine, and they're pointing at people who'd like to kill me. Then I like guns a great deal. In this case, I'd like to place an order for as many guns—and people to use them—as are necessary to ensure I return safely from my overseas business trip, and to subdue any particular element that dislikes the way I run Angelus Genetics. Am I talking to the right party, Mr. Presley?"

Elvis grinned. "You are, sir."

"Good. And just so we are absolutely crystal clear, you need to be completely successful in this venture, or the first task of your replacement will be making sure you and your colleagues disappear."

"I'd hoped our work cleaning up the mess in Atlanta would be proof enough."

"Never hurts to remind the service provider what's at stake." The doctor waved a hand, shuffling toward the garage exit. Elvis followed.

"Atlanta was petty cash," Dr. Hauser said. "If they're coming for me in Bali, I want a small army to meet them. See Jennings' people for the money, like last time, and get enough hitters so you can eliminate this threat without breaking a sweat. I want no mistakes this time."

"Not a problem. Can we expect any help from the Indonesian army?"

"For what I'm paying their prime minister, I certainly hope so. But let's face it, they're not exactly the U. S. Marines, are they? Or should I say former Marines?" He glanced at Elvis' companions. "I'll arrange for some speedy jets to get you and your first team where you need to go. Obviously, you can't all fly to Bali with us on our plane, but I'll accommodate two of you. The others will travel on jets that are just as good and just as fast. How soon can you be ready?"

"I took the liberty of making some arrangements in anticipation of this meeting going well. My people can board a plane within the hour, with a not-so-small army to follow by this time tomorrow morning."

"We might not have that long. And what about this Greyhound character? Think he's already in the air?"

Elvis' jaw dropped.

"You're not the only one with contacts, Mr. Presley. Nor are you, Miss Jackson and Mr. Michael. This is serious business, and I do my homework. You go airborne when my plane does, understood?" The old man turned and leaned close to Elvis, his stale coffee breath permeating Presley's nose. "This situation ends only when a few bullets come to a stop in the back of The Greyhound's skull. And anyone who worked with him—or even considered working with him—needs to die, too. Slit the throats of their sleeping children and then burn the house down. I want my message delivered in the absolute harshest terms possible, so no one ever tries anything like this again."

Presley stood, staring at the tiny man, not speaking.

"Too rich for your blood, Elvis?" The doctor wiped a drop of spit from the corner of his mouth.

"No. Just . . . not what I was expecting, sir."

"Good." Dr. Hauser's shaking hand let go. He walked away, his cane pounding the garage floor with each step. "Then The Greyhound won't expect it, either."

* * * * *

"My head won't stop pounding." The Greyhound rolled over and squeezed his eyes shut, pulling a pillow over his eyes to block the light. "What did you give me?'

"Steroids," Maya said, crossing the hotel suite and coming to the bed. "Among other things. The new mix seems to help the others for extended periods, but it's a daily routine."

She took his pulse and temperature. Both were normal for a change.

"Steroids, huh? Well, if that's what it takes." He sat up, pushing the sheets aside. "I have to tell you, aside from the headache, I feel great. Like I finally have energy again."

Maya watched him stretch. "It's an experimental mix, and it's expensive, even to a big-time hedge fund manager like you."

"Former hedge fund manager. Now I do this. How much?"

"Five thousand a dose, and you need several doses a day, but the results are encouraging."

He stood and walked, flexing the muscles of his half-naked torso. "It's worth it. If you can get me a version that doesn't come with the skull splitter, I'll take a month's worth."

Maya picked up an oxygen sensor and blood pressure monitor, carrying them to him. "Sit down so I can get your vitals. I said the drug is new. It doesn't have a version without a headache side effect yet."

He sat in the chair by the desk, holding his arm out to her. "I'll still take a month's worth." He drew a deep breath as she wrapped the blood pressure cuff around his arm. "Where's Dominique? I have some traveling to do."

"She split for work. Hold still."

He frowned. "I told her to quit. She knows I have enough money to take care of whatever she needs."

"She needs to stay connected. Her sources bring in half of our information, so let her."

"Yeah, yeah." He looked around the room. "What about Britt? Where's he?"

"Getting breakfast. We weren't sure when you'd wake up, and we were hungry."

The Greyhound stared at her. "How long have I been out?"

She waited until the blood pressure cup had deflated before she replied. "Long enough to make us think you might not wake up again."

"That's amazing. I haven't slept more than three hours at a time in months." He stood again, pacing around the room like a panther. "I really feel strong. This mix may be the one."

"You say that every time. It has other side effects, like irritability, but I'm not sure we'd notice that one. Plus the usual anger flashes and rage that come with steroids." She scribbled some notes on a pad. "But with proper dosages, we can keep you running for a week at a time at this stage, maybe more. That's what we're seeing in the tests."

"A week? Why didn't you tell me about this sooner?"

"You haven't been around, and it's a trial drug. I can't just grab a jug of it and board a plane. I've been stealing a dose here and there on the side and having a private lab make more for me in secret. The bill for that has been big. Even you'll think so."

He went to the closet and grabbed a suitcase, tossing it on the bed and opening it. "Doesn't matter. If we own the patent rights, we'll make it back." Returning to the closet, he clutched an armful of shirts and pants against his chest, carried them to the suitcase, and dropped them in. "And money won't matter to me if I die from not having your special cocktails. So get me a month's worth. I have a plane to catch."

* * * * *

The Cessna bounced from turbulence. DeShear grabbed the headrest of the seat in front of him to stabilize himself from the jolts. "I have to admit, I thought I'd like Hawaii more. But the airport looked great out the window. I almost saw a palm tree, I think. Very . . ." He glanced at the cheat sheet. *"Indah."*

From her seat at the front of the plane, Cammy took a bite of a donut and flipped him off.

"Don't make jokes." Lanaya opened the laptop again. "The black screen site has gone dark, and that message is scary to me."

"I know," DeShear said. "I'm sorry. Look, you said Double Omega died, so this could be a hoax of some sort—"

"It'd be the first in the history of the site."

"Okay, well, whoever The Greyhound is, he or she will be running into a lot of armed FBI agents if they try anything."

She shook her head. "Nobody can access the site unless they know the codes, and those are extremely secure. Greyhound may be a code name for the group behind the murders of the Angelus employees."

"But what I was getting at is, if your friend is dead, somebody's posing as her. If it's not a hoax, it's either intended to scare you out of coming, or it's a warning to be very careful if we come. So . . . who has access to the site?"

She leaned back in the seat and stared at the plane ceiling. "At our peak, there were a few dozen users. We asked questions before admitting anyone, and security held up tight. Up until a few months ago, I felt very good about the site."

"What happened a few months ago?"

"Get ready," Camilla said. "Seatbelts on. We're going up again for the next leg. We land in Bali in about two hours."

Lanaya knitted her hands. "Hamilton, if it's been breached, then who knows what information has been compromised?"

"Okay, calm down." He placed a hand over hers. They were trembling. "Let's go over the facts. It doesn't matter if The Greyhound is headed for Indonesia. We wanted him there. That helps us. Next, whoever he brings, we never expected him to come alone—and Cammy has a ton of heavily armed people on our side to guard us."

Lanaya nodded. "I suppose that's true."

"So somebody was trying to help you with that message. That's a good thing. It's not the dead girl posting messages from beyond the grave, so the question is, who is it really? But as long as we're in the hands of these fine folks with all the weaponry .

. ." He pointed at the others on the plane. "I think we'll be okay."

"My brain knows all that, but my heart won't listen." She sighed. "It keeps worrying and beating fast. I think the pounding in my chest is so loud, it's keeping everyone on the plane awake."

DeShear smiled. "Yeah, well, if you weren't worried, you wouldn't be human. Just . . . close your eyes and focus hard on something else. Like your kids. Getting them ready for bed on a school night, making them brush their teeth, fighting with them for five more minutes of TV. Focus on that. See if you accidentally fall asleep. We have a big day ahead of us."

"My youngest always does that." She curled up in the seat, resting her head in the leather cushion and facing him. "Every night, it's 'Five more minutes, Mom? Pleeeease?'"

"Typical kid." DeShear shook his head, chuckling.

"I miss them, Hamilton."

He put his arm over her shoulder and patted her on the back. "You'll see them soon, don't worry."

"Promise?" she whispered, closing her eyes.

"Promise."

CHAPTER 23

She stared at the picture. It hadn't faded. Neither had the memories.

Sitting in her car, the woman tapped a cigarette out of the teal-colored pack and placed it between her lips. Her trembling fingers dug through her purse and found the butane lighter. With a flick, the little flame appeared. She held it to the tip of the cigarette and inhaled, heat and bitter smoke flowing over her tongue and down her throat, filling the insides of her lungs.

She still wasn't used to it. Never would be, probably.

Smoking can kill you. She'd heard that how many times over the years? She'd said it, too. Didn't matter. It was a habit of necessity, and had been for quite some time. One does what one must.

She breathed out, the smoke cascading across the steering wheel of the Mercedes and into the windshield, rolling slowly outward over the dash board.

Her father used to lower the driver's window a little when he smoked. That was when she was a child, and doctors in TV ads actually recommended certain brands of cigarettes over others. "More doctors smoke Camels than any other cigarette," the black and white ads proudly boasted. Men in white jackets sat at desks puffing away; elegant ladies wearing strapless gowns and pearls blew streams of white past their lipstick, then smiled at the camera.

Dad always cracked his window so the cigarette fumes would escape as he drove. The smoke obeyed, too, curling upwards from the glowing tip of the cigarette and dancing in the sunlight before getting sucked out near the side view mirror. But the smell lingered anyway, and the children all got plenty of second-hand smoke during the long drives. When they jumped into the pool at the Holiday Inn that night, their young faces would turn up and frown as the water unlocked the smoke smell from their hair and ran it down their cheeks.

She wore her hair down to her butt back then, so hers smelled the most. But they were kids. They didn't know any better. Children don't know about the dangers of the world, and they aren't supposed to.

Children.

She stared at the picture. "Children are a precious gift—of constant worry," a friend had joked a few weeks after her oldest was born. "Welcome to parenthood."

Sleepless nights filled with feedings, or diaper interruptions in the middle of dinner, those were nothing compared to worrying if the baby's reflux was preventing her medicines from fully being digested, or waking up every hour to see if her fever had subsided. After the divorce—she married too young, to her high school sweetheart—it was just the two of them, a young mother and her daughter, and the bond between them grew, but the concerns multiplied. Worrying if she was growing fast enough, learning to ice skate as well as the other kids in her class, worrying about good grades and making friends at school and talking to boys. When life dealt her a good turn and she was able to go back to school, she still worried about her baby. About teaching her to drive and calling before curfew and applying to colleges and getting a good job out of school.

A gift of constant worry? It wasn't so. The worry ends.

She glanced at the clock on the dashboard. A few more minutes.

She took another puff, the tip of the cigarette glowing. Closing her eyes, she eased her head into the soft leather seat and blew the smoke out, letting it fill the car.

The face from the picture smiled in her mind, growing from toddler to adult in the blink of an eye, but she used to play and laugh with her two young brothers. The three children were close, as siblings should be. Loving.

The picture was the last one taken with all three together. Her babies. She couldn't bear to look at the more recent pictures that displayed only two of her children. That wasn't fair, she knew, but the pain was still too much. Too intense. Too raw. Pain like that never goes away. A parent learns to live with it, but it's always there, raising its volume occasionally to stab at the heart and break it all over again.

The other two said they understood, and they did. They shared the loss. But they didn't really. Not as fully as she did. They couldn't, at their age.

Another look at the clock. How much time should she let pass? She allowed herself fifteen minutes for smoke breaks, at mid-morning, to establish the pattern. But today she sat in the car past the allotted time. The cold weather seemed too refreshing to pass on, so she stubbed out her cigarette and cracked the window, allowing the icy breeze to float through the car.

She hated smoking. But habits are habits.

As she slid the picture back into her wallet, the voice of Dr. Hauser came to her. She hadn't noticed him pull in; normally Marcus would have been there hours ago. In the corner of the garage, he and another man spoke, with a man and a woman nearby, watching.

Their conversation was quiet from that distance, but the words carried through the concrete garage. They were too far away to hear everything, but she could hear enough.

All she saw was the face of her daughter, the oldest, smiling from the photo. The last photo she had of her family together.

She slid down in her seat and listened as the men spoke.

Killing a child is a terrible thing. Threatening to kill the other two surviving children will get most parents to agree to anything.

For a while.

Then the hands of fate work their magic. Fighters gotta fight, and she was a fighter. If she hadn't been one before, she became a fighter after her daughter's murder.

The death of a child will do that, too. Especially when you got the kid a job at your company.

The conversation ended. The old man limped across the parking garage, pounding the concrete with his cane. The noise echoed through the cold, still morning like shots being fired at a gun range.

When he was gone, she sat for a while, staring at the clock and wondering how long to wait before she entered the Angelus Genetics headquarters building. Five minutes more, maybe ten. Or possibly she'd run an errand to pretend she hadn't been sitting in the parking lot at all.

Ten minutes might not even be enough, but Dr. Marcus Hauser was a very important, very busy man. He wouldn't be sitting in the lobby watching for her, and she wouldn't mention where she'd taken her break. No one would ask, but if they did, maybe she could say she walked around outside for a few minutes. She'd done that before on cold days. No one would question it.

Ten minutes, then, and a short walk after. That should do it.

It took an eternity for the ten minutes to pass, but when they did, she got out of her car and exited the far side of the garage, away from the spot with the sign that said "Reserved for the Chairman of the Board, Angelus Genetics."

She circled around to approach the front doors from the other side, as if she'd been walking. Simple and effective.

The wind picked up, tossing her hair, her heels clicking and clacking over the hard sidewalk. Drawing a deep breath, she approached the big glass doors and checked her reflection. Normal, and yet nothing of the sort. Not anymore. Not for a long time now—Hauser had seen to that. But she was functional, performing her job as before to all eyes who cared to watch, and that's what mattered.

Pretending to be a smoker so she could escape the corporate walls and covertly pass information along to others about the illegal side of Angelus Genetics, that was simply a habit created of necessity, and had been for quite some time.

One does what one must.

She pulled the heavy door open and stepped inside, smiling at the receptionist. The young man in the headset smiled back, then punched a button on the phone console and waved at her.

"You have a call on line three, Dr. Carerra."

CHAPTER 24

The jet had barely touched down at the Ngurah Rai airport before the agents were up and moving. The man seated in front of DeShear stood and stretched. "Time to put on our party dresses for the big dance."

The door opened and the humidity of the island swept into the plane, like entering a bathroom during someone else's shower. A United States Marine Lieutenant in khaki green camo gear boarded the jet. He matched the image on his phone to the woman standing in front of him. "Welcome to Bali, Bureau Chief Madison. I don't know how much local interaction you and your people will have, but the fine people of Indonesia primarily speak Indonesian—although many speak decent English. Be advised, fair skin and American accents will stick out. Enjoy your lunch, and good luck."

The Lieutenant left the plane, followed by the agents. DeShear and Lanaya exited last, with Camilla.

"You two stay with the team." Camilla put on her sunglasses. "The other agents will be landing in a moment. I need to rendezvous with a representative of the Indonesian government."

DeShear squinted in the bright light, holding a hand up to shield his eyes. On the shadeless airfield, the sun was hotter than a summer swamp. "You meeting anybody I'd have heard of?"

Camilla scrolled through pages of maps on her phone. "Dina Wulan, special assistant to the prime minister."

"Nope. Never heard of him."

"Her."

A Mercedes limo approached, flying the red and white flag of Indonesia from the side of its hood. A Marine waved to Camilla as he led several people toward the vehicle.

"Looks like this might be her now," Camilla said. "I'll see you two back at the hangar."

DeShear followed the agents from his plane across the scorching tarmac to the Delta hangar as another Cessna jet pulled up. A small jet landed on the runway behind them.

"Hamilton," Lanaya hurried her pace to stay next to him, looking around the airfield. "Are you the least bit nervous?"

"I'm definitely a little out of my element." He spoke loudly, to be heard over the whine of the jet engines. "But that's not unusual in my line of work. How are you holding up?"

"Oh, very nervous." She rubbed her arms like she was chilly. "Death threats tend to do that to me."

He stopped and put a hand on her shoulder. "We'll be okay while we're with these guys." He pointed to the group of agents assembling in the hangar. "Focus on what Camilla told us. When we get to the lab, it'll be our job to notice what's out of place."

"She said that was my job."

"I get to help you." He smiled, patting her shoulder. "We're a team."

The hangar was hot and stuffy, but it offered a way to get out of the blazing sun. DeShear wiped his brow, glancing around. Dust blew in from every hole and crack in the aging airplane garage. Across the runways, the trees of the thick jungle swayed in the breeze.

Folding tables and chairs had been set up to allow the team members to eat. DeShear approached a table where a Marine laid out small bags. "Are these any good?"

"Best chow in the world, sir."

"Really?"

"Yes sir. Much better than dog chow or cat chow—but it's still chow."

"People chow, huh? Great." He took two of the rectangular bags from the young man. The next table offered unchilled bottles of water. He grabbed two and took a seat next to Lanaya, handing her a bottle and an MRE. "Lunch is served."

A woman in camouflage approached them. "Ms. Kim?"

"Yes," Lanaya said.

"These are for you." She handed Lanaya an large manila envelope. "From Bureau Chief Madison."

"Thank you." Lanaya opened the envelope and pulled out a set of blueprints. "It's the plans for the Angelus Genetics lab here, dated from before they left Arizona. I bet they didn't stick to these."

"Maybe not," DeShear said. "But we can get some current satellite images and see what's changed. Let's have a look at your laptop."

A Marine captain in green fatigues called out from the front of the hangar. "Listen up. The buses for Bureau Chief Madison and her teams will report in five. Be ready to move."

DeShear waved at him. "Captain, we need wifi."

"Hot spot in the rear office, sir. But we still leave in five."

"Got it." DeShear stood, turning to Lanaya. "Let's see if we can get an overview image of the facility and take screen shots to review it on the bus. Maybe load it into my phone if we get a chance, too."

The IRS agents remained seated, studying spreadsheets on their laptops, while a crowd of FBI people gathered near the hangar exit.

"Come on." Lanaya stood. "We'd better hurry up and find that hot spot."

* * * * *

The Mercedes stretch limo cruised around the perimeter of the airport. Inside, a small woman in a dark gray business suit extended her hand to Camilla. "Ms. Madison. It is very nice to meet you. I trust our accommodations have been satisfactory so far."

"Yes, madam assistant director." Camilla shook hands and settled back into her seat. "The IRS is very grateful for the cooperation of your government, and the Vice President sends his regards."

"Ah, yes." The assistant nodded. "A good golfer, your Vice President. It must have been very difficult to lose to the Prime Minister, without appearing to do so, the last time they played."

"Well," Camilla said. "Our Vice President was once a diplomat, ma'am."

"I see." She folded her petite hands in her lap. "Can you tell me what your plans are for your stay? I understand you brought many people with guns. The country of Indonesia does not want trouble with our friend the United States."

"Of course not. We are only here to conduct an audit."

"Does an audit require so many people and weapons? Our friends to the north are nervous about so many jets landing. It almost appears to be an advance team before an invasion."

Camilla took a deep breath. "Those concerns are understandable. In this case, we need to move fast, but we fear the subject of the audit, a U. S. company, may object to our presence and offer some resistance. We intend to make an impression with a show of strength to them, nothing more." She swallowed hard. "I'm sorry, I was told your government was informed of all this."

"Sometimes things have a way of changing. In my position, it's best to keep informed. You are planning quite a show, as you say."

The car stopped. The uniformed driver got out and opened Camilla's door.

"I will relay your words to our Prime Minister," the assistant said. "Do your best to see that the show of strength remains a show only. Indonesia does not want a war."

CHAPTER 25

As his escort vehicle bounced its way along the road to the genetics lab, Dr. Hauser's phone rang. He checked the screen but didn't answer, scowling at the driver instead. "Can you find any more potholes to hit? Don't you people know how to pave a road?"

Wiping his brow with a handkerchief, Dr. Hauser pressed a button on the phone and held it to his ear. "Dina, how are you?"

"Welcome again to Indonesia, my friend. All of Bali welcomes you. Was your flight enjoyable?"

"I'm afraid not. These old bones don't travel as well as they used to."

"A pity," Dina said. "Perhaps a visit to one of our many waterfalls will renew you, Doctor. Some are said to contain the powers of magical healing. Remember, the one in Nungnung is not far from your facility."

"You tell me every time I come. The pictures look beautiful—a giant river that takes a long, steep drop into a vast pool, surrounded by lush tropical foliage. Very pretty."

"And magical. People write their problem on a piece of wood from the *pala* tree and throw it in the river, because whatever goes over the falls is never seen again."

"But it's still located in the hills at the end of a long footpath, right?" He stared at his cane. "And ever since I've taken to needing a walking stick, places like that will remain a longer jaunt than I care for. Maybe you can arrange a tour of it for one of my next trips. We can ride in one of those military helicopters my company convinced Uncle Sam to give you."

"Excellent suggestion, Doctor."

A low-hanging palm tree branch slapped the side of the car as it passed. "I understand you've had some other American visitors arrive today, Dina. What of our friends?"

"A Miss Madison of the IRS has landed. She brings many agents from FBI and ATF. Many small jets, with big jets coming. We are, of course, concerned. We value our relationship with all of our friends—the American government, and of course our generous business friends who bring jobs to this country."

Hauser frowned, raising his voice. "The IRS is trying to embarrass me and my executives to our shareholders. Well, I have a small army arriving at ten A. M. tomorrow." He jabbed the car seat with his index finger. "Then we'll see this Miss Madison and her little band of bookworms tuck their tails between their legs and run home."

"Please choose your pejoratives carefully, Doctor. Words such as 'army' are very distressing for the people I report to. Indonesia does not want a war."

"Figure of speech." The doctor leaned back, tugging his linen *guayabera* shirt to send puffs of air across his chest. "I simply mean I have a business to run, and I don't need distractions like this. I'm sure your boss understands."

"My superior reads words in American newspapers like the New York Times, that tell the world Indonesia is still a semi-dictatorship, and that your company is engaged in illegal activities here. Of course, we both know neither of these things are true, and that your IRS will not find anything at your facility to the contrary."

"You have my word. News reports are merely a pack of lies and gossip, written by morons hoping to get a Pulitzer prize. Whoever can embarrass the biggest fish, wins. We should do it like you, with more government control of the press. Then nothing would get out that we don't want out."

"Of course, Indonesia has a free press now, Doctor."

"Uh huh. But either way, tomorrow morning, my ar—my set of *auditors*—will land. And shortly after that, a speedy resolution of these unpleasantries will occur."

"Do you expect Miss Madison's people to wait? We were told—"

"I don't care what they do." Hauser dabbed his upper lip with the handkerchief. "I'll stall them with presentations about our operation and its vast importance to the world of science, but a bunch of number crunchers won't have the technical expertise to begin to understand the intricacies of the genetic selection process. Following the presentation is a fancy reception and dinner at the Viceroy. I want to appear friendly and cooperative, but perhaps you could arrange for the power at their hotel to go out, so there's no air conditioning and they can't sleep. Cranky auditors tend to want to go home quickly." He chuckled. "But either way, their report will end up saying whatever we want."

"And if it doesn't?"

"Oh, we have plenty of friends in Washington, as we do here. We can get an IRS report slow-walked to the point that a snail would look speedy by comparison. Maybe even bog it down until a new administration gets elected. One that's more open-minded about our operations."

"As always, you have thought of everything, Dr. Hauser."

"Glad I could offer you and the people of Indonesia a lesson in strategic planning, Dina. Feel free to come to the dinner tonight. It should be quite elaborate by third world dictatorship standards."

"I'm afraid I'll be working late tonight, sir. Our friends to the north and elsewhere have expressed concerns about all of this. Indonesia does not want a war."

The car came to a stop in front of a set of tall, iron gates. Men with machine guns blocked the entrance. Behind them, a series of huge warehouses spanned over acres of cleared jungle.

"I understand. Go hold their hands. Tell them, sometimes you simply have to do what needs to be done—and often the best choice is clear, but unpleasant."

An attendant looked at the driver's credentials, and the gates opened.

"And don't worry, I'll take care of things at my lab."

* * * * *

The blueprints were unfolded over a filing cabinet in the hangar's small office. DeShear stared at the pages, rubbing his chin. "On paper, the genetics facility doesn't look as big as I thought. I'm not sure what I expected, but not this. A building or two? Seems kinda small."

From her seat at a nearby desk, Lanaya glanced up from her computer. "I didn't think they'd match, but I didn't expect them to be this different, either." She pointed to the overhead images on her screen. "I count twenty buildings, all over a hundred feet long. That's a far bigger campus than any research facility I've ever seen."

"How big was the one in Arizona?"

"Two buildings that size, with an annex. A lot like the blueprints."

"So they used the same format to get a toe in the door, and then expanded." He shrugged. "I guess that makes sense. The labor's cheaper here."

"Hamilton, with that many buildings, they could house every genetics lab in the world. What we want is in those buildings, I'm certain of it. But they're so big, and there's so many . . . And I'm sure there's security."

A Marine opened the office door. "Time to go, folks. Your ride has arrived."

"Thanks, private." He nodded to Lanaya. "Grab a screen shot."

She frowned and tapped the keyboard. "I'm not sure what good it'll do. Who knows how often the Indonesian government allows these satellite images to be updated."

"It's a start. We'll learn a lot more once we're able to get on site and start looking around. 'Improvise, adapt and overcome,' right, private?"

The young Marine smiled. "Oohrah, sir."

* * * * *

The escort vehicle carrying Dominique Carerra and some other Angelus board members pulled up to the Viceroy hotel. Its expansive, elegant white façade and columns were a sharp contrast to the jungle nearby.

A uniformed attendant opened her door. "Welcome to the Viceroy Bali, Miss Carerra."

"It's Doctor Carerra," she said, sliding out of the car.

"How clumsy of me. My apologies, madam." The man bowed and greeted the other board members by name. "Bali welcomes you all. Please, follow me. Your suites have been prepared, and our staff will attend to your baggage."

A red helicopter approached, with an "Air Bali" logo painted on its side. It swooped in and landed on the helicopter pad across the drive. The attendant waved to the pilot before returning his attention to his guests. "This way, please."

The lobby of the grand hotel was lavish. Its dark bamboo ceiling stretched upwards three stories in an elegant cone shape, towering over the white marble floor below. Each suite was equally impressive. The massive beds looked out onto stone balconies and the lush landscape beyond.

A young bellman followed Dr. Carerra into her suite, her suitcase riding on his shiny brass cart. "Shall I unpack for you, madam?

"Thank you, no. I can manage." She inspected the room. It had one phone on the nightstand, and a large stone ashtray on the coffee table. "But I'd like a pack of cigarettes. Salem lights, if you can find them."

"That will be no problem, madam."

"And then I'd like to walk the grounds and stretch my legs. Can you recommend a running trail?"

"I shall have the concierge call your room, if it pleases madam." The boy said. "She will know the best path to recommend."

"Very good." She tucked a bill into his hand. "Thank you."

"Thank you, madam." He bowed, his eyes widening upon seeing the denomination of the bill. "I am Rafi, and I am assigned to this floor. If you need anything, please do not hesitate to call."

"Thank you, Rafi." She strolled to the balcony. "I shall need some things from time to time during my stay. And please have the concierge call me about a trail."

The young man bowed again, backing toward the door. "Right away, madam."

When the door closed behind him, she opened her laptop and scanned the Viceroy's many scenic hiking paths, to locate the one that ran closest to the nearby Kamandalu Ubud hotel. She made a mental note, shut the computer down, and powered off her cell phone. Crossing to the bed, she reached behind the nightstand and unplugged the room phone.

She grabbed a pair of sneakers and some running clothes from her bag and entered the marble bathroom to change.

* * * * *

"Dr. Carerra!" A board member waved at her from the bar. "Will you join us for a drink before we head over to the facility?"

A rotund man passed her in the lobby, answering for her. "Dressed like that, I'm guessing the answer is no, Patel. But Dominique, isn't this weather too hot for a run?"

Rafi appeared, carrying a teal-green pack of cigarettes in a clear plastic bag marked Viceroy Bali. "Madam, as you requested."

"Thank you." She took the cigarettes and slipped them into the hip pocket of her sweat pants. "And thank you, gentlemen, but I'm going to try to exercise my way out of jet lag. A nice, long trail through the hills sounds good."

Patel strolled into the lobby from the bar, smiling. "That's a strange combination, Doctor Carerra. Cigarettes and running?"

"A good habit to cover a bad one." She patted the enormous stomach of the man next to her. "We all have our vices, don't we Dr. Bruner?"

The men chuckled.

"Yes," Patel said. "I was about to treat myself to some carrot juice in the bar. I take your point, Doctor."

"Enjoy your run, Dominique." Bruner waved a hand, ambling toward the bar. "See you at dinner."

The bellman walked to the bell stand.

"Rafi," Dr. Carerra said.

The boy whipped around, snapping to attention. "Yes, madam?"

"The concierge never called me." She walked toward the front door. "Let's see about a running trail."

CHAPTER 26

DeShear's phone vibrated in his pocket. As the bus rumbled along the broken asphalt, he slid it out and checked the screen.

Text message.

Pressing the icon, the app opened. The sender information said Name Unknown, with no number displaying, but their message was short and clear.

Check black screen site.

He sat back, raising his eyebrows. Not a lot of people knew about the site, and even fewer knew he had knowledge of it. Could be a trap.

Next to him, Lanaya sat with her hands in her lap, one massaging the other, a distant look on her face. The last message hadn't been a threat, so maybe this one wasn't.

He chewed his lip and looked at the phone screen again. The message was gone.

Bolting forward, he clicked the app again. There were no messages.

The jungle rolled past as the bus rocked back and forth, sending dust clouds out in its wake. DeShear had never seen a message disappear that way. Not a regular text message. Not without manually deleting it himself.

Its quick disappearance meant whoever sent it didn't want anyone else to see it. How they made it happen, he didn't know.

It's a move of fear, though. Not strength.

He nodded to himself. "Lanaya, can you get a signal here? For your computer?"

She lifted her eyes, blinking as if to remove a fog. "What?"

"Can you access your black screen site right now?"

"No, I don't think so." She glanced at the computer. "I thought they said there'd be no access on the bus."

Swaying and jolting with every pothole, he faced the front of the bus, holding the seat in front of him as he stood. "Cammy. Any way to get wifi out here?"

Camilla turned in her seat and looked at him over her shoulder. "I can let you access my hot spot, but out here it'll be slow. They might have wifi at the lab."

He went down the aisle, holding the seat tops with each bumpy step. When he reached Camilla, he brought his face close to her ear. "I'm not sure we can wait until we get to the lab."

"What have you got?"

"Not sure yet. Can you link us in?"

Camilla rose and followed him to the rear of the bus. Opening her phone, she found the laptop signal and watched for it to connect. "All set. It's a weak signal, but it's there."

DeShear faced Lanaya. "Check your black screen site."

"Why?"

"Just check it."

She tapped on the keyboard, bringing up a series of password pages. Each required a code before allowing the user to move on to the next. When she finished, a new window opened and a tiny message icon appeared on the screen. Next to it was a gray box with a blinking cursor, and next to that were three white boxes. The rest of the screen was black.

"Man, you're making me feel old." He shook his head. "I wouldn't know what to do on a website like this."

"That's entirely the point," Lanaya looked up from the screen. "It's only to be accessed by people who know how. For example, normally, you'd type a password or command where the waiting prompt is, right?"

"Sure," DeShear said.

"If you do, it'll lock you out, shut down the site for a few hours, and permanently ban this computer's IP address. The ban keeps hackers from autosearching web addresses. Nobody can afford a sextillion new IP addresses merely to see what's happening on this little site." She pointed to the three white boxes. That tells me my hidden password dock is in the third quadrant."

She slid her finger over the mouse pad until the cursor arrow was in the lower left corner of the screen. It flashed a top hat like the guy in monopoly wore, then disappeared.

"I now have five seconds to enter a code."

Her hands hovered over the keyboard.

"Uh." DeShear shifted in his seat. "You'd better hurry."

She didn't move, her face blank.

"Lanaya . . ." He leaned forward.

She dropped her fingers onto the keys and typed rapidly. None of the letters or numbers were visible. When she finished, a blue window opened.

"You don't really have five seconds. You can't start typing before three seconds have elapsed."

"Good grief," DeShear said. "This site's gonna give me a heart attack and I'm not even using it."

"That's also the point. It has many hidden features to keep secrets private. The message won't appear for thirty seconds. That's so anyone who accessed this screen would think there was nothing there, or they'd hit a glitch. If they type any key stroke in that time, it locks them out. By shutting the site, it lets every valid user know a breach was attempted. Traffic usually slows down for a day or two after that. But . . ." She shrugged. "There are so many people quitting the site lately, it doesn't matter. They're so paranoid it's been accessed by Angelus, it's nearly a ghost town, and fewer users means those that remain have a greater chance of being spotted. I'll probably have to quit soon." She set her hands in her lap. "Here's the message."

Kamandalu Ubud hotel, room 502
- Double Omega

Camilla looked at DeShear. "What do you think?"

"I think somebody calling themselves Double Omega warned us not to go to Indonesia." His gaze went to Lanaya. "Now they know we're here, they'd like to chat."

"Don't go," Camilla said. "If they're using the name Double Omega, it's obviously somebody from Angelus."

"A team leader or project manager, I'm sure." Lanaya knitted her hands again. "If they know the name Double Omega, they know everything."

"Hold on," DeShear said. "It could be an outsider she told things to before she died. Even if it *is* someone from Angelus, we're still alive, so they might be a friend. There's no other reason to reach out. I think the first message was trying to help, too."

Camilla shook her head. "Dash . . ."

"Look, these people killed executives and high-ranking people. They'd never make murdering us a priority over knocking off the board members. And they could just wait until we were in our hotel rooms tonight and whack us then. There's no reason for the killers to schedule a meeting and leave that kind of trail." He peeked at the driver, then looked back to Camilla. "Can we detour this bus to the Kamandalu Ubud hotel?"

"It's not exactly on the way, but yes, we can take you."

"Just get us within a half mile," DeShear said. "We'll walk the rest. I trust your agents, but I don't know about a local driver. Who knows what his annual income is. A tipoff about us to someone at Angelus could go a long way to improve his finances."

Lanaya typed on the laptop. "About seven thousand dollars."

"What?" DeShear said.

"In Indonesia," Lanaya pointed at the screen. "The average annual income is about seven thousand dollars.

Camilla shook her head. "No wonder Angelus moved their lab."

"Well, then," DeShear said. "A little cash will go a long way here, and Angelus has a mountain of cash."

"Dash, listen. You and Lanaya have set me up with a nice sting operation to expose a multinational corporation and their fraudulent business practices. Money laundering, tax fraud— that's all good for me. What's your goal in all this now? It's not to make the IRS look good."

"I want to stay alive." Lanaya closed the laptop, her hands shaking. "Angelus employees are dying at the hands of someone who wants vengeance, and my name is on that list. My life has become a mess of hiding and running, and I've endangered my family. By coming here, we thought we'd have a chance to expose what Angelus is up to but also draw the killers out." She glanced at DeShear, lowering her voice. "That they'd come for the Angelus board."

"They will." He nodded. "They'll come. It's too tempting for them not to. Either at the hotel or somewhere at the lab, the killers will try to make a move—and soon. If they know anything about what's going on, they're expecting a bunch of IRS accountants to be here. Cammy, all you have to do is ask the FBI to keep their eyes open, and as soon as the killers try to strike at the board, have the feds grab them. They aren't expecting that. Then we'll go to the press and expose Angelus Genetics and all of their illegal operations."

"Okay," Camilla said. "So how does going to the Kamandalu Ubud hotel help any of that?"

"I don't know." DeShear pounded his fist into his other hand. "But if this message is from an employee at Angelus, they're risking their neck to send it to us. It might be a good idea to find out what they think is so important."

* * * * *

The long driveway of the Kamandalu Ubud was smooth and even, as was the public road it connected to, but the scorching heat from the jungle had already worked on DeShear and Lanaya as they walked the half mile to the hotel. By the time they were near the front entrance, his shirt was clinging to his chest.

"Next time I tell somebody to drop us a half mile from a hotel in Indonesia and we'll walk the rest of the way," DeShear panted, "you smack me."

Lanaya dabbed her forehead and neck with a handkerchief. "Do you suppose we march right in and knock on the door to room 502?"

"If we're not supposed to, I'm sure our new friend has figured out some way to let us know that." DeShear wiped the sweat from his face with his shoulder. "Ready?"

"No!"

Smiling, DeShear put his hand on the hotel's front door. "Just act natural, like we're staying here. Hotel elevators are usually on the far side of the lobby, past the front desk. Walk with determination and act tired."

"I am tired."

"Then it won't be difficult to act that way."

The Kamandalu Ubud was a beautiful hotel, with an extravagant air. The lobby was large and spacious; the service staff friendly. Each greeted the couple as they walked by. DeShear returned their hellos; Lanaya stiffened more and more with each one.

At the elevator, she exhaled sharply.

"What?" he said. "Were you holding your breath?"

She shook out her hands like she was flinging water from them. "My breath, my nerves, my heartbeat. Who knows what we're walking into, Hamilton?"

He folded his hands in front of him, eyeing the row of lighted numbers above the elevator. "We'll be fine." The doors opened. He stepped in and pressed the "five" button on the service panel.

As the lights glowed with each passing floor, Lanaya's hands rubbed faster. The doors opened and DeShear led the way down the hall. At room 502, he stopped, glancing at Lanaya. She rolled her shoulders and took a few short breaths, then wiped her trembling hands on her thighs.

"Okay." She nodded. "Go ahead and knock."

DeShear raised his hand to knock on the door. The latch went down with a sharp mechanical ratchet, and the big door swung open. Standing in the entry was a woman with dark, curly hair, dressed in a sports bra and sweat pants.

Lanaya gasped, turning white.

"What?" DeShear took a sideways step from the door. "What is it?"

"She—she's on the Angelus board." Lanaya backed away. "They've got us."

"I recognize you, too, Dara." The woman stepped forward. "Please come in."

Lanaya held her hands up, shaking her head. She stumbled backwards, bumping into the hallway wall.

"I think you knew my daughter," the woman said. "On the black screen site, she went by the name Double Omega."

Lanaya pressed herself into the wall, sliding to the floor. Her breath came in short spurts.

The woman looked up and down the hallway. "I'm not here to hurt you. Is that what you think?"

"What . . ." Lanaya shrugged. "What . . ."

"Come inside before someone sees us." She held her hand out to Lanaya.

DeShear stood by, watching, unsure what to do. He swallowed hard. "I think it's okay. If she had wanted us dead, we'd be dead by now."

The woman kneeled by Lanaya, whispering. "I want what you want, Dara—the end of Angelus Genetics and its horrendous activities. But people are coming here to kill you, and if you don't listen to me, the only thing that will be ended is you two. Now hurry. There isn't much time."

DeShear helped Lanaya from the floor and onto the couch in the room.

"Mr. DeShear, I'm Dominique Carerra. Lanaya is right, I'm on the board of directors at Angelus Genetics."

DeShear cocked his head. "You called her Dara."

"I know several of her aliases, and I know why you're here. I've been following you through the black screen site." Dominique bit her fingernail. "But now things have gotten . . . out of control. If you're trying to expose Dr. Hauser with an audit, it won't work." She threw her hands out. "Did you think he wouldn't protect his investment? This laboratory facility is the single most valuable asset Angelus Genetics owns. It's worth hundreds of billions of dollars. This IRS situation you created has caused him to arrange for hundreds of armed killers to be here tomorrow. They'll defend the laboratory and stall any inspections. You don't know him. He's not going to allow anything to jeopardize his work. My daughter and my husband were both lost because of his insidious vision, so I have to be careful while I protect what's left of my family, but I can still help you bring him down."

Dominique stared at them, both of them staring back.

"Hauser has grown rich and arrogant. He thought a few guns at the front gate of the facility here would be enough to keep its secrets safe—and for the most part, he's been correct up until now.

He's only been untouchable because he seemed too powerful to oppose. Once that dynamic changes . . ." She shook her head, then peered at DeShear. "Do you still have your phone?"

"Yes," he said.

"Then take pictures. Bring them back to me and I will get them to the media. The drone rooms are the key. I would do it myself, but Hauser will be watching me. I got you these." She dug into her hip pocket and handed them two green plastic cards with a gold-colored chip imbedded in each, and a green Angelus Genetics ID card. "Security will take your picture when you enter the lab. They'll issue you a red temporary ID card for the duration of the IRS audit, which they think you're with. A green ID is executive level access."

DeShear took the ID. His driver's license picture from the Florida DMV had been used for the image.

"These can't get you into every building, but it's the best I could do. The drone rooms require a yellow ID, a top security clearance. For that, use this." She pulled up the leg of her sweat pants and unstrapped a long, thin, black metal case. She placed it on the coffee table.

DeShear picked it up. The case was about the size of two watch boxes laid end to end, and heavier than he expected. Velcro straps had been fitted to it.

"Inside is a strong electromagnet that will deactivate the locks on the far buildings—there, you'll find the drone rooms. Wear it on your leg, Mr. DeShear, as I did. I don't think they're going to be frisking people on the IRS accounting team."

She went to the door. "Wait here a few minutes after I leave, so we aren't seen together. Remember, get the pictures, and get them to me. I will get them to the press."

Holding the heavy case, DeShear looked at her. "I had a hard time believing all this, and I've been in the middle of it. Will the press take your word for it?"

Dominique's face fell as she turned to him. "I'm on the board of directors for what's about to become the most despised company in the history of the world. Trust me, if you bring back pictures of the drone rooms, every news agency on the planet will believe every word I say."

"And the drone rooms?" he asked. "Is that where . . ."

"The drone rooms," Dominique sighed. "Are where you will see the worst depravity the human mind is capable of creating."

CHAPTER 27

DeShear walked to the cabs at the end of the long Kamandalu Ubud driveway. The first two were Toyota Camrys; the next was a Mercedes. "Hello." He waved at a small cluster of men smoking under a *pala* tree, then pointed to the Mercedes. "Whose cab is this one?"

The closest driver stamped out his cigarette. "Please to go in order, sir."

"Sorry." DeShear shook his head. "I'd like this one. I'll give the cars ahead of it ten American dollars to let the Mercedes go first." He waved the bills at them. "Deal?"

Two of the men rushed forward to take the money. A third hurried to the Mercedes.

"Thank you." DeShear clasped his hands together at his chest, bowing. *"Terima kasih."*

He crouched down in the back seat as the Mercedes neared the front of the hotel. Lanaya walked out the front door and went quickly to the curb, gripping her hands in front of her. "Stop right here," DeShear said to the cab driver. "Let this lady in, but don't get out to open the door."

She climbed into the back of the cab, rigid and shaking, staring straight ahead. The driver pulled the car around the curved driveway and back to the main road.

"Okay," DeShear sat up. "When we get to the laboratory, Cammy's group will have already gone in. Hopefully, the Mercedes will help us look a little important, and we'll proceed as though we're supposed to be arriving later than the others did. I'm sure someone will take us to them."

Lanaya leaned to DeShear, whispering in his ear. "Should we talk openly in front of the driver?"

"They can't all be spies for—" He stopped himself. "Well, they can't all be spies."

When the cab arrived at the gate, a short, thin man in a beige uniform approached. The driver rolled down his window, and the steamy jungle heat rolled in. A bronze plaque on the tall limestone columns bore the name Angelus Genetics.

Getting inside was the key to everything else. DeShear pretended to busy himself with his phone, watching carefully while trying not to appear to be watching at all. Next to him, Lanaya sat rigid, knitting her hands.

The attendant had a long, oval face, with narrow slits for eyes and a jaundiced complexion— not at all like the locals. He glanced at the Americans and nodded to the guards at the gate, saying nothing. Two men walked to the center of the entrance in silence and pulled the iron gates open.

As they passed, DeShear looked at them. The gate area was open to the sun, yet they seemed unfazed by the heat. They bore the same yellowish complexion as the attendant, but with rounder faces and an obvious underbite. Their jaws stuck out, not like a boxer getting ready to take on his opponent, but like a child pretending to be a chimpanzee. It gave them a dull, unthinking expression.

"They're undernourished," Lanaya whispered, as the cab passed through the gate. "Not well fed, by the look of them, and certainly not eating a balanced diet."

That hadn't been the case with most of the people they'd seen in the airport and hotels. Indonesians were noticeably skinnier than an average American, but these men would look gaunt compared to anyone DeShear had met in the country so far.

The cab bumped along a dirt road that was lined with banana trees. They swayed in the breeze as the Mercedes stirred up a dust cloud to greet them. Prior traffic had settled so much tan silt on the leaves, the roadway looked like a black and white movie of itself. Dark shadows cutting between dirt-coated palms were the only colors.

At the end of the road, the laboratory rose up out of the jungle—a giant, windowless blue steel rectangle rising thirty feet into the air. A hundred feet long, it stood like a castle wall, imposing itself on the foliage and daring anything to try to pass. In the center, a large white sphere jutted upwards, an eye staring at the heavens.

The cab pulled in front of a pair of black doors. The sign mounted next to them was painted in red: "All visitors must pass through security." Above the doors, a black sign contained the word "Security."

From the front, the entire building appeared to have no other doors or windows. Behind it stood dozens of identical buildings. They spanned four across, and at least ten deep, separated by the wide ribbon of the dirt road. No weeds, not a single blade of grass, grew alongside the structures.

DeShear glanced at the meter and counted out some money. He handed the cash to the driver as Lanaya got out of the car.

As DeShear exited, the driver clasped his hands together at the chest, nodding. *"Berhati-hatilah,"* the man said. "Be safe, my friends."

It was a friendly gesture, but it made the hairs on the back of Deshear's neck stand up. He shut the door and the cab sped away, disappearing in a cloud of dust as the jungle swallowed it up. Facing the glass doors, an emptiness crept into DeShear's stomach.

The worst depravity the human mind is capable of creating.

He stood next to Lanaya, staring at the entrance, not at all sure he wanted to see what waited inside.

A blast of cool air rushed over his face as he opened the door. The lobby inside was white and spotless, four gleaming walls and not much else. A stainless steel counter bearing several computers occupied one corner of the space, with a black glass door behind it. To the left was a camera on a tripod, with a series of colored screens next to it.

DeShear took a few steps into the cold room, his footsteps echoing off the empty walls. Across the room, stationed midway between the camera and the counter, was a large, black metal door marked, "Authorized personnel only." In the door was a thin rectangular window with criss-cross wire mesh inside it.

Other than that, the room was empty—and completely silent.

The uneasy feeling intensified its grip on DeShear's gut. He took a deep breath and tried to shrug it off. If he let himself appear bothered by the situation, Lanaya would get even more worked up. He looked at her and shrugged. "It's security. Gotta be a security guy around here somewh—"

An overhead speaker announced a message in a woman's voice. *"Tunggu disini."* Her tone was calm and pleasant. "One moment."

The speaker repeated the twin messages after about ten seconds. As it started a third time, the glass door behind the counter slid open, and the message stopped mid-sentence. A small, black-haired man entered the room and pointed to the camera. *"Kamu berdiri di sana."*

A large Caucasian man with square shoulders and a square jaw appeared behind him. "Are you with the audit?" His accent was American.

"Yes, thank you," DeShear said, approaching the counter.

The big man narrowed his eyes. "You're late."

"We had other business to attend to first. For the audit."

"Like what?" The man glared at DeShear, not moving.

DeShear held his breath for a moment, searching for the way to deliver his words. He did not want a confrontation, but he didn't want to explain further, either. "IRS business." He said it flat and even, as though he was telling the man what the date was. Information, nothing more.

The man's eyes went from DeShear to Lanaya, then back again. With a grunt, he nodded to his associate. The smaller man walked to the camera.

"Stand with your back against the red screen," the American said.

DeShear nodded at Lanaya. She swallowed hard, massaging her hands as she followed the instructions.

"That's good," the big man said. The camera clicked twice. "Okay. Next."

DeShear replaced Lanaya in front of the camera. Two clicks later, the small man returned to the counter. The glass door slid open and he went inside.

"Wait here," the American said, going into the back room. The glass door quietly closed behind him.

The uneasiness tightened its grip on his gut. DeShear shoved his hands into his pockets and checked around the room. The low hum of the fluorescent lights was the only sound. Strolling to the large metal door on the far wall, he peeked through its tiny window.

DeShear jumped back, his heart in his throat.

On the other side of the glass was a large machine gun, held by a huge man in camouflage fatigues. The man held the gun to his chest, his eyes blank and cold, staring right at DeShear.

The security officer reappeared, carrying two red plastic IDs. He slinked a lanyard through each and tossed them onto the gleaming countertop. "Put these on. Step to the door."

DeShear and Lanaya slipped the lanyards over their heads.

"Where do we find the others?" DeShear asked.

"Wait for the buzzer," the security officer said. He called out over his shoulder. *"Buka kunci pintu."*

A buzzer sounded from inside the metal door, and the lock opened. DeShear put his hand on the pull bar, ready to see the huge machine gun and the hard face of its owner on the other side. He took a breath and yanked the heavy door open.

Inside, the small, black-haired man from the security counter was alone in the room.

The windowless space was about twenty feet by twenty feet square, like a two-car garage, with opaque white walls—but without the intimidating man and his machine gun.

Odd.

The far side held another black steel door. Beside it, a silver-colored ball protruded from the wall.

The small man scowled and pointed at it. *"Tunggu di sana."*

DeShear stared at him.

"Di sana." He repeated sharply.

Lanaya crept toward the door. DeShear followed. A rectangle was etched on the metal ball, with the silhouette of a head and shoulders in the upper right corner. He lifted his ID card, keeping his eyes on the black-haired man.

"Iya nih, iya nih," he growled. *"Baik."*

DeShear slid his ID card across the ball. The lock tumblers in the second door clicked. He turned and pulled the second heavy metal door open, revealing a long, white hall with black flooring. As he walked through the doorway, Lanaya swiped her card over the reader and was right back on his heels.

The faint, sterile smell of cleaning solvents filled the hallway, the way they do in a doctor's office. Halfway down the hallway, he stopped at a door and tried the knob. It was locked.

"What do we do?" Lanaya asked.

"They're here somewhere, behind one of these doors." He swallowed hard and walked another thirty or so feet to the next door, trying it.

Locked.

"What if they're not here?" Lanaya whispered. "They could already be—"

"They're here."

As he approached the next room, a tall man in a white lab coat stepped out. He said nothing as he held the door open.

When DeShear reached the entry, he peeked inside. Camilla's audit team was seated on folding chairs watching a presentation by a gray-haired woman in a lab jacket. At the back of the room, Camilla stood with her arms folded.

"Ah, there is the rest of the team," the lecturer said. "Let us continue." The lights dimmed as the screen behind her illuminated with the words Angelus Genetics in blue.

"As I explained earlier, the compound consists of a mere eight buildings, each connected to an airlock and each with its own security passcode. Our workers are put into sterile cleanroom suits, similar to hospital scrubs. They wear shirts, pants, masks, boots—like a surgical team, as will all of you. Our sites operate at 99.97 percent decontamination, the highest in the industry. Next question, please."

An agent raised her hand. The woman pointed at her. "Yes?"

"We saw at least four more buildings when we arrived. What are the others?"

The lecturer smiled. "Dr. Hauser has generously leased some of the buildings on the site to a school for underprivileged children, an orphanage, a shelter for the homeless, and an animal rescue facility. Of course, these are done at no charge in order to assist the people of Indonesia in the greatest way possible."

DeShear walked to Camila.

"Welcome back," she whispered, keeping her eyes forward. "You missed over an hour of the most thrilling, paint-drying lectures I've ever had the displeasure to sit through—and I work for the IRS. Did you get what you were looking for?"

"Slight change in plans," DeShear said.

"Do I want to know what?"

255

"We're splitting from your team to get pictures. I think it's better if you don't know more at this point."

A few rows in front of them, another agent raised his hand. "Do you work with living genetic tissue?"

"That's a common misconception," the lecturer said. "Our procedures are largely done with computer models." A slide appeared on the screen— a young man with his face to the lens of a huge electron microscope. "We utilize a minimal amount of genetic material, as allowed to us by the World Health Organization, whose embryonic protocols were agreed to in Geneva in 1999 by . . ."

DeShear leaned to Camilla. "Did they count heads on the way in?"

"They don't have to." She held up her red plastic identification card. "We swiped these IDs through readers at the doors."

"Okay." He handed Camilla the cards they'd received a moment ago. "Take these and scan them for us on the way out."

Camilla slipped them into her pocket. "How will you be able to get out, then?"

DeShear chewed his lip. "I don't want to get into details and jeopardize what you're up to. You have a legitimate function here, so the closer you stick to that, the better—but make sure those cards get scanned on the way out. We don't want anyone to come looking for us. Are the FBI agents present?"

"Front row and back row."

"Good. We'll meet you at the reception tonight."

"Listen, Dash—"

"We'll be fine." He winked. "You know me."

Camilla grumbled. "That's what worries me."

An image of a laboratory appeared on the screen as the lecturer continued. "Workers pass through the first two rooms in this hallway for their decontamination process, and then they enter the labs in their cleanroom suits, through sealed airlocks. You will be permitted full access to the site, wearing the same protective gear and accompanied by members of our security team, as well as one of our geneticists who can answer any of your questions."

She slid her hands into her lab coat pockets and smiled as the Angelus Genetics logo reappeared on the screen. "As we said earlier, we wish to comply with all of your requests, and conclude your audit quickly and to the satisfaction of all."

CHAPTER 28

The short, round man stopped his golf cart with a screech, jumping out and rushing to the open door of the large jet. "Welcome back, sir! All of Jakarta welcomes you!" The scorching heat lifted from the tarmac, casting mirage-like reflections over the runway and sending up heat ripples that distorted the view of anything further than fifty feet away. Behind him, a private team of baggage handlers pulled open the plane's cargo hatch and unloaded suitcases.

A brown-haired woman in ripped blue jeans stepped off the jet first. Standing in the shadow of the jet, she clutched a bottle of water and twisted back and forth, stretching. Next came a tall, muscular man, wearing a blue blazer and sunglasses.

The tall man smiled and shook hands with his friend. "Thank you, *temanku*. Was it any trouble arranging for us to come in this plane?"

"Oh yes." The little man winced. "The Concorde has been banned here for many years. Much trouble has been caused by your loud arrival." He put his hands over his ears and made a face. "Sonic booms over Jakarta are not popular."

"This isn't a Concord." The American patted the side of the big plane. "It's better—a prototype from a company based out of Denver, and it flies at Mach 2.2. Knowing an investment banker or two has its privileges. They had one of these in New York, and four and a half hours later, here we are. Not too bad."

"Yes, but very loud."

"Well, our friends had a head start and I needed to catch up. How much money will it take to make anyone's issues about the noise go away? One hundred thousand American dollars?" He walked to the baggage cart and pulled off a blue suitcase. One of the baggage handlers rushed forward, but he waved them away. "Thank you, it's all right. I've got it."

His friend shrugged, massaging his hands. "That much money will most certainly take care of our friends in the government, but—"

He looked away, scowling. "Two hundred thousand, then."

The man clasped his hands in front of his chest, bowing. "As you wish, sir."

As the other suitcases were loaded onto the baggage tram, the little man and the American seated themselves in the golf cart. The woman took a seat behind them.

"Where is the helicopter?" the American asked.

"Right this way, my friend." He set the cart in motion, with the baggage tram following. They drove past several terminals and out toward the tree-lined edge of the airport property. Behind a chain link fence, a half dozen red Air Jakarta helicopters sat inside painted circles. Next to those stood another half dozen, in various colors. The golf cart came to a stop in front of a black six-seater. The pilot gave them a thumbs up, setting aside his clip board and moving his hands over the console. The whine of the shiny black turbojet quickly overwhelmed any other sounds nearby, as the big overhead blade crept into motion.

The American leaned forward, shouting to his little round friend. "*Teman*, I have something for you." He stepped out of the golf cart. The little man followed. Hefting the blue suitcase, the American placed it at the feet of his *teman.*

"By dawn, I will need the helicopter refueled in Bali," he shouted. "And this jet needs to be ready and waiting to leave again."

"It will be done. And I have something for you as well." The little man walked to the golf cart and pulled out a small, polished wooden case, the size of a box that would contain expensive silverware. "As you instructed, a high intensity air pistol—extremely lethal at close range. From China, but high-quality, and very reliable. But . . ." He shook his head. "My friend, I'm afraid a second noise infraction so soon may take more than another two hundred thousand dollars to correct."

The American lifted the suitcase and shoved it into his friend's chest, scowling. "There's a million dollars in cash inside that. Make it happen!"

"This is a mistake," the woman said. "You're throwing too much money around."

He grabbed the wooden case, glaring at her. "Get on the helicopter."

She climbed on board and sat in one of the plush blue seats, buckling herself in. The American threw the rest of the bags onto the floor in front of her, then grabbed the side rail and hauled himself into the cabin.

"It's my money." He sat, heaving the door shut. "I'll do what I want with it."

"It's going to raise eyebrows. You're putting the operation at risk like you did with that stunt in Canada."

He whipped around to face her, his eyes narrowing. "Maya, you disappoint me." Heat rose in his cheeks. "First, you hold out about a new medicine by saying you can't contact me. Then you get insubordinate with me in public and embarrass me in front of my friend."

"I'm just saying—"

"That is enough!" he shouted, his face growing redder with each breath. The veins throbbed in his neck. "One more outburst and I swear, I'll . . ." His hands trembled.

She backed away, pressing herself to the helicopter door, but also remaining defiant. "Stop it. You need me."

"Do I?"

"The medicines. You—"

"You told me you stole them and you had them made by private laboratories. It's fair to say when I check the receipts for the many, *many* things you've purchased, I'll get the names of those labs. Was there something else?"

"You—you're tired." She spoke in a soothing tone. "From your trip. We both are. You don't mean it." She placed her hands at her sides. "It's the new drugs. I—I told you, they contain steroids, but some of the new components are like steroids amplified—one of the side effects is being short tempered and irritable. They'll come and go, but—"

"I've never felt better." He glared at her. "But I don't kid myself, either. There's not much time left. Your drugs are going to give me a week, maybe more, but I know what waits for me after that. This work needs to get finished, and if I have to spend a little bit of money to make it happen, I don't want to hear about it from the likes of you. Do we understand each other?"

"Excuse me," the pilot said. "We are ready to depart for Bali. Please put on your headsets and make sure your seat belts are fastened."

The American took one of the headsets from the overhead clip, thrusting a second set at his companion. "Maya, I asked you a question," he growled. "Do we have an understanding?"

"Yes, Tristan."

"See, that's been part of our problem all along." He gritted his teeth. "We're too informal, too relaxed. We're getting sloppy. *'Tristan?'* This isn't a friendly tea party, this is business—so maybe we need to start acting like employer and employee.

Now, I'll ask you again. Do we have an understanding?"

She spoke softly, not taking her eyes off him. "Yes, Mr. Carerra."

CHAPTER 29

Camilla looked at herself in the mirror as the other female agents changed. Clad in a white jumpsuit from head to foot, including sewn-in booties, and a hood that surrounded all but her eyes, she brushed a damp strand of hair off her forehead. "I should have opted for the three-piece set."

"It's not better," one of her agents said rising from the locker room bench. Wearing the white scrub pants and shirt, similar booties, and a hood, she held out her arms and walked stiff-legged toward the mirror. "I look like a snowman."

"Well, Frosty." Camilla stuffed her clothes into a locker. "It's all for a good cause. Let's go. I hear the next room is even more fun." They passed several others coming from the showers.

"Make sure you're not entering the cleanroom with any cosmetics, lotions or sprays of any sort on your person," the lecturer told them for the second time.

Camilla and the agent walked around the corner to the locker room entry, a glass door with a large rectangular button next to it. Each entry they passed had a box of white latex gloves mounted on the wall, with hand sanitizer nearby. After they put on the gloves, they tucked them under their sleeves as they had been shown. Camilla elbowed the button to open the door. A whoosh of air blasted her head as they entered the small airlock. They waited for the door to shut behind them, then opened the second door. Another whoosh of air. On the other side, they passed a large bin labeled "Disposal for Gloves." As long as they hadn't touched anything in the airlock, they didn't need to replace their gloves, but the bins were everywhere. As the second door shut, the airlock made a sucking sound.

The gray-haired woman from the lecture stood at the front of the room. "You may sit anywhere. This room is completely sterilized every four hours." She strolled in front of a row of chairs, moving toward the podium. "I apologize for these inconveniences, but we must preserve the integrity of the sterile laboratory environment."

Camilla stared at her white-gloved hands. "I'm sure you get used to it after a while."

"Indeed," the woman said. "Only the front entry of every building contains the airlock, so all personnel must pass through the front entry to gain access to any building. Our workers joke that after they get home, they walk through the front door and reach for gloves they are not wearing, to throw them in the bin." She picked up some papers from the podium and tapped the edges, lining them up. To her left, a row of windows gave a view of a long hallway. Beyond them, another set of windows allowed a look at the outside. The large blue buildings of the strange campus stood, one after the other, spotless and clean, next to the dirt road that separated them. Each had a red sign out front, "Cleanroom Suit Required For Entry."

"When the others join us, we will begin our tour," the lecturer said. "And then you can return to your hotel to prepare for tonight's reception."

"Actually, I'd just as soon miss the gala and shorten this tour." Camilla approached the front of the room. "We have a lot of work to do, and we haven't been provided the on-site financials yet. We can split my group into teams and have some of them do the tour while the rest of us—"

The woman held up a hand. "The numbers will only make sense when you understand the facility and its many intricate functions. It's best that you—" She glanced at the window to the hallway. "Oh, we have a special treat."

An old man in a business suit stood next to several people wearing cleanroom attire. The gray-haired woman walked to an intercom unit mounted by an emergency exit, and pressed the button. "Good afternoon, Dr. Hauser."

"Good afternoon." He pointed his cane at the auditors passing through the airlock. "Are you treating our guests well?"

"Of course, sir."

"Fine, fine." His eyes passed across the men and women next to Camilla. "Ladies and gentlemen, I welcome you—and I welcome the opportunity to share the monumental scientific achievements we perform here on a daily basis. Angelus Genetics is truly changing the world. Enjoy the tour. I look forward to seeing you all tonight at the reception."

Camilla waved a hand. "Dr. Hauser—"

He leaned on his cane with both hands, shaking his head, his eyes on the intercom. "Please. I'll be happy to entertain any questions you have at the reception. Until then, you are in good hands. Thank you."

The intercom made a popping noise as he turned away, hobbling down the hallway.

Camilla leaned toward the agent next to her. "Make a note. The lecturer specifically said cleanroom suits have to be worn everywhere in this building, no exceptions, and in all buildings marked with the red sign out front. Why does everyone else have to wear these moon suits when he doesn't?"

"Hmm," the agent said. "So much for the integrity of the sterile environment."

"It's just a hallway, but no exceptions means no exceptions. My trainer at the IRS once said, when people are doing what's supposed to be their routine, pay attention to what varies. The things they don't remember to do every time are being done as a show for you."

"Why would he not wear the cleanroom suit?" the agent asked. "Where's he going, if this audit is allegedly the biggest thing in his life right now?"

Camilla folded her arms.

He's going to check on whatever actually is the biggest thing.

She sauntered to the glass, peering through the two sets of windows. The old man exited the building and climbed into a black golf cart. The others, still dressed from head to toe in white, joined him, and they drove away. In the distance, a few people dressed in full cleanroom attire entered the side door of another building with the red sign out front.

They aren't using the airlocks.

She whispered to the agent, "Without drawing attention, get a male agent to bring DeShear over here. You go get Ms. Kim. They're probably still in the locker rooms."

Let's find out where Dr. Hauser goes.

* * * * *

The desk clerk at the Viceroy Bali smiled at The Greyhound. "Welcome back, Mr. Huntley. How was your flight?"

"Fine." He smiled back, stepping to the counter. "I've brought a guest." He glanced at Maya, who sat on one of the overstuffed couches, her phone to her cheek. "I hope you'll be able to accommodate her with her own room. Adjoining mine, if possible."

"Of course, sir." The young man leaned over his computer keyboard. "We have a suite reserved for you, but if I may move sir to another floor, I can most certainly have your guest be next door."

The smile left The Greyhound's lips. "We're very tired, so I suppose that'll have to do for now."

"Very good, sir." The clerk typed for a moment, then placed the key cards on the counter. The Greyhound waved at Maya, who pushed herself up from the couch and walked over.

"Here are the keys," he said to her. "Go get settled in. I'll be up in a moment."

She took the plastic cards as a bellman approached with their bags.

The Greyhound turned back to the desk clerk. "And now I'd like to speak with the manager."

The clerk's face fell. "Sir, I'm happy to—"

"The manager. Now."

"Of course, sir." The clerk nodded.

Maya's jaw dropped. "Tristan—"

"It's fine." He turned to her, putting his hands on her shoulders. "Really, I'm not upset at all." He lowered his voice, smiling. "Go upstairs and relax. Please. This will only take a few minutes."

She watched his face for a moment. "Okay." Walking across the marble lobby with the bellman in tow, she pressed the elevator call button.

An older man appeared at the counter. "Mr. Huntley, how good to see you again. I understand there is a problem. How may I be of assistance?"

"Mister . . ." he read the manager's nametag. " . . . Rahmat, is it? Do you have an office where we can speak in private?"

"Of course, sir. Right this way."

The manager led The Greyhound down a hallway, past a door that opened into the service area. Huge carts of towels awaited the laundry machines, and a man in blue coveralls folded cardboard boxes, stacking them near the dumpsters.

"Here we are." The manager stood beside an office door, holding his hand out.

The Greyhound stepped inside and scanned the room, his hands going to his suitcoat pockets. A sturdy wooden desk and two chairs filled most of the space, along with several filing cabinets and a potted plant. There were no security cameras, and there hadn't been any in the hallway, either.

"Please sit." The manager eased the door shut. "I'm sure whatever the issue, we can—"

The Greyhound was upon him, handkerchief in his fist, thrusting it over the manager's nose and mouth. The man pushed back, but was unable to break The Greyhound's iron grip. Struggling until he needed a breath, the manager reluctantly inhaled the ether. His eyes rolled back in his head as his arms sagged; then his body went limp and he collapsed to the floor.

The Greyhound held the cloth on the manager's face until he was sure the man was unconscious, then rifled through the man's pockets. Attached on a retracting belt lanyard, with a dozen metal keys attached, was a plastic card—the manager's master room key.

The Greyhound unclipped the lanyard from the belt, slipping it into his pocket.

He stood, wiping his brow as he stared at the man on the floor. The Greyhound had no perspiration. A steady heartbeat. He stared at his hands—no trembling fingers.

Stay in control.

He nodded, taking a deep breath. The new version of the drugs had side effects, but now that he was aware of them, he could maintain his composure.

He opened the door a crack and peered down the hallway. Nothing. The service area was vacant, too. Stooping to grab the manager under the shoulders, he dragged him to an empty laundry cart and dumped him in. After enough towels from another cart had covered the unconscious Mr. Rahmat, The Greyhound administered the Propofol.

In six or eight hours when the manager woke up, he'd remember nothing.

The Greyhound returned to the office, locked it from the inside, and pulled the door shut from the hallway. Straightening himself up, he smoothed out his jacket and walked through the service area and into the big lobby, heading for the elevators.

* * * * *

"Cammy," DeShear whispered, his cleanroom suit covering everything but his eyes. "What's up?"

"The chairman of Angelus Genetics just went for a ride in a black golf cart," Camilla said. "If you hurry, he'll still be at whatever building he went into. I think you might use it as a starting point for your little side venture."

Lanaya peeked out the window, massaging her hands.

"Any idea how we can get around outside without being stopped?" DeShear asked.

"Have a look." Camilla peeked over her shoulder, keeping her voice low. "Others are walking around out there, dressed the same as us, and nobody seems to care. The security bit may be a ruse, but either way, if you move quickly and stay hidden between the buildings, you can probably go wherever you need to go."

He stared out the window. "I'll be darned."

"Wait for the tour to start, and as soon as we move from one building to another, just stay behind somewhere until the coast is clear. Maybe in an airlock, or duck behind an AC unit or something. Best I can think of at the moment."

"It'll be fine." DeShear said. "If there are other people out there wearing these moon suits, who'll know the difference? All that's visible is our eyes."

"Okay then." Camilla looked at him. "And if you get caught . . ."

"Don't worry." He took a step backwards, toward the rear of the room. "You knew nothing about it."

* * * * *

Dr. Hauser waited while one of the members of his party opened the door for him.

"I'm a bit concerned, sir," the man said, entering the warm, dim room. Ventilating fans turned overhead, while circulation pumps hummed below. "All these strangers, poking their noses around the facility. It's not a good idea."

Hauser waved the cane at him, hobbling down the shadowy center aisle. The stainless steel shelving was thirty inches wide and forty feet long, reaching thirty feet into the air. Each was spaced exactly thirty inches apart, for maximum capacity in each building.

"We'll keep them busy with the tour until it's time to go to the reception," the old man said. "Tomorrow morning, this audit nonsense comes to an abrupt end." Hauser squinted at the rows and rows of high shelves, his eyes adjusting to the low light.

"By the time they're done showering and suiting up again, I'll have my own private army here to meet them." He walked up to a shelf, inspecting one of the thousands of fluid-filled containers housed on each. Reaching past the long lines of surgical tubes running in and out through the container lids, he tapped the glass, staring at what floated within. "My people arrive at ten A. M. Then we'll see what happens with this little audit."

CHAPTER 30

"Please remember, stay with your guide." The gray-haired woman walked between the agents, her back stiff and her nose in the air, as she handed out white clipboards. "Use the airlock entrance at the front of every building. A new cleanroom suit will be provided to you as needed during the tour. Any—"

"Agents." Camilla addressed her group, looking right past the lecturer. "This is an inspection. It is part of an official audit. If you have questions that are not answered, direct them to me immediately."

"As I was about to say," the lecturer scowled at Camilla, "any questions will be handled by the guide assigned to your individual group."

Camilla raised her voice. "Any area of this property that you are not immediately granted access to, detach from your tour at once and report to me."

The lecturer's voice raised to a shrill pitch. "All visitors must remain with their group!"

Camilla glared at the woman. "Then you'd better grant immediate access to anything my people want to see."

A hush fell over the room. The agents watched the standoff in silence, their bureau chief's words hanging in the air.

A smile forced its way across the gray-haired woman's lips. "I shall see to it that all requests are handled in accordance with Dr. Hauser's generous instructions to us that you be accommodated fully."

One of the guides in a cleanroom suit ambled forward, reading from his clipboard. "The first eight agents, please step this way. We will be exiting through the airlock." A cluster of agents dressed in white moved forward. "This way, please."

Camilla lagged behind. The lecturer addressed her. "Which group will you be with, Ms. Madison?"

"I haven't decided yet. Do you have a suggestion?"

"The septic facility is that way." The old woman turned to walk away.

I'll look for your office there. Camilla offered her most professional tone. "If you'll excuse me, I have an investigation to conduct—and if attitudes don't improve around here, I'll be requesting additional time for a much more thorough and cooperative examination."

"Request what you like." The woman continued walking. "Your work here will come to a speedy conclusion soon enough."

"I'm in charge of the audit here." Camilla squared her shoulders. "It'll go on as long as I see fit."

The lecturer wheeled around, her eyes ablaze. "It will go on," she yelled, her voice echoing off the white walls. Catching herself, she lowered her voice. "It will go on for exactly as long as Dr. Hauser decides." She smiled again. "And not a moment longer."

An agent put her hand on Camilla's shoulder. "Boss . . ." He held a clipboard with a site plan in front of her. She straightened her spine and took it, flipping pages and staring at them until the lecturer exited.

The first group of agents filed out of the room. DeShear walked up to Camilla. "What was all that?"

"That," she winked, "was me making sure all eyes are on me and not on you. I'll go with the next group. You go with the one after that. First time they go around a corner, split off."

"Got it." He returned to Lanaya. "How are we holding up over here?"

She sat on a side bench, her fingers trembling as she held her clipboard. Squatting in front of her, DeShear took one of her hands and held it between his. "I think you're getting calluses from all the massaging you've been doing to these."

"I should think that's a far sight better than an ulcer or heart attack." She swallowed hard. "But I'll be all right."

He patted her hand. "I know you will."

DeShear debated about whether or not to tell Lanaya more about the sketchy plan. Additional information might help her calm down, or it might give her another thing to stress about. He opted for the "less is more" option and said nothing, taking a seat next to her on the bench.

Camilla's group moved forward with their guide.

DeShear stood. "Let's stand a little closer to them as they leave." He tapped an agent on the shoulder, whispering. "Get the group to come forward so it's not as easy to eyeball who's with what guide."

The agent nodded, rising. A moment later, the two groups were next to each other at the airlock. DeShear stood behind Camilla's group first, then slowly moved back to his. As the door opened and her team entered, he stepped aside at the last minute. The door shut in front of him, and he slid between the others on his team.

Their guide came forward, staring at a clipboard with a map of the facility on it. "As soon as they are out, we'll go." He raised the clipboard, pointing to a blue square at the front of the facility. "Our first stop is in records. I understand you folks like numbers. We have a lot of them there."

A chuckle went up from the team members.

The guide walked to the airlock door. "This way, please."

DeShear's group crowded into the space. The rear door shut and the door to the hallway opened, complete with the windy re-pressurization. The guide led them toward the exit. "Stay together, please."

DeShear put his hand on Lanaya's shoulder, holding her back and letting the others pass. The hallway had no security cameras.

Strange, for a facility that's supposed to be so security-oriented.

He clutched his white clipboard and peered out the windows, inspecting the other buildings. There were no visible cameras where they'd normally be—over doorways and on the corners of the buildings.

"Lanaya, did you see any mention of security cameras on the blue prints?"

"No, but that's not unusual." She clutched her clipboard to her chest. "Things like that are often added later. Why?"

"I don't see any." DeShear rubbed his chin. "They could be hidden, but part of the effectiveness of security cameras is letting some be visible so people know you have them."

They stepped outside, the heat mugging them in their cleanroom suits.

"This way," the guide said. "Stay together, please."

The prior group had gone to the right and were already a hundred feet away, waiting to enter the next building through its airlock. The guide for DeShear's group walked straight ahead, raising his clipboard and pointing to a blue square two buildings down and to the left.

As they walked, they passed utility fixtures. Large pumps, high-volume air handling units, and massive electrical boxes lined the blue exterior walls.

Plenty of space to duck behind.

The group neared the end of the first building. "As you can see, we have a first-rate facility," the guide said. "All construction was done using the highest possible standards . . ."

DeShear tapped the nearest agent on the shoulder. "Be sure this tour is the last one to finish today. And I mean, late-to-the-reception last."

The agent nodded.

When his group turned the corner, DeShear took Lanaya's arm and kept walking straight ahead. She blinked rapidly, her spine frozen as he drew her to an electrical closet, pressing both of them to its side.

"What now?" she whispered, plastering herself against the building.

DeShear pointed. "We move as fast as possible to that next building and take a spot in the exact same place. Got it?"

Her eyes went wide. "Do I run?"

"Walk fast." He peeked out from the electrical box, looking up and down the path. "Act like you're inspecting the roof. If someone sees us running, that'll attract attention." He gave her a nudge. "Go!"

Lanaya jumped out onto the dirt path, walking briskly. DeShear followed, gazing at anything upwards as he covered the ground between the buildings.

No visible cameras, but they still might have them.

Reaching the tall metal closet at the next building, the pair slid around next to it.

"Can we hide in these things?" she asked.

"It's high voltage stuff. I'd rather stay out here." DeShear glanced around. "Actually, I think it's time we got inside a building. Any thoughts on that? Do any of these big blue boxes look interesting to you?"

She shook her head. "On the blueprints, they had generic labels—but I'm sure those have changed since construction ended." She brushed the dust off a pipeline with her finger and inspected the label. "This is potable water. That one's 'gray' water— people have showered with it, or something similar." She looked up to where the pipes disappeared into the wall. "Doesn't look like anything interesting goes on in this one. I'd say the newer buildings, in the back, would be where the good stuff is."

The sound of a diesel motor echoed down the alleyway.

"Stay back," DeShear said, pressing himself to the wall.

She squeezed her eyes shut. The engine noise grew louder, the ground under their feet vibrating. A huge white tanker truck rolled by, sending up a cloud of dust.

Lanaya fanned her face. "So much for our cleanroom suits staying clean." She stuck her head out and looked at the back of the truck. "Well, now. That's interesting."

"What?" DeShear said, leaning forward. The dust trail obscured his view of the truck, except for the top of its big white tank.

Lanaya tucked her clipboard under her arm. "Let's follow that."

"Okay, but why?"

"That's a refrigerated dairy truck, Hamilton." She crept out onto the dirt road, putting a hand on her hip. "I can't think of a genetics lab in the world that uses milk in its protocols."

* * * * *

Holding his breath, The Greyhound held the big pellet gun next to his cheek, his hands trembling as he slid the manager's key card across the door lock. The latch for Dr. Bruner's room disengaged, and the door opened easily. The Greyhound tiptoed inside, ready to assault the obese board member.

Easing the door shut with latex glove-covered hands, he studied the scene. The shade curtains had been drawn, making the room dim. The aroma of food reached him from the room service cart by the desk. Empty plates and an empty bottle of wine littered the surface. On the bed, a thin brown-skinned girl stirred, curling away from the hairy back of the enormous fat man snoring next to her.

The Greyhound crept toward them, grabbing her dress from the floor. He tapped her shoulder. The young girl mumbled something incoherent and rolled over. As her eyes fluttered open, she recoiled with a gasp. Her tiny jaw dropped open as she stared at The Greyhound in his ski mask.

He lifted a finger to his lips, handing her the dress and pointing to the door. Her eyes went to his gun. "Go." He whispered. "*Pergi*. Now."

The girl nodded, taking the dress and wrapping it around her as she slid from the mattress. She bolted across the grand room, stooping to pluck a small purse from under the chair, then flung open the door and raced down the hallway.

The sound of the heavy door slamming shut awakened the fat man. He grunted, patting behind him without looking. When he didn't find his companion, he sat upright.

A long, slow wheeze escaped Dr. Bruner's lips as he stared down the barrel of The Greyhound's gun.

"Where is your phone?" The Greyhound asked. "Don't speak, just point."

The man swallowed hard, gesturing to the desk with a shaking hand.

"Thank you." The Greyhound went to the desk and picked up the phone. He tossed it onto the bed. "Open it."

Bruner's pasty complexion turned whiter as he stared at the phone.

"Open it, or I'll shoot you in the head and hold your dead finger to it, and open it anyway."

He grabbed for the phone, fumbling as he picked it up.

"Press the texting icon."

Dr. Bruner panted, pressing a button. The screen came to life.

"Put it on the bed and slide it to me."

The doctor complied, his large torso rocking forward to shove the device a few inches closer to the intruder.

"Thank you." The Greyhound picked it up, leaning back on the edge of the desk as he thumbed through the texts. "Ah, here we are. 'I am taken sick. Will miss reception dinner, but will be back in action tomorrow morning.' Hmm." The Greyhound pressed the top of the text message to see its recipients. "This went out to the other board members."

Bruner nodded, his mouth hanging open.

The Greyhound raised his gun, aiming at the doctor's forehead. "You've saved me the trouble of worrying about who might come looking for you if you missed dinner." He stood up, stepping closer to his cowering victim. "And you're sick all right, judging from the age of the escort you hired."

The fat man stammered, his mouth unable to form words.

The Greyhound pulled off the ski mask, staring into the eyes of his victim. "You thought you'd gotten away with it. You and the other Angelus board members. The executives, the project managers—you all thought you could hide your secrets in the jungle, but you can't. Some secrets refuse to remain hidden."

He fired. The large air gun bucked in his hand, making a sharp *pfff* noise as the pellet burst forth. The doctor jerked backwards into the pillows. His arms and legs flailed as he struggled to get his bearings.

"These are as lethal as a gun, and every bit as fast. Two to the side of the head will kill you. That's what I came to do." The Greyhound leaned over the man. "Now that we've met in person and I've seen your recreational pursuits, I'm even more convinced of my decision."

Bruner gurgled, grabbing aimlessly, his head swaying back and forth until he sagged into the mattress.

"Good thing for you I'm in a rush. I have several other appointments this evening, with colleagues of yours." The Greyhound tossed the phone back onto the bed, putting the barrel of the gun against the fat man's temple. "I hope they're less distasteful than this one's been."

* * * * *

The tanker truck drove to the far end of the complex, a straight line down the path Lanaya and DeShear were on, then turned left.

"I think we should move a little faster through here." Lanaya's words huffed as she walked. "We don't want to lose that truck."

"Agreed. And . . ." DeShear took her clipboard and stacked it with his, reaching up to slide both onto the top of the next electrical closet they passed. "I think the IRS auditors are the only ones carrying those."

At the end of the building, they peeked around the corner and scurried across the gap. Lanaya shook her head. "I've been in a lot of genetics labs in my day, Hamilton. I don't think this place has much in the way of security."

"Maybe not in the traditional sense." The image of the big man with the machine gun flashed in his mind. Again, he decided less information was better for his client. "But let's not guess wrong."

When they reached the end of the row of blue buildings, DeShear stood next to one of the electrical boxes and looked back over his shoulder, counting the buildings. Twenty. Much more than were visible at the front. The road was wider here, too, and paved with asphalt. By setting each building a few feet further away from the dirt road than the next, it was impossible to see them all from the front of the complex.

An error in construction, or an easy way to allow visitors to only see what you wanted them to see?

He answered his own question when they rounded the next corner.

CHAPTER 31

The Greyhound slid his personal key card across the hotel lock and thrust open the door to his room. The interior door to the adjoining suite was open. He tossed the air gun onto the bed and unbuttoned his shirt, yanking its tails from his beltline. "Maya, when is my next dosage due?"

"Depends." Dr. Carerra stepped into the doorway between the two rooms. "When was your last one?" Leaning on the door frame, one of her hands dangled at her side while the other rested on her hip.

"Dominique," he whispered, rushing to her. He pulled her close and buried his face into her shoulder, his hands sliding along her back. The long, dark curls of her hair brushed past his face. "Oh, I've missed you," he said.

She slid her hands inside his shirt, wrapping them around him, squeezing him as if she never wanted to let go. A soft moan escaped her lips.

Leaning back, he took her face in his hands and crushed his mouth to hers, devouring her warm, full lips. He kissed her again and again, tears coming to his eyes. Pressing his cheek to her face, he rocked back and forth in the doorway, his hot breath rushing over her neck. "You left New York without saying goodbye."

She stroked the back of his head, running her fingers through his hair. "I had to maintain appearances in front of the others. I've missed you, my love. I can't stand being away from you." She closed her eyes and kissed the back of his neck. "Especially not now. Maya said you were having mood swings. Anger and rage."

"I'm handling it." He drew a deep sigh, pulling away from her. "And the work is almost done. Soon—"

"Okay. Shh." She pressed a finger to his lips, shaking her head. Her voice fell to a soft whisper. "Not now. Let's talk of other things. There's plenty of time to discuss all that later."

"I wish you were right." He stepped away to face the window. The Bali skyline glimmered in the afternoon heat. "Doing . . . this, these things—" he turned to her. "It's not how I envisioned spending my last remaining days."

She closed her eyes, leaning her head back. A tear ran down her cheek. "I . . ." she sniffled, staring at the ceiling. "I wish I could do more for you."

"Don't say that. You did what you could. Everyone has. The latest version of the meds have made me feel better than I've felt in months. That can't be a bad thing."

"No." She shook her head, mascara streaming over her cheeks. "It's not."

"Be strong." He went to her, taking her in his arms. "We need you strong, this team we've assembled. And later . . . I mean, after . . ." He gazed into her eyes. "Our boys will need you to be strong. You'll be all they have left soon."

"But one in five survive. We have to think about that. You could—"

"Don't believe the stats from the cretins that created this nightmare. Don't pin your hopes on a lie."

"The numbers . . ."

"Numbers don't bleed." He walked to the window, leaning on the frame. "They don't cough all night until their ribs ache and their throats are on fire. They don't vomit blood and pass out in the shower from the hammering pain of a migraine. They don't cry as child after child parades by in a nonstop blur of hospital visits that only end at the morgue. Numbers . . ." he shrugged. "They give the wrong people false hope. And any numbers from Angelus are lies."

She crossed the room to him, stroking his back. "You said you were feeling better."

"It takes bigger and bigger doses and more each time." He lowered his head. "That's the fine print. Three injections a day become six, become nine. Pretty soon I'll be shooting up every fifteen minutes just to stay awake."

Wrapping her arms around his naked torso, she pressed her cheek to the warm skin of his shoulder. "They're working on the longevity."

"I'm working on longevity, too. It's all I have left. That, and you—and a little more work. Then I can go. I'll know I did what I could, regardless of the personal costs."

She lifted her chin to rest on his shoulder. He leaned his head against hers, both of them staring out the window. A gentle breeze swept across the landscape, making the palm trees dance and sway. "Do you remember how we used to be?" she asked. "Before we started our life together? When we first met?"

"I think about it all the time." He put his hand on hers. "The pretty young intern who got invited into the big prospectus meeting."

"I was there to take notes. Not even notes—I was the backup to the note taker."

"I remember blue eyes and long dark hair. A pink glow on tan cheeks, from a weekend at the beach. And a smile that lit up the room."

"I remember a tall, confident hedge fund manager, holding court over all the big, powerful people at the company. And they all listened. You owned the room."

"You wore a green silk blouse." The tip of his finger traced the curves of her French nails. "Green, with little white flowers on the bottom of it. I barely made it through my presentation." He turned to face her, chuckling as he leaned back against the window frame. "I couldn't keep my eyes off you. Then or now. You showed me how to love again. After I lost Megan, I never thought I'd care for another woman that way, or want a family. You gave all that back to me."

She rested her head on his smooth, firm chest. "I still have that blouse. I take it out of the box in the hall closet sometimes and daydream about how things used to be."

"Tell me."

"I think about things I wish I'd done differently. Like not getting Sadie the job at Angelus, or not even going to med school. Not saying yes to Keenan when he proposed after high school. Lots of what ifs."

He pulled his head back so he could see her face. "I think sometimes if we took out the bad things in life, it might take away the good things that came after. Our paths led each of us to the other. For better or for worse."

"Mostly better." She snuggled against him. "Hug me."

He put his cheek to her hair, closing his eyes and pulling her closer.

"Tighter," she whispered. "One day soon, I might not be able to do this, and I want to remember."

He took a deep breath and let it out slowly. "Remember me how I was before this started, not who I've become. The me from a few years ago."

"I'll take you now and then, and with mood swings and 'roid rage, with any negative side effects and any other changes." She sniffled, looking into his eyes. "I'll stand by you, as you take vengeance on people who did unspeakable things to you and others, and I'll keep working night and day to find a cure." Tears welled in her eyes again. She swallowed hard. "I'll take any of it over a long, slow, irreversible, slide toward death—but only if you will, too. If you'll fight with me—for you."

He lowered his chin, easing his forehead to rest against hers. "The drugs may keep me on my feet, but I fight every day because you give me the strength."

* * * * *

DeShear stared at the wall of bamboo trees. The wind crashed their tall, thin trunks together, sending knocking sounds down to earth, like musical sticks or hollow blocks hidden somewhere high up in the long green leaves.

But through the noise of the wind and the trees, the distant sound of children reached his ears.

He caught glimpses as he walked. Running, laughing, singing, sitting, the sun shining bright on their t-shirts. There were hundreds, maybe more. Bits of color flashed through the foliage. Red, white, green, blue—clothing of every color, every shape, every size; some faded, some new—all adorning the mobs of children in the big field.

To his left, the road cut a hole through the barrier trees. He walked to it, his eyes on the distant children. It was a pleasant sound, a soothing one— and a nice difference from the undertone of the rest of the campus.

A cluster of girls made a circle and danced. Another group played jump rope. Beyond them, soccer and ring toss. Tumblers and jumpers and mad-dashers playing tag, he stared in disbelief at the throngs of children at play.

It had been many years since he'd paid attention to that sound, or cared to remember it, and it warmed him inside. "This must be the orphanage, or the school," he whispered, mostly to himself. "Or both."

Lanaya stood next to him, her jaw hanging open. "There are so many."

"Halo."

DeShear turned to see a wrinkled old woman approaching from the blue buildings. The tanker was parked next to the building behind her. She waved at DeShear, donning a dark colored head scarf and a semi-toothless grin. *"Halo, teman-teman saya."*

"I'm sorry," DeShear said. "I'm new to speaking Indonesian. I speak very little." He put a finger to his chest. *"Saya . . . tidak berbicara."*

"Ah." She held her arms out at her sides as she walked, her long, dark dress frayed at the hem. *"Parlez-vous français?"*

He shrugged. "Sorry. American."

The old woman took his hand, patting it. She looked up at him with brown eyes that were fading to a milky white, gently pulling him toward the playground. "Come. You can see." She pulled again, and he followed. "Come."

Her steps were short and hobbled, but she moved quickly. She swept her free hand outward at the field full of children. *"Indah.* Beautiful, yes?"

Still holding the old woman's hand, DeShear nodded. "Where did they all come from?"

Lanaya walked behind them, saying nothing.

The field was even bigger than he'd thought. Easily a few hundred yards away still, it spanned close to a half mile in each direction, a strange, green playground chopped out of the jungle. A thick line of bamboo bordered it on all sides.

It's not a fence. Where would they go—and why would they leave? It's a visual barrier. This area isn't meant to be seen from the ground.

DeShear's host stopped but still held his hand. She smiled as she viewed the children. *"Semua ciptaan alam itu indah."*

He caught "beautiful" again, but that was all. "Do you work in the school, ma'am?"

"I am *saudara*," the old woman said. "Sister."

"Sister? Like a nun?"

She pulled him along, walking along the bamboo wall. "Come. You can see."

"Where is the orphanage?" DeShear said. "The buildings for the school? This way?"

The old woman hobbled over the grass. "Come."

DeShear followed, towed at a quick pace by his elderly host, nearing the hundreds of children. It was as if an entire grade school had been released at one time. Kids of all ages were scattered everywhere. He passed by a tall metal pole with speakers on top.

That must be how they call them in from recess.

As he got closer, the groups were easier to see. Not all of the children played. Many sat watching, or sat on the sidelines *not* watching, as others played.

Lanaya stayed on the road as DeShear dropped the sister's hand and walked toward the children. Clad in the cleanroom suit from head to toe, his taller white frame stood out in sharp contrast against the green of the field.

An errant kick launched a soccer ball in his direction. A small, barefoot boy galloped after it, running in a lopsided way. "Bola, bola."

The ball rolled close to DeShear. He walked forward to retrieve it, but the boy was faster.

"Bola." Panting, the child called after the ball, plodding along with his hands outstretched. "Bola."

DeShear's stomach lurched at the sight of the child. The boy had the same jaundiced color as the guards at the gate. The same half-open jaw. He was shoeless, with messy hair, and his dirty clothes fit poorly and had holes in them. His curved spine forced his right side down onto his hip. He didn't run lopsided because he had no shoes; he ran that way because that was the only way he could run. His head was too large for his body, giving the appearance at a distance of being younger than he was. The face of the child was thirteen, maybe older; the body, maybe five or six.

The boy picked up the ball and ran back to the game, moving in his unbalanced lope. "Bola . . . bola."

A sick feeling rising in his gut, DeShear inched closer to the hordes of children.

The sickly look was present on many faces. Some were missing legs or arms. Boys playing soccer without shirts displayed massive surgery scars on their backs. Children with shirts had blood stains seeping through around rectangular bandages.

He stumbled forward, his heart in his throat, taking it in, unable to stop himself from seeing what the field presented.

A girl with no arms smiled at him, her dress a tattered rag. Next to her, another girl sat on the ground, her eye sockets shriveled and empty.

"What's happened?" DeShear said, his voice trembling. "What's happened to all of you?"

The girl with no eyes turned her face to him. Her words flowed slowly from her hanging jaw. *"Apakah kamu punya permen?"*

"What?" DeShear swallowed hard, his voice breaking. With tears welling in his eyes, he took a step toward her and extended his hand.

"Permen?" Another girl echoed. *"Permen."*

The children swarmed in on him, hands out, clamoring at his cleanroom suit. *"Permen?"*

DeShear's jaw hung open, his breath coming in short gasps. They were all deformed in different ways. Misshapen heads, missing teeth, missing limbs. Some sat on the grass, staring off at nothing. Others limped forward, fresh bandages on their backs or abdomens.

He didn't want to breathe. He didn't want to see. But it was everywhere, all around him. Every child he saw had a different malady.

They were too thin, too dirty, too short, too ragged. They were undernourished, with sickly yellow skin. Their faces looked at him, but few had much glimmer of awareness in their eyes. They were less like children and more like . . . newborns. Alive and functioning, doing human things, but not engaging in the recognition and intelligence that even a one-year old displayed. They were slow and disengaged, not really seeing, not really hearing.

Dozens crawled toward him over the grass, dragging their legs behind them, not a wheelchair in sight.

"Permen. . . permen."

They mobbed him, gently pawing him, idly chanting.

"Permen. . . permen."

"Sister!" DeShear turned to the old woman, the force of the mob of children pushing him this way and that. "What is it? What do they want?"

Lanaya stood with her hands over her mouth, tears welling in her eyes.

"Permen." The old woman held a wrinkled hand up to her brown, weathered face, pinching her bony fingers closed and pointing them at her mouth. "They ask, 'Do you have candy?'"

Candy. DeShear gasped, his words no longer leaving his mouth, his knees wobbling. Dozens more children pushed forward from all areas of the field.

The old sister clapped her hands three times. The children stopped, the field going silent. All eyes were upon her, each child standing completely still. A strigidae owl screeched in the distance.

"Biarkan dia dating," the old woman said. The children near DeShear stepped and bumped, moving backwards to clear a path for him, back to the where the sister stood on the road.

He waited, unmoving, not yet ready. His heart pounded as he yanked the hood of his cleansuit down past his face, staring at the old woman and choking on his words. "What's happened to them?"

"Parosesseen." She turned and pointed a brown, wrinkled finger. The bamboo wall came to a corner and turned, exposing more blue buildings.

Above the doors, a sign said "Processing."

CHAPTER 32

"Ms. Madison?" the young agent asked. "They're calling for us to go back to the main building and depart for the hotel."

Camilla glanced at her watch. "Thanks. I'll be right there."

"Yes, ma'am." The young woman turned to go.

"Hastings," Camilla said.

The agent stopped. "Yes, ma'am?"

"Any word on DeShear or Ms. Kim? Have any of our people seen them at all?"

"No ma'am. Not since we started the tour."

"Okay. Thanks." Camilla stared down the dirt road, the sun hanging low in the sky, as the agent joined the others. Camilla took one last view of the many large buildings before heading toward the rest of her group, a long line of white-suited agents in front of them.

"Excuse me." Camilla trotted to their guide. "I need to arrange for a hired car."

The man kept walking, not looking at her. "We have orders to take everyone to the hotel."

Camilla stopped, putting her hands to her hips. "Orders?"

"I mean," the guide stopped, facing her. "Our orders—our instructions—were to see that you are all safely returned to your hotel." He worked a smile onto his face. "So you may have enough time to prepare for this evening's reception."

"Uh huh. Well, I have another meeting first, so I need a cab. Have one sent to the front of the security building. Now. And I'll be taking several of my staff with me."

"I'm sorry, ma'am," the guide said. "But—"

Camilla narrowed her eyes. "Do you want me to miss a video conference with the Vice President of the United States? Do you think that's good business for your employer?"

The man's jaw dropped. "No."

"Then call me a cab, and do it quickly." Camilla pointed. "I want it at the front door before I get there. Understood?"

"Yes, ma'am." The guide walked away quickly, then broke into a run.

The young agent leaned close to Camilla. "We have a meeting with the Vice President?"

Camilla turned to her. "I asked if he wanted me to miss a meeting with the Vice President." Camilla grinned. "I didn't say I had one. Grab some other agents and have them mill around my cab as everyone boards the buses, so it's not obvious whether DeShear and Lanaya went with me."

"Yes, ma'am."

"Okay." Camilla said. "If you get asked, they did."

* * * * *

"How is security?" Maya asked, sliding a needle into The Greyhound's arm.

"There isn't any." He looked away from the syringe, focusing on the tube taped to his other arm.

Dominique picked through a series of bottles in a padded suitcase. "That's not entirely true. My good friend Dr. Hauser arranged for security, but apparently only for himself. A few of the men with him are soldiers from the Indonesian Army, dressed as civilians." She stood, walking to the bed. "I suppose the rest of us are on our own—although he made it clear during the conference call with the board that wouldn't be the case."

Maya administered another injection and inspected the IV drip. "What about your strength? How are you holding up?"

"Good." The Greyhound stared at the tubes carrying drugs into his arm. "And so is my attitude. If I didn't lose it on that pervert Bruner, I'm not going to."

"Did you want to?" Dominque looked into his eyes. "Was there any inclination toward rage?"

"Are you analyzing me, Doctor? I was focused on the job. I already knew—"

"It's important to understand." Maya stood, crossing the room to the bag of bottles. "As these treatments get more frequent, the inclination to react harshly will increase."

"I can keep it together."

"Tristan," Dominique leaned forward. "She's trying to say you might not realize you're going too far. These drugs affect your emotions and reactions."

He chewed his lip. "I . . . I was dispassionate. I knew what I was there to do, and how I was going to do it. I knew Bruner wasn't going to suffer much, so when I saw the girl, I wanted to get her out of there and get it over with."

"No feelings of rage?" Dominique asked.

"No."

"Any feelings at all?"

"Not like before." Behind him, the sun touched the tops of tall buildings in the distance. "Look, I know what you're thinking. You're worried I'm getting de-sensitized to it, to the killing. Well, I am. And I think I need to be. If I thought too long about what my task is at any given moment, I'd hesitate—and then I might make a mistake. That could cost all of us. But if you want to know how I sleep at night, well . . . not very good." His eyes went to Dominique. "And not all the vomiting is from the sequence breaking me down, okay?"

She nodded. "Okay."

Maya pulled the IV tape from his arm and removed the needle, pressing a ball of cotton to the injection site. She tore a short piece of white tape and pressed it over the cotton.

"Tonight, I can get several of them here in the Viceroy. The rest, I'll get tomorrow at the facility.

I'll wear one of their moon suits, and whenever any of them separate from the group, I'll be ready."

* * * * *

"Come. You can see." The little woman hobbled toward the second set of buildings—the ones marked Processing. "Come. I will show."

"Hamilton." Lanaya grabbed his arm, wiping the tears from her eyes. "I heard rumors about this— I read about it on the black screen site. But . . ." She swallowed hard, looking out over the masses of children. "I—I don't think I really ever conceived that they'd . . ."

He took her hand, squeezing it gently. "I understand."

"They're . . . they're children." Her words caught in her throat. "Little children. Babies. And they're chopping them up."

"And we're going to stop it. All of it." He leaned forward, frowning. "We're going to make this madness end."

She nodded, drying her eyes.

DeShear handed her his phone. "Can you take pictures? And maybe some video? Let's focus on finding things that will get the newspapers to help us end all this."

She took the phone and stared at it, her voice a whisper. "Yes."

DeShear glanced at the old woman.

"Come." She walked toward the processing building. "I will show."

An eighteen-wheeler truck was parked at the rear of the second facility. Behind it, in the distance, stood a bulldozer and a back hoe.

Breaking ground on their latest building.

The nearest side of the building was lined with oval tanks. Pipes ran from them and into the building. Red warning signs had been mounted on the front of each one.

DeShear pointed. "What do you think those are for?"

"It's a surgery facility," Lanaya sniffled. "Those will be gases for operations and medical functions. Oxygen, nitrous oxide, carbon dioxide, nitrogen. That sort of thing." She lowered her voice. "Why do you think she's showing us all this?"

He lifted the ID card from the lanyard around his neck. "It's an executive level pass. She probably does this all the time for the big wigs." DeShear trudged along, glancing over his shoulder. "Probably figured that's what we were doing all the way down here. To her, we're VIPs."

The processing facility had no airlock. They opened the doors and went right in.

Cool air swept over his face. A few overhead lights were on in the massive building, illuminating the glass rooms below. Each was about twenty feet square, and maybe twenty feet high, with an operating table in the center and a rack of lights over it. Several tray tables were nearby, and a long row of gurneys lined the corridor.

DeShear walked up to one of the operating rooms, his footsteps echoing through the empty facility. Beside him, the old woman smiled. "It is here. Very good, they take bad parts out of the children."

"I—I can't believe it," DeShear's shoulders slumped, his breath fogging the glass. "They tell them they're sick, and then . . . they chop them up and sell off the pieces."

The faces of the children, asking for candy, clouded his vision. Their scars and deformities blocked his view of the surgical machinery in front of him. "That's why they look jaundiced." He turned to Lanaya. "They're not underfed. They can't process the nutrients."

She stared at the operating room, her eyes unfocused and vacant. "You take out a liver, or a section of intestine, or some knee cartilage . . . I'm not sure the recipient asks where it comes from. They're told cadavers, for some of it. Recent car crashes and the like." She inched closer, placing her hand on the glass. "They . . . they have no idea."

"How many organs can a—" DeShear exhaled sharply.

The back hoe.

His heart raced as rage welled inside him. "Where's the back exit?" he shouted, running down the aisle. "How do I get out of this place?"

He sprinted past room after room of operating tables, fear growing in his gut, his eyes scanning the walls. When he found the exit sign, he didn't slow down. He threw both hands into the door's crossbar and slammed it open. Racing across the short span of asphalt, he hurled past the truck and up a small hill. When he reached the top, the bulldozer and back hoe were visible again.

The ground was churned and uneven, like a recently plowed field. The wind shifted, bringing the smell to him, assaulting his nose and making him choke—but he forced himself to keep going.

At the bulldozer, he stopped, panting as he gazed over the big hole. To his right, the back hoe rested silently, its shovel posed in midair, ready to continue its work the next day.

Below it, the tiny faces.

Gasping, DeShear sank to his knees, almost unable to speak, the breath going out of him. "No. Please, no."

Row after row of small bodies lined the hole, dusted with lime to kill the smell and speed decomposition.

Blank eyes stared up at him. Their young faces were empty and gray. Some had been wrapped with a loose sheet; others were nude, their play clothes probably saved for another child.

He stood on the edge of the hole, shaking his head, unable to fathom the minds that could do such things. There were so many bodies stacked in the rows, they seemed not to be real.

But the smell made it real. The stink of rotting meat, and the buzz of the flies. The half-buried bodies, some with dirt resting on their open eyes and mouths, next to the feet and hands of their little playmates, that was all too real.

"Hamilton!" Lanaya made her way up the small hill. "What is it?"

"No." He jumped up, the soft brown dirt sinking under his feet. He fell to his knees. "Stay there. You don't need to see this."

"I have to take pictures."

He got up and ran to her. "Don't. I'll do it." He took the phone. "Go. Go now."

She stared at him for a moment, then nodded, backing away.

He faced the hole in the distance, then looked at the mud under his feet. This, too, had been recently filled. He was standing on the graves of other children.

He winced, stumbling backwards, looking for an unturned patch of ground, not wishing to further desecrate the burial site.

For hundreds of yards in all directions, there was none.

CHAPTER 33

DeShear paced back and forth in front of the tanker truck as the old woman looked on. "How can you be a part of this, smiling and walking around like it's not happening? What is wrong with you?"

She shook her head. "Not to understand."

He gritted his teeth, pointing at the play field. "Those children are being slaughtered. Killed. Don't you care?"

"Killed?"

"Yes. Those kids, right there. Aren't they your responsibility?"

"They die, you say. I make them alive." Her tone was calm and even, her hands held in front of her. A teacher, teaching. "When I come here, they not play. They not sing. They sit, like dog, in rooms. I make this."

DeShear shook his head. "You . . . you . . ."

"Everyone die. You, me. I cannot stop the bad. But I can make better, this." She waved her hand toward the playground, a thin smile on her lips. "For some good, for them. Do you understand? I help them come from baby to now, and know some joy of the world."

"Babies? Where do you have babies?"

"We have. Come. You can see."

She led them back to a building near where the milk truck had been.

"I don't know if I want to see anymore." Lanaya shuddered.

"Well, you have to." DeShear scowled. "And so do I. We're in this thing. With the pictures I just took, we have enough to bring this whole place down, but the people at the top have a plan for that. They'll deny, they'll obfuscate. They'll say some low-level person in charge went rogue. I want proof that they knew all along, so there's no escape for the freaking monsters who did all this."

The sister hobbled past the sign demanding everyone wear cleanroom suits to enter, pushing open the door. She held it for them. "Come. Here is."

DeShear checked the battery on his phone. More than fifty percent. Hopefully, more than enough.

The room beyond the open door was dark. He looked at the old woman. "The babies are in here?"

"Yes. Come." She brushed past him into the dim room. "You can see."

DeShear took a few steps into what appeared to be a library or warehouse, pausing as his eyes adjusted to the dim light. It was almost as hot inside as it was outside. That hadn't been the case in the operating building. Lanaya entered the room and let the door close, shutting out most of the light.

Rows of shelves were visible, but not much else. A steady, low hum filled the air. He scanned the ceiling, where large circulation fans turned slowly, their massive blades black against the fading light of the sunset sky. A gear engaged somewhere in the back, with the whir of an electrical motor, and the concrete floor under his feet vibrated.

Pumps. Fans.

He walked down the center aisle, between the shelves, and opened his mouth to ask the sister where the babies could be in such a place. It was sterile and dark, but warm.

A fine bead of sweat formed on his lip. As he went to wipe his shoulder across it, Lanaya turned on the flashlight from his phone, shining it downward to light the floor.

The glint off the glass was the first evidence he had that anything was even in the room but the shelves. Clear, rectangular containers rested end to end, with hoses running across the tops, each diving down to the shadow floating inside.

He stepped forward, his mouth open and his guts in a knot, as he reached out to touch the container and convince himself that what he saw was really there.

Inside the glass, attached with surgical tubes, was a human baby. They floated, not fully formed, looking part human, part fish, with large, round heads and curled, translucent bodies, floating in a silent pool. Their eyes, formed but not seeing. Tiny organs were visible through the undeveloped skin.

Hands with fingers reached outward at him. Tiny feet pulled close, as if to offer protection from whatever might come in the darkness.

He panted hard, his hands shaking as he moved to the next container. It held another fetus, as did the next. They were like aquariums, spanning as far as he could see. The shelves went to the ceiling, and from front to back in the room, with just enough space to step in between them and maneuver.

He shook his head, his gaze going down the row as far as the light from the phone allowed, shimmering off dozens and dozens of containers.

Babies. They're growing fetuses here.

He looked at Lanaya. She stood by the first row, staring at the glass. They were larger there. Farther along, maybe by a few months. The ones by DeShear were smaller. He walked down the aisle in silence, peering at the smaller and smaller residents of the containers.

Pictures.

"Lanaya," he said.

"I'm on it." She wiped away a tear and held up the phone, hitting the video record button. The front light came on as the phone started recording. She gasped, quickly aiming the beam at the floor. "What about the brightness of this light? Will it hurt their eyes?"

"I don't know," DeShear said, swallowing hard. "I think it might. You figure, these would normally be inside some layers of skin and muscle."

He leaned back, scanning the ceiling, forcing himself to concentrate. There might be special lighting. He didn't want to gather evidence and blind thousands of victims in the process.

Thousands.

They grow them here until they're big enough, then take them to processing and start carving them up.

Nausea gripped him. He shook it off and counted the shelves he could see. There were more than a dozen and a half on each side of the aisle, reaching to the ceiling. Each had an occupant, as far as he could tell. There'd be no reason to have hoses going into a container if there wasn't. There had to be tens of thousands of fetuses, possibly more. Maybe a hundred thousand.

"Sister, are there any lights in here? One that won't hurt the eyes of the babies?"

"Light, yes. Here. I will show." She walked past him in the nearly-dark room. DeShear followed, with Lanaya behind him, cupping her hand over the phone. Only part of the light went past her fingers, but it was enough to act like a small flashlight.

At the back wall, the old woman turned. About ten feet down the aisle, a panel of knobs and switches was mounted on the wall. "Here is light."

Lanaya raised the beam, still covering it, allowing the reflected light to illuminate their way. Her hand glowed red, showing the bones within, like the skin of the fetuses.

DeShear studied the panel.

The front door opened, and the room was bathed in orange light from the setting sun.

"This way, gentlemen." A man's gravelly voice boomed forth into the room, accompanied by a sharp, intermittent *clack* of hard wood hitting concrete.

DeShear crouched, grabbing Lanaya's arm and pulling her downward. He put a finger to his lips and nodded at the camera. She held it to her chest and shut off the light, snapping the side button down to "mute."

The old woman watched with an expressionless face, not moving from the panel. She curled a wrinkled finger at her two guests, tiptoeing further down the row to the corner.

Several men could be heard in the room. DeShear took Lanaya's hand and slinked toward the old sister. She rounded the corner and stepped into a small wooden closet—mostly empty, but big enough to house all three of them, and unable to be seen from the front of the room.

"Haskins, get the lights." The gravelly-voiced man said. "My friends, here is where the real magic of our facility resides."

Footsteps came down the aisle, toward them. DeShear held his breath, hoping the man found the light panel and nothing else. Next to him, the sister stood, unwavering.

A figure rounded the corner. DeShear eased his head back, balling his fist as the silhouette neared. The man stopped halfway down the row and snapped some switches. A dim, pink glow washed over the room as the assistant went back to the others.

The man with the gravelly voice spoke again. "The room will get slightly brighter over the next few minutes, but your eyes will quickly adjust. We also have still images we can show you of any specimens, and I can bring infrared and ultrasound equipment in if you should so require."

DeShear crouched, inching out from the wooden closet and peeking at the group that had entered the room. There were six total, three facing him and three facing away.

Two of the men appeared to be Asian, with black hair and dark eyes. A third man was tall and blonde. Of the people facing away from him, two wore cleanroom suits. The other had gray hair and was hunched over, dressed in a dark business suit. He gestured with a cane as he spoke.

"We call this the Fetal Development, Retention and Obstetric Nutrition Enclosure," the old man said, his gravelly voice rumbling over the glass containers. "Its nickname is the drone room, because it resembles a beehive—and we have been so very busy. Each human embryo here has been developed from our stock, genetically selected to be free of almost every form of human suffering, and housed in our proprietary synthetic amniotic fluid, much like that of a real human womb. We have four such buildings on site, and each contains over a million live specimens in various stages of growth. As your eyes adjust to the special lighting, feel free to look around."

"That's Dr. Hauser," Lanaya whispered. "The one with the cane."

"There are concerning rumors," one of the short, black haired man said. His accent was decidedly Asian, possibly of Chinese descent. "I have heard they die early."

A man in a cleanroom suit waved a hand. "All developmental sciences have challenges—"

Hauser stepped in. "Any of these specimens not developing adequately are terminated. Fetuses determined to be inadequate for any reason can be selected for terminus prior to introduction into the synthetic utero habitat you see here, while others are terminated in infancy. We have very strict standards. By age five, we will have completely purged these lines of any deficiencies. We are, of course, working on those challenges, but my understanding was you required stock that was already beyond childhood."

"No, we hear *adult* have short life span."

"Ah." Hauser said. "You may be referring to some nasty rumors about an earlier series we developed decades ago. The group was about seventy-three percent male, and they typically lived almost to age sixty. Fine specimens, the Gammas. Very smart, very strong. Athletic. But we no longer . . . that line is no longer produced."

"I see. At present, we have no use for that," the short man said.

"Of course not." Hauser swept his cane at the rows of containers. "But what you want is here, for every client you have, whatever their needs. We can grow and harvest any internal organ, for you to ship worldwide. We can provide your customers a subservient work force or any type of worker you desire. And in a year or two, we can open a facility in your country."

"We would be grateful. Cambodia is a poor country with many needs."

Hauser nodded. "High tech jobs, with laboratories and shipping. The construction of a large campus, like you've seen here. These are all good for Cambodia."

"Our current interest is in females." He held up a handful of pictures. "Where can we inspect these?"

The man in the cleanroom suit checked his clipboard. "I believe what you want is at recess now, on the playground, or we can take you to the school when recess is over."

"Yes, we pass on the way here." The short man shook his head. "But no school. My employers have no need for them to be educated. No reading or writing."

"Not a school to educate, my friend," Hauser said. "Simply a way to ensure a child remains obedient. Training."

"Obedience training?"

"Yes, of a sort."

The door opened again, and another group of people entered.

"Dr. Hauser," a security guard said, stepping forward. "These are the Norwegian representatives you wanted to see. They've just arrived."

"Ah, excellent." Hauser extended his hand. "Please, join us."

The security guard stepped back, allowing Dr. Hauser to shake hands with the Norwegians. "Sir, this is Ms. Pederson," the guard said. "And her associate Dr. Karlsdotter. He had a question about longevity, and I was unable to properly answer."

"We were just discussing that," Hauser said. "The Gamma sequence. It's merely an unfortunate circumstance, really, in a line of embryos we developed years ago."

The woman nodded, making notes as Hauser talked. "Why does it happen?"

"We don't completely know. In the same way pre-birth babies develop organs for nine months, hormones and DNA coding says 'stop' at birth. Yes, they still develop, but not like before. They move from creating organs and systems to growing and maturing them. Upon a genetic marker, similar to ones that cause gray hair, the organs in the Gammas stop regenerating. Since it's all organs, blood, et cetera, it manifests itself as massive and virtually simultaneous organ failure. Like cancer, its cause isn't completely known. And also like cancer, its cure isn't yet known. It's as though their bodies do a pre-birth for nine months and then a pre-death for nine months."

He walked along the aisle, leaning on his cane with each step, deep in lecture mode as he passed rows and rows of the containers. "Modern science doesn't actually know why people die of old age, except to say their bodies wear out. We simply view this as an accelerated version of that. Like a tire that is said to last fifty-thousand miles, for some cars that would be ten years, but on other cars it might only be five. With the Gammas, we don't know where the extra mileage is happening, we simply see that it does. It could be partially explained by the faster metabolism genes that were brought forward in that line."

He turned, punctuating the air with his cane for emphasis. "Life begins with rapid growth, and then slows. We don't ask why. Puberty happens at roughly the same age all around the world, based on nothing other than a predetermined DNA time stamp that says it's time to stop being a child and start becoming an adult that is able to reproduce. Menopause also occurs at a predetermined time, within a few standard deviations, because the DNA time stamp says it's time to no longer have children."

The doctor limped back toward the group. "In the Gamma individuals, death occurs at roughly age fifty-five for a similar reason." He shrugged. "A predetermined DNA switch in them simply said stop. But as I say, it's no longer an issue."

The Norwegian woman looked up from her notes. "I believe that alleviates any concerns we had, Doctor."

Her associate nodded. "We are ready to place our order."

"Fine. Right this way." Hauser headed for the door, his cane popping fast as he moved across the concrete floor. "The paperwork will only take a moment. And then, if you'll excuse me, I have a reception I must attend."

"I believe we are ready, too, Doctor," the Asian man said. "Subject to a satisfactory inspection of the stock."

"Excellent!" Hauser chuckled. "I may have to open a bottle of champagne."

The others laughed, following him to the door.

"But to be clear . . ." The Norwegian woman held the door for her elderly host. "After the Gammas, you were able to detect the flaw in subsequent lines, and remove it?"

"Gammas are not produced anymore." Dr. Hauser lumbered outside into the fading light. "And none exist today. You have my word on it."

CHAPTER 34

The Greyhound stood shirtless at the edge of the bed, studying the clothing laid out there. "Quite a selection."

"Best I could do." Wearing a fluffy white robe, Dominique sauntered from the bathroom, her hair wrapped in a towel. "One maintenance uniform, and one from the dining room staff. What else do you think you'll need?"

He sighed, going to the dresser and taking out a pressed, folded dress shirt. "A fast car, a reliable gun—a reliable machine gun would be nice, or even two—some good timing, good luck, and good strength." Opening the top drawer, he sifted through the silk neckties. "Did I say good luck?"

"The best luck is being prepared." Dominique came up behind her husband and slid her arms around his waist, kissing the back of his shoulder. "And you are certainly that."

321

"Tristan?" Maya knocked on the partition door. The Greyhound turned around and kissed his wife, then went over to the door and opened it. Maya held a notepad in one hand, a cell phone in the other, examining the screen. "I have some good news. The lab says the half-life for this latest batch of meds is testing better than previous ones. Initial field tests show as much as twenty percent better endurance."

The Greyhound slipped his shirt on. "I feel it. We talked about that in New York, remember?" He lifted his chin, inspecting himself in the mirror as he pushed a gold cufflink through a stiff white cuff. "I'd say it's more potent, with a longer range, and less of a downslide after."

"If we can flatten the peaks and valleys," Maya said, "so there's no crash between cycles, we'll really have something."

"That's great news, Maya." Dominique sat on the bed and folded her hands in her lap, her voice low. "Thank you."

Tristan finished buttoning his shirt, tucking it into his pants, his tone equally somber. "You're a great chemist, and a good friend, Maya. If I haven't told you that before, I should have." He glanced at Maya as he picked up the shoulder holster, sliding it over one arm and then the other, the strap running across his back. "You've saved my life more than once, both of you." Taking the air gun from its polished wooden case, he slid it into the holster and smoothed the wrinkles from his shirt.

From the bed, his wife gazed at him, her face drawn.

"I . . . should probably go." Maya took a backwards step toward her room. "You two have preparations to make. Good luck tonight, Tristan."

He forced a grin. "I'll see you in New York very soon."

He didn't fully believe the words he said, and neither did anyone else. It was more of a wish than anything. All three knew there was a very real possibility they'd never see each other again. The expression on Dominique's face said it all—a wife sending her husband off to war, possibly never to return.

In a few hours, it would all be over, one way or the other. Hauser and the board would be dead, or The Greyhound would be.

He put on a windbreaker to cover the gun and the fancy shirt.

"Do you have a plan for Hauser?" Dominique asked.

"I'll get into the reception, and an opportunity will present itself. He'll go to the bathroom or he'll step into the hallway to take a phone call. Then I'll take him down and make him disappear. I'll ambush the others in their rooms tonight."

"The phone call." She nodded. "Hauser's always doing that—stepping out so no one can overhear him. But he'll have bodyguards with him."

"Leave that to me." He shoved a handkerchief and the ether bottle into his pocket, along with the Propofol and a few syringes. The last item was a small container of pepper spray. "As for the rest, the less you know, the better. For your protection."

"Don't do that. Don't act cold. Not now."

A sad smile crossed his face. "My love, I said goodbye an hour ago—unrushed, unworried, a perfect moment—because I knew there wouldn't be a chance to say goodbye properly when I had to leave." He chose his words carefully, making sure his voice didn't waver. "If that's the last time I hold you, I'll remember it forever. And if we see each other again—"

"Stop." She lowered her head, wiping her cheek with the sleeve of the robe.

He went to the bed and sat, taking her hand in his and looking into her teary eyes. "If we should see each other again, we'll cherish that goodbye, and share another one at a different time." He swallowed hard. "I hope that's the case."

Squeezing her eyes shut, she pressed her face to his chest.

He held her, enjoying her warmth through the soft robe, brushing his hand up and down over her back as he inhaled the aromas from her shampoos and bath soaps.

On the dresser, a series of chimes played on his phone.

He kissed the top of his wife's head. "It's time."

She hugged him a moment longer, then let her hands fall to the bed. The Greyhound stood and stuffed a few garments into a canvas bag, picked up his phone, and headed to the door.

* * * * *

DeShear and Lanaya reached the security station after the sun had set, but its interior lights were still on. Sweaty and tired in their cleanroom suits, they approached the building. At the back door, DeShear pressed the intercom button.

The voice of the security guard came over the speaker. "You're late."

"Yep." DeShear said, leaning on the button. "You gonna buzz us in?"

"The others went through a long time ago. You were supposed to stay with your group."

He glared at the intercom. "Clearly, we did not."

It remained silent.

Lanaya huffed. "Does he expect us to spend the night out here?"

"He might."

She frowned and pressed the button. "See here, young man. Who do you think you're talking to? We are board members of Angelis Genetics, with executive level passes. If we wish to stray from our group, we shall—and with not a word of admonition from a security guard in the process! Do I make myself clear? Now open this door before we're late to the reception."

The door buzzed. As they opened it, the tall square-jawed American guard ran toward them. "I'm so sorry, ma'am! I thought you were with the audit team." He opened the next door for them. "I really apologize. It's been a long day, and—"

Lanaya stormed past him, with DeShear following.

"My good man," she said, "it's one thing to have a long day. It's quite another to be rude."

"Yes, ma'am."

She stopped, putting her hands on her hips. "I shall keep this between us this time, but remember, you are a representative of Angelus Genetics. I'll expect better from you in the future. Now if you'd be so kind as to call a cab for us."

"There's one waiting, ma'am. The IRS woman insisted. But . . ." The guard folded his arms.

"Yes?" Lanaya stared at him.

"Ma'am, I'll need to collect your ID cards." He eyed the lanyard with the security pass.

DeShear held his breath. If the guard inspected cards every day, he would know DeShear's was doctored.

The guard stared at Lanaya.

She narrowed her eyes, holding up her ID badge. "We'll be keeping these."

He let out a loud sigh and reached behind the counter. The door buzzed. "Yes, ma'am. Enjoy your evening."

Lanaya marched through the front door and headed for the taxi, climbing in with DeShear on her heels.

"Nice work." He chuckled.

"Thank you." She fanned her face. "I nearly wet myself."

The cab bumped along the dirt drive, heading from the lab campus to the hotel. DeShear pressed his phone to his head, holding his other ear shut so he could hear over the road noise. "We got him, Cammy. We caught Hauser talking about committing euthanasia, and we have pictures of a mass grave site on his property, filled with the bodies of children."

"What?" Camilla said. "I can't hear you, Dash. You're breaking up."

DeShear raised his voice. "I said—"

His phone cut out. He looked at the screen. There was no signal and only three percent battery life.

"Crap!"

A moment later, the screen flashed with an incoming call from Camilla, but it immediately dropped and lit up with the message "call lost."

"Is there any juice left in your phone?" he asked Lanaya.

She shook her head. "What do we do?"

"Driver, do you have a cell phone?

The man shrugged, peering at DeShear in the rearview mirror. "No English, sir. I am only speak Indonesian."

DeShear held up his phone, pointing to it. "A power cord? Anything?"

The driver shook his head. "No phone, sorry. I take to hotel, yes?"

"Yes." DeShear slumped back in his seat, pulling his cleanroom suit hood off. "Hotel."

* * * * *

The Greyhound waited in coveralls behind the dumpster until a truck pulled up to the Viceroy loading dock. A man with a rifle stood at the back of the hotel; another at the side. Both were dressed the same as The Greyhound. As the service crew came out to unload the vehicle, he joined them. Hefting a box onto his shoulder, he lowered his head and carried it inside.

He followed the man in front of him to the kitchen and set his box on a stainless steel counter, lingering as the others returned to the truck. When they were gone, he walked in the opposite direction and ducked into the restroom. He unzipped his coveralls and balled them up, slipping them into the trash can in the corner, then smoothed his hair.

The wait staff jacket and dark pants would work well enough inside the reception.

* * * * *

Near the Christmas tree in the Viceroy hotel ballroom, Camilla sipped ice water, tapping her hand against her thigh. There had been no word from DeShear yet. Something may have happened. If it did, what then?

She distracted herself by watching one of the hotel staff plug a cell phone into a projector cable. Slides about Angelus Genetics appeared on screens lining the walls. After a second cord was attached, holiday music came over the ballroom sound system.

Her phone pinged. Pulling it from her purse, she read a text from DeShear.

On our way.

She strolled around the room, trying to focus on mingling with her agents as they awaited their host, telling herself if DeShear and Lanaya were on their way, they were probably okay.

* * * * *

Dominique took one last look in the mirror, pressing her hand to her stomach to ease the butterflies. She slipped her key card into a small handbag, adjusted the strap on her shoulder, and headed to the door.

When she opened it, Dr. Hauser was smiling at her from the hallway.

Her stomach lurched. She fought the urge to slam the door in his face and throw herself against it.

"Hello, Dominique." Hauser brushed past his two bodyguards. "May I escort you to this evening's reception?"

She swallowed hard. "Uh, of course, Marcus." Then, a smile. "It would be my pleasure."

"Excellent." He extended his arm. "This way." They walked down the hallway together, his cane setting the pace. At the elevator, one of the body guards pressed the button. The doors opened, and the foursome stepped inside.

As the doors closed, Hauser leaned his cane against the wall and pressed the button to the lobby. "You know, my dear Dominique, you disappoint me."

Her heart pounded. Would the body guards attack her now that she was out of sight in the elevator? Why hadn't she brought a weapon?

She fought to keep her breathing steady, staring straight ahead.

"You are an amazing creature. So smart." He patted her arm. "But I knew you only did my bidding out of fear, and that can only take things so far." He pulled a piece of paper from his pocket and gazed at it. "How are your children—the boys? Are they behaving while you're away? Not giving your mother any trouble, I hope."

Her hands shook, her voice wavering. "They're fine."

"Ah. Good." The paper crackled as he unfolded it. "They have school in the morning, tomorrow, and baseball practice after." He looked up. "Baseball, in December?"

She said nothing, holding her breath, unable to stop her heart from racing.

"And you will call them at your mother's, on their tablet, after baseball—as you do every time you travel." He folded the paper and put it away. "I'd like that to continue. I'd like for you to call them tomorrow. I'd like for them to answer and speak with their mother. I'm sure they'd be disappointed if that didn't happen. Of course, I'm sure you'd be heartbroken if you called and *they* didn't answer. If your mother said they weren't there, and she didn't know where they were."

A shudder ran through her. "Please don't."

"Why, I admire the effort you make to call them every day. In fact, I want you to call them tomorrow, and the day after that, and greet them with loving arms upon your safe return."

Tears welled in her eyes. "Please . . ."

He squeezed her arm, his gravelly voice growing stern. "It would be terrible if anything were to happen to your young sons while you are out of town, so I've asked a friend to keep an eye on your children during our stay here. A friend of these gentlemen."

"Marcus, y-you know me. I would never—"

"I've been watching the entire time, my dear. I know everything. You leaked confidential information on our company through a black screen site. You're working with a psychopath called The Greyhound. You may even be responsible for this IRS debacle." He gritted his teeth. "It infuriates me that I took you in as a lowly intern, and helped you soar to great heights, and—I've given you so much! I helped you become a doctor, put you on the board of Angelus. I had great hopes for you. But . . ." He lowered his voice. "I don't pretend I haven't taken much from you as well. Your daughter leaked information, and she paid a high price—but you paid it as well. I don't deny that, and it turned you against me. Among other things you disagreed with." He looked her in the eye, his gaze growing cold. "But just as you've taken from me, with the lying and sharing secrets, more can always be taken from you. So let's both hope nothing happens while I'm here in Indonesia. Because if something were to happen to me, something most assuredly will happen to your lovely children."

The bell rang. The elevator doors opened to the lobby. A large, lighted Santa greeted them from the far side of the room.

Hauser dropped her hand and leaned on his cane, hobbling across the shiny marble lobby.

"Dina!" Hauser shouted, waving his hand at the Special Assistant to the Prime Minister. "You made it. How good of you to come. You're in time for my speech."

The woman smiled and clasped Dr. Hauser's hand.

Inside the elevator, Dominique fell against the wall, shaking and clutching her stomach, barely able to keep from sliding to the ground.

CHAPTER 35

The woman from the lecture walked briskly across the ballroom, passing a long table of dignitaries. Various board members from Angelus Genetics were seated next to representatives of the Indonesian government, the slide show of Angelus Genetics PR images projected onto screens behind them. In the center of the long table, a microphone awaited.

The lecturer leaned forward onto the lectern. "Ladies and gentlemen, thank you all for coming." She tapped her note cards, looking out over the gathering. "Angelus Genetics would like to welcome our guests from the United States Internal Revenue Service, the Federal Bureau of Investigations, and the Federal Marshal Service, as well as representatives of our host nation. This reception is being held in the hopes that we can get to know each other better and come to some understandings about our business here in Indonesia. To that end, I have a slide presentation prepared . . ."

Camilla groaned to herself. A few of her agents groaned quietly nearby.

"But first, we have a special treat for you. The chairman of Angelus Genetics would like to welcome you. Ladies and gentlemen, I give you Dr. Marcus Hauser."

She stepped away from the microphone, clapping. A polite applause went up from the assembled agents and others in the room. In the back corner of the ballroom, far from the doors, a man in a wait staff jacket carried a tray of hors d'oeuvres. As Hauser lumbered toward the lectern, the server set the tray on one of the many round tables in the room, and walked quickly toward the rear exit.

* * * * *

DeShear and Lanaya pushed the front ballroom doors open and rushed inside. Hauser's gravelly old voice boomed over the speakers as DeShear walked through the crowd of agents.

"Happy holidays, everyone. Thank you all for coming." The old man cleared his throat. "I can't say I'm happy you're here, but I look forward to addressing your concerns and putting this awkward audit behind us. I hope you'll all be home for Christmas."

"Dash." Camilla's voice came from behind DeShear. "What happened to you?"

"Cammy, you won't believe what we found." He glanced over both shoulders and lowered his voice. "I tried to tell you this earlier, but the call dropped. We heard Hauser talking about conducting human trafficking and euthanasia, and I saw a mass grave site on the far side of the campus where there's supposed to be a school. He's in it up to his eyeballs."

Camilla's jaw dropped. She put her hand on his shoulder, directing him to the back of the ballroom. "You saw mass graves?"

"Mass graves, organ harvesting facilities," DeShear said. "I was in a field where there had to be thousands of children buried. They're using a freaking bulldozer to cover the bodies. And Hauser knows all about it. We overheard him when he was pitching some clients."

"That's incredible." Camilla put her hand to her forehead, glaring at Hauser as he spoke.

"Get some lights and I'll take you there right now." DeShear said. "It's all just sitting there, a whole second campus."

"Ms. Madison, if I may." Lanaya leaned in close. "I want this company stopped, believe me, but it may be best to move quietly. Dr. Hauser is very smart and very well protected by the Indonesian government. The Prime Minister would be hugely embarrassed by word getting out about mass graves and human trafficking. An IRS audit of an American-owned company? That, they can weather. Euthanasia, organ trafficking—those things are another matter entirely. If the Prime Minister is in on any of this, I fear they may try to hush it up. They could even hold us as spies or some such thing while they move the evidence."

Camilla waved to a few of her agents. As they approached, she put a hand on Lanaya's shoulder. "Don't worry. With proof of a mass burial site, I can call the Vice President and get the U. N. here in about twenty-four hours. Nobody can move a mass burial site that fast."

The two agents stood by Camilla. "Get word to the team leaders that I need to see them, but they need to move quietly." The agents departed. Camilla turned back to Lanaya and DeShear. "When I get the U. N. here, the press will follow. That spells the end for Angelus Genetics. We can seize everything they have, and they won't be able to say a word about it."

DeShear pounded a fist into his hand. "Good. Hauser needs to go down."

"Hold on," Camilla said. "It's not that fast. Lanaya is right. Hauser's being protected, and the Indonesian prime minister won't want that being exposed on his watch. We need to move carefully, and if we tip our hand, Hauser might walk."

"How does he walk from something like this?" DeShear's face grew hot. "He's in too deep. We saw him talking about it. Go arrest him right now, in the middle of his stupid speech."

Camilla put her hands out. "For me to do anything, we need direct proof that he violated U. S. laws. Otherwise Hauser will say he didn't know anything about it. He'll blame it on a rogue manager, climb onto a jet, and ride it all out somewhere else. That's how these multinational corporate big wigs play the game."

Lanaya groaned, putting her hands to her face. "He could open up shop in a new country and be right back in business."

Camilla nodded. "We need direct evidence that shows he knew about the killings and human trafficking. It won't be in the company ledgers, but if we find evidence of money laundering, we can squeeze some lower level players and work our way up to Hauser. That'll take weeks, and if he even thinks we're getting close, he'll bolt."

"But he talked about euthanasia." DeShear shook his head. "We both heard him."

Camilla shrugged. "Right now, it's your word against his."

Lanaya shot upright. "No, we—"

Camilla held up a finger. "We need to do it right, so he can't weasel out of anything. Let me call this in. That lady at the table is the Special Assistant to the Prime Minister. She's here to show Hauser is connected. We'll need hard proof that he—"

"We have it!" Lanaya whispered, holding up a phone. "Where's a power cord?"

At the front of the room, Hauser dug in his pocket with one hand and waved at the group with the other. "Now if you'll excuse me, duty calls. So, Merry Christmas, and enjoy the party." He stepped away from the microphone, holding his phone to his ear. As he headed for an exit, two large men followed him.

* * * * *

The Greyhound was waiting for them.

Hauser left the ballroom, speaking quietly into his phone. "The Cambodians closed on an order for three hundred today, and signed a deal for a thousand more as soon as we can get them ready." He looked around. "Hold on, I need to move to where there's more privacy." He walked toward the men's restroom, pointing at one of his bodyguards. "You make sure no one comes in." He nodded at the other. "You, come with me."

The bodyguard opened the restroom door. Hauser went inside to continue his conversation, the other large man following him.

On the other side of a bushy potted plant, The Greyhound pulled out the ether, splashing some onto his handkerchief. He palmed it in his left hand and walked toward the restroom, his right hand around the container of pepper spray in his pants pocket.

"Sir," he said to the bodyguard. "You're with the reception. May I get you anything from the bar?"

As the man opened his mouth to reply, The Greyhound yanked the pepper spray from his pocket and released it into the bodyguard's eyes. His hands shot to his face as he shook his head, backing up into the wall. Before he could call out, The Greyhound was on him, shoving the wet handkerchief into the man's face. The bodyguard twisted away, but The Greyhound held fast, keeping one hand crushed to his target's face and wrapping the other one around his throat. The man launched himself backward, slamming into the wall to crush his assailant. The Greyhound winced, the air going out of him as sharp pains exploded through his rib cage.

The handkerchief was his only chance. He gritted his teeth and forced the cloth harder into the man's face, tightening his grip on the bodyguard's throat. The lingering pepper spray burned The Greyhound's eyes as he fought to keep the handkerchief in place.

Inches from him, the men's room door flung open. The other bodyguard stepped out, his gun drawn. The Greyhound leaned his shoulder into the wall and shot a foot out, catching the gunman in the jaw. The man's head snapped back, and he sprawled onto the carpet.

The bodyguard's thick arms came at The Greyhound again, swatting at his ears and eyes, as the man tried to get a grip on his attacker. The bodyguard groaned and clawed, then heaved himself into the wall again. Blind and struggling for air, he caught his attacker's collar. The Greyhound kept his grip, struggling to hold the ether over the man's face. The bodyguard grunted into the cloth, flinging his head. He let go of The Greyhound's collar and put both hands on the arm that choked him. He grunted, bending over and falling to his knees, twisting and turning, but unable to shake loose his attacker. His hands slipped off, but he grabbed again—slower. The Greyhound stood behind his target, sweating as he forced the cloth to stay in place. The bodyguard groaned and swayed, his movements growing clumsy. The thick fingers finally went slack and slid off The Greyhound's arm.

The bodyguard's hands dropped to his sides, and he slid to the floor.

The Greyhound stood over him, panting. His eyes watering, he blinked hard and glanced up and down the hallway. No one had come around the corner in the melee. He grabbed the big man by the arms and dragged him into the ladies' room, returning a moment later for the other bodyguard.

As the restroom door shut, The Greyhound opened the bigger man's jacket and relieved him of his gun. It was a military-style weapon, probably from the Indonesian army. He tucked it into the back of his belt and moved to the second man. Same style gun. He tossed the weapon into the trash.

He moved quickly, sweat dripping off the tip of his nose. Hauser wouldn't stay in the men's room too long without his bodyguards, and he may have already phoned for help.

Standing, The Greyhound peeled off the wait staff jacket and unholstered his air gun, laying it on the sink. His own jacket and shoulder holster went into the trash; the air gun went into his hand. His eyes still burning from the spray, The Greyhound pulled out his shirt tails to hide the weapon tucked in his belt and stepped into the hallway. He took a deep breath, readying himself to enter the men's room.

He looked almost like any other guest at the hotel now, and a man walking into a men's restroom wouldn't normally raise any concerns—except to the old man inside.

He pressed the air gun against his thigh so it wouldn't be immediately visible to a casual onlooker. He stared at the restroom door. Hauser might be armed, too.

The Greyhound chewed his lip, his pulse racing. If he could act casual for a few seconds when he stepped inside, like he was a normal guest entering the restroom, that might be all he needed. He placed a hand on the restroom door.

A two or three second advantage.

That was all he required for the air gun to quickly and quietly do its job.

CHAPTER 36

Lanaya looked around. "Is there a plug? Anything?"

"Up there." Camilla pointed to the lectern. "The audio and video for the ballroom are coming from a cell phone. Use that."

Clutching the phone to her chest, Lanaya viewed the nearest screen. Holiday music accompanied slides of the Angelus propaganda. Her eyes wide, she faced Camilla. "Are you sure?"

Camilla gritted her teeth and pointed at the phone. "Is the proof on there or not?"

"It is."

"Then let's go." Camilla headed for the lectern. "Jingle Bells can wait."

* * * * *

The Greyhound held his air gun tight as he stood by the restroom door, his thoughts racing.

Hauser is in here. He might be hiding in a stall, or he might have a gun—and start shooting the second this door opens.

I can't just kick open the door and use the bodyguard's weapon to open fire, because the noise will draw attention. Hauser can make all the noise he wants, though. Whoever comes will protect him.

Right now, he's probably on the phone calling for help—and that help will be here in minutes, or even less time.

So . . .

He leaned close to the heavy door, ready to give it a hard push.

It's time to go in.

He shoved the door open and leaped inside, his gun raised at arm's length. As the door crashed into the inside wall, The Greyhound scanned the room, peering down the barrel of his weapon.

Tile. Sinks. Stalls. Urinals.

The room appeared empty.

He has to be in one of the stalls.

The Greyhound lowered himself to one knee. The bottoms of the toilets were visible under the short stall walls, their shadows falling on the tile floor. In the far stall, the shadow was larger than the others. He kept his gaze on the shadow as he crept into the room.

The shadow moved.

The Greyhound leveled the air gun at the stall door. "You can come out, or I can shoot holes in the door until you come out."

"You can't shoot." The old man's gravelly voiced wavered, echoing off the tile walls. "There are five dozen FBI agents across the hall. The noise from a gun will have them here in—"

The Greyhound squeezed the trigger, sending a pellet blasting through the stall door and into the tile wall. A golf ball-sized hole appeared in each, a cloud of splinters and plaster falling to the floor.

"Okay," Hauser said, his voice wavering. "I'm coming out."

The latch on the stall door *clacked* as it unlocked, and the door inched outward. The tip of the cane touched the floor, followed by one foot, then the other, as the old man stepped off his toilet seat perch. "I'm unarmed." Hauser's voice trembled. He stuck a hand out of the stall, waving it.

"I'll need to see both hands, doctor. Now come on out."

"My cane. I can't walk without it."

Then how did you climb up onto—

Hauser leaned out the door and fired a gun. The deafening blast echoed off the tile as a white and yellow flash burst from the barrel. The Greyhound slammed backwards like he'd been hit by a linebacker. Red exploded from his shoulder, a searing crash of pain surging through his arm and chest.

He fell into the wall, gasping and trying to raise his gun. The muscles wouldn't respond. His weapon clattered to the floor. Blood gushed from his wound.

* * * * *

"That's gunfire!" Camilla shouted. She bolted from behind the lectern. "FBI, let's check that out. My people, secure the room. Get the civilians and dignitaries to the far wall, away from any windows and doors."

A group of FBI agents headed for the door, followed by several Indonesian soldiers, splitting into two teams. The commander barked orders to secure the perimeter. Guns drawn, the agents pressed themselves against the walls as their leader threw the door open and leaped into the hallway. "We're clear! Move, move."

The agents funneled through the door, splitting left and right into the hallway.

DeShear turned to Lanaya. "That could be our killer. You got this?"

She fumbled with the projector's connectors. "I think so."

"Okay." DeShear bolted for the door.

"Dash, don't!" Camilla shouted.

It was too late. He was gone.

* * * * *

Blood streamed from The Greyhound's shoulder. With his other hand, he reached behind his back for the pistol.

"I wouldn't." Hauser's cane fell to the floor as he limped forward, keeping his gun pointed at The Greyhound. "I'm not a killer, but I'll make an exception if you pull out a gun."

"You're worse than a killer." The Greyhound winced, fighting the pain. "You're a mass murderer."

"And you're not?" Hauser smiled, inching closer. "How many people have you killed? Twenty? More?" He took another step, balancing carefully. "But you justify it because you disagree with them.

You don't like their ideas. Well, I disagree with you and your ideas."

The Greyhound gritted his teeth, gasping as the pain pounded his shoulder.

"It's over." The old man took another step toward him, putting the tip of his gun to The Greyhound's head. "You lost, and I won, because I always win."

* * * * *

A large woman in an evening dress stood in the hallway, trembling. DeShear shouted at her. "Where's the shooter?"

She pointed with shaking hands. "M—men's room."

The FBI commander squatted in the hallway, his gun trained on the men's room door. "Team one, go." As two agents raced to the bathroom door, the commander called down the hallway. "Team two, check the lobby for additional threats."

DeShear took a position behind him, leaning in close. "Have somebody find an interpreter in case the shooter doesn't speak English."

"Carson," the commander shouted. "Grab one of the hotel staff that speaks English." He glanced at DeShear. "Are you armed, sir?"

"Not yet."

"And Carson—get a weapon for the bureau chief's friend."

* * * * *

The gun shook in the old man's hand.

The Greyhound winced as the pain from his shoulder throbbed. Sweat formed on his brow. "Not so easy, close up—is it? You prefer your victims small and helpless."

The doctor shrugged. "The trembling is a byproduct of an adrenaline surge—from when you shot at me—and nothing more. If I wanted you dead, you'd be dead right now."

A bead of sweat trickled down The Greyhound's cheek.

"It's easy to kill a man," Hauser said. "Killing his ideas takes time and effort. I know you have others working with you. Seeing you humiliated in public as your efforts are disgraced, that's how you kill a movement."

* * * * *

The agents took positions on each side of the men's room entrance. "You! In the restroom! Throw down your weapon and come out."

"I went into the ladies' room." The woman backed down the hallway, a hand over her mouth and her eyes wide. "There are two bodies in there!"

"Watkins!" The commander shouted. "We have an unidentified threat in the ladies' room."

Another agent raced forward, two others on his heels. "On it."

A gravelly voice came through the restroom. "I'm Dr. Hauser. I've been attacked."

"Doctor Hauser." The commander shouted, moving to the men's room. "Where is the gunman?"

"I shot him. He's on the floor."

The commander frowned, facing DeShear. "There's a lot of bodies piling up in this hotel. How big a threat is the old man?"

"Small," DeShear said. "Unless you're a kid."

The commander nodded. "Doctor, we're coming in. Lower your weapon."

He pressed his hand to the door and opened it. Inside, an old man with a gun stood over a younger man with blood seeping from his shoulder. "I got him," Hauser said. "I got The Greyhound."

An agent rushed past the commander and relieved Hauser of his gun. Two others took The Greyhound's weapons and lifted him to his feet.

"Get an ambulance and get something to restrain that guy," the commander said, pointing to The Greyhound. "See if any of the soldiers have handcuffs. If not, get some zip ties from the kitchen. Anything to hold him until the local police arrive."

The men dragged The Greyhound out of the restroom and toward the lobby, leaving a dotted trail of blood along the floor. DeShear stepped to the wall so they could pass.

This was the big killer. The one we were all afraid of.

The Greyhound hung his head, staggering as the agents helped him walk.

Doesn't look like such a threat now.

"Doctor." An agent took Hauser by the shoulders. "Are you all right?"

Before he could answer, his own voice boomed from the speakers in the ballroom. A conversation between Hauser and another man filled the air.

"Any of these specimens not developing adequately are terminated . . ."

"Let's get you to a hospital, sir," the agent said, taking the doctor by the arm. "We'd like to get you checked out and make sure you're okay."

Hauser shook the man off, limping toward the ballroom. As if in a trance, he moved forward, frowning, his mouth agape.

"... *others are terminated in infancy.*"

"What is that?" Hauser shouted, throwing open the ballroom door.

Lanaya stood at the lectern, all the screens filled with a video—a distant image, shot between shelves and over the tops of surgical tubing and glass containers—of Dr. Hauser and the Cambodian man.

"*By age five, we will have completely purged these lines of any deficiencies.*"

"Stop it!" The doctor's face turned red as he yelled at the screen. "Turn it off!"

The lecturer watched, her mouth open, as the doctor continued into the ballroom. Two FBI agents held her, keeping her from going to him.

"*... my understanding was you required stock that was already beyond childhood.*"

Hauser's eyes darted to every screen, his arms flailing. "No! Stop it! Turn it off." He glanced wildly around the room, his gaze falling on the Special Assistant to the Prime Minister. "Dina! I can explain!"

She reached into her purse and took out her phone, holding it to her ear—and turning away from Hauser.

"Dina!"

Hauser limped to the center of the ballroom, viewing every screen, his image plastered on all of them. He leaned on the back of a chair, his head sagging.

The men onscreen continued their negotiation.

"Our current interest is in females. Where can we inspect these?"

"I believe what you want is at recess now, on the playground . . ."

Panting, Hauser stood upright and smoothed his shirt. "Madam Assistant, I . . . I am an important person in this country. The—the Prime Minister, he instructed you . . . to show me every courtesy."

Dina lowered her phone and looked at the doctor.

Hauser swallowed hard. "I wish to leave Indonesia. Tonight. Right now. Earlier, you offered me a helicopter. I'd like you to take me to it."

"What!" Lanaya shouted. She turned to Camilla. "You're in charge. Don't let him walk away."

Camilla stepped forward. "I'm sorry, Dr. Hauser, but the FBI has the authority to ask you as many questions as they want, and the IRS will insist on getting those answers before you leave."

"No, no, no." He shook his head, waving his hands. "Forget all that. I am not on U. S soil, so you have exactly zero authority. I was willing to sit still for this ridiculous audit, but my patience has run out. By ten o'clock tomorrow morning, I'll have my people here to put an end to your little witch hunt. Then we'll see who has authority." He pounded the table, pointing a finger at Camilla and narrowing his eyes. "Tomorrow morning, your so-called audit ends, Ms. Madison. And then you go back to the United States with your tail between your legs!"

Camilla folded her arms. "They're not coming."

"What?"

"That big army you hired to swoop in and stop us," Camilla said. "I got a phone call from somebody who overheard a conversation in a parking garage, where you hired a bunch of killers to come here and disrupt a federal investigation. Your army of thugs got stopped at the airport in Tampa. It seems the ATF and FBI had an issue with so many people and weapons being moved illegally out of the country, so they're all discussing it." She shrugged. "Well, the agents are. Your mercenaries are behind bars. And so is your lawyer—who hired killers at your direction. So, nobody's going to be riding in like the cavalry to save the day."

"What—who?" Hauser's face turned white. "That's a lie. I never told anyone—"

"Yes, you did." Dr. Carerra stood up. "I heard it all in the parking garage, Marcus. I called the FBI, and they were kind enough to put my children in federal protective custody while I came here to watch you sweat."

"Dominique!" Hauser gasped. "I'll—I'll sue! I'll destroy you. I'll take everything you own, and then I'll burn it to the ground!

"I don't think you will." Camilla smiled. "A lawsuit would require you to set foot back in the United States—where I have a lot of subpoenas waiting for you."

"It's over, Doctor." Dominique made her way around the dignitaries' table. "Your company is over, and your power is over." She walked past him, heading to the exit. "You're over."

His jaw hung open as she passed.

"But my audit isn't." Camilla strolled to the lectern, picking up the cell phone. Its cables swayed as she held it over the projector. "I have an agent out front hiring every cab on the hotel property, and we're going to have them turn on their high beams and drive me to the land behind your second campus." She set the phone down and glared at him. "I think pictures of what's buried there accompany this little video of you and your Cambodian client."

Hauser got to his feet. "I don't know what you're talking about. I have no idea what's buried out there, and I'll deny I ever knew. You don't decide when things are over, I do. That's the benefit of dual citizenship. I'll find another Third World dictatorship to park my laboratory in, and Angelus Genetics will keep going. Nothing's going to change. In fact, I think I'd prefer living in Paris or Stockholm, or perhaps somewhere in China."

He backed away from the table, looking at his friend Dina. "A facility in Cambodia could be open within six months, Madam Assistant." He snapped his fingers. "But, as a friend of the Prime Minister, I'd prefer we stay here. I'll simply have to consider my options."

She shifted on her feet.

"Now what about that helicopter, Dina? I'd like to leave. Now."

She put the phone back to her ear and stood for a moment, whispering. A few seconds later, she nodded and slipped the phone into her purse, looking at Camilla. "It is the wish of the Prime Minister that his very special friend, Dr. Hauser, be allowed to leave immediately." She turned to Hauser. "My car and driver are out front. You will be escorted to the airport, where the Prime Minister's helicopter will be standing by to take you to his private jet. You may take it anywhere in the world you wish to go."

"No!" Lanaya screamed. "He can't be allowed to just leave!"

"I'm sorry." Dina's face was firm, displaying no emotion. "Indonesia wishes no trouble, but my orders are that he be allowed to depart immediately."

Hauser smiled, lifting his chin. "The Prime Minister's private jet." He limped to the door. "I think a quick trip to Switzerland may be in order."

Lanaya turned to Camilla, tears in her eyes. "That's it? He gets to walk away?"

"What's buried out there isn't going to go away," Camilla said.

Hauser stopped, peering down his nose at her. "Of course it is. The fact is, Ms. Madison, aside from a few people in New York and Washington DC, nobody will care this audit ever happened. In a few years, most Americans won't remember what all the fuss was about. But." He wagged a finger at her. "Right now, millions of shareholders of Angelus Genetics have lost a lot of money—most are little people, who will feel it in their retirement accounts." A smile stretched across his thin lips. "The Wall Street Journal has been begging for an interview. I think I'll give them one—and I'll make sure they know who caused all those people to lose so much money." He turned, hobbling toward the exit. "Life has different lessons to teach us all. You learned that you are ineffective, and I learned that dual citizenship is worth several billion dollars."

He chuckled as he passed through the door, not looking back. "Good evening."

CHAPTER 37

DeShear followed Dr. Hauser down the hallway and across the ornate lobby of the Viceroy hotel. He stood by a Christmas tree at the entrance as the vehicle for the Special Assistant to the Prime Minister rolled up. The young driver hopped out and opened the car door for his "very special" passenger. The old man entered the vehicle, the door shut, and the car drove slowly down the long driveway. The moonlight illuminated the *pala* trees there in a silvery glow, as the car turned left and disappeared down the main road.

DeShear stood inside the hotel doors, gritting his teeth.

It was no longer his battle. He'd done what he could, from protecting Lanaya to bringing down a killer. Angelus Genetics had suffered. The Greyhound was in custody.

But it was a hollow victory. He'd learned too much in the past few days to be satisfied with these results.

Across the lobby, The Greyhound sat in a chair under a large wreath, an attendant bandaging his bloody arm while two FBI agents looked on. One pointed to a set of handcuffs being held by a nearby Indonesian army officer. "Hey, shooter—these pretty bracelets go on your wrists when he's finished wrapping your arm."

The Greyhound said nothing, slumping forward in the chair, his head hanging.

Siren blaring, an ambulance sped to the front door and screeched to a stop. The agents put their hands under The Greyhound's arms and pulled him to his feet. He winced in pain.

"Serves you right," the agent said. "I heard they found another body upstairs, a big fat guy. And the manager went missing after he met with you." He shoved The Greyhound forward toward the ambulance. "Is that more of your handiwork?"

"Nick," the other agent said. "Take it easy."

"No, screw this guy, Jake."

Nick shoved The Greyhound again. He banged into the side of the ambulance, groaning and sliding downward. He turned and leaned his back on the vehicle, his eyes closed and his head sagging.

"Hey!" Jake jumped in front of Nick, blocking him from assaulting their prisoner again. "I said take it easy. We don't get extra points for killing the—"

The Greyhound sprung up and raised his hands high over his head, crashing them down on the back of Jake's neck. Swaying sideways, Jake slumped to the ground.

The other agent pulled his gun. The Greyhound swung his leg in a roundhouse kick, crashing it into the agent's forearm and sending him sprawling onto the sidewalk.

From his vantage point in the lobby, DeShear bolted toward them. "Hey!" he shouted, raising his weapon. "The killer's loose!"

A second kick from The Greyhound landed on the side of the agent's head. Jake's eyes rolled back and his body went limp. The Greyhound scooped up the agent's gun and raced down the long driveway.

DeShear sprinted out the door after him, several agents and army soldiers following.

The Greyhound was fast, covering the driveway at an amazing speed. DeShear was barely able to keep up. At the tree line, The Greyhound darted across the main road and disappeared into the darkness of the jungle.

DeShear hit the main road at a full sprint, the jungle coming up fast. A small hole was visible in the bright moonlight—a running trail. Palm fronds and brush hung low over the dirt path. Ducking his head, DeShear thrust through the wet leaves, their long green fingers slapping at his face.

"DeShear!" the agent called behind him.

"I'm on him," DeShear yelled over his shoulder. "Split up and see where these paths come out."

He bounded over the dark path, unable to see beyond a few feet. His heart raced, knowing The

Greyhound could be waiting for him anywhere ahead, but his gut said the killer intended to run—and running was DeShear's game. He hurled himself down the trail, legs churning, heart pounding. The path turned and climbed, narrowing as outcrops of rocks extended from the sides. DeShear's shoulder caught the edge of a stony outcrop, bouncing him away and nearly causing him to lose his balance. He stopped to right himself, gasping in the still night.

He held his breath until his lungs ached, listening to hear the fleeing killer somewhere ahead. Thumps and cracking branches reached his ears. The killer was still running.

Pulse pounding, DeShear lurched forward down the path. Ahead, the trees opened to a clearing. He slowed his pace. He'd be an easy target there, even for a wounded man. He couldn't count on the killer getting tired or missing a shot.

DeShear crouched, gasping as he checked left and right. A smooth rock jutted out from the thick, wet jungle. Sweat dripped from his nose as he slid behind the rock, his eyes darting around the clearing.

He inhaled fast and hard, trying not to make much noise, then took a deep breath and held it.

No twig snaps or brush being swatted aside. The killer had stopped.

DeShear exhaled quietly, his heart thumping. Several trails met in the clearing, but a cloud had moved over the moon, making the view hazy.

Which trail had the killer taken?

A gunshot came from his left, its muzzle blast lighting the trees like lightning. Before he could react, the rock pinged next to him, ringing in his ear and covering him in grit. He threw himself to the wet jungle floor, his weapon next to his cheek, holding his breath and waiting.

Branches crashed together as the killer fled, racing down the trail. DeShear leaped to his feet and followed.

The path sloped downward now, twisting and turning, jarring his knees as the ground dropped in the dark. He crashed into rocks and trees that sprang up out of nowhere, slipping on a dirt trail that grew muddier with each passing minute. His face scratched and stinging, he raced onward, his anger and adrenaline fueling him.

The trail turned, moonlight illuminating his way. Ahead, a tall shadow darted past the trees.

I'm gaining on him.

DeShear growled and pumped his legs harder, limbs and vines whipping his cheeks as he sped down the path.

Trees loomed ahead again, and the trail went dark. He rushed forward, gun raised, ready for another ambush. As he crashed through the palm fronds, he looked for a place to take cover.

His feet went out from under him. The trail dropped downward, and he fell, face first, into the mud, sliding several feet until his shoulder slammed into a tree trunk.

DeShear rolled over, panting, gun drawn, ready to shoot anyone who appeared. The jungle was quiet. He put a hand out, found a rock to lean on, and got to his feet. Dripping with sweat and wincing from the pain, he scanned the underbrush.

The roar of water came through the dense jungle. Somewhere to his left, water surged through the brush, cutting its way through the dark hillside. It was loud and constant, a river or more—probably what the trail was originally designed for. Tourists, seeking a scenic trail to walk or run on, not a killing zone.

The noise of the surging water lessened his ability to hear the man he was following. His world just got a little more dangerous, but if it did for him, it did for the killer, too. He peeked over his shoulder. Any FBI agents or Indonesian soldiers following him wouldn't be able to hear verbal directions now, but that might be a good thing. Whatever they could hear, the killer could hear—potentially giving away DeShear's position and making him a target.

He leaned forward into the brush, pushing aside a large cluster of leaves. The path worked its way downward through the thinning foliage. A scenic trail would have water views if it was this close to the water, but that water sounded too fast and too loud to get close to.

He crept over the path, hunching down to be a smaller target if anyone was going to shoot.

Another gunshot pierced the night air. He heard it, and saw the reflected flash off the wet leaves near him. It missed, not even coming close, but it told him the direction of the killer—and that was all he needed.

He's shooting blindly. He doesn't know where I am.

DeShear could no longer hear footsteps or someone making their way through the brush. Not over the noise of the rushing water. But he could follow a shadow down a trail. Keeping low, he moved fast, using the moonlight as his guide while he could, and keeping the river on his left.

DeShear's heart pounded as he raced forward, calculating the killer's options. There were only two directions, and really only one. The killer couldn't very well come back toward him if he intended to get away; somewhere behind DeShear, FBI agents and Indonesian soldiers were coming. He couldn't go left; the river would drown anyone that tried to enter it. And he couldn't go right—up a wet jungle cliff in the dark? No chance.

The killer's only option was forward—downward, moving along the same path he'd chosen in the clearing. His only escape was to outrun them all, and bleeding from a gunshot wound, that was unlikely.

DeShear gritted his teeth and pushed another clump of leafy branches out of his way. The ground sloped downward more sharply, with a row of short, straight lines appearing through the dark.

Steps.

It was definitely a tourist trail, then. DeShear moved quickly over the wet steps, climbing down through the thick foliage. He looked ahead, trying to see through the brush. A shadow moved. DeShear stopped, holding his place and not trying to find cover. The incline was too steep, and any sudden movements might give him away.

He waited, gun drawn, watching the shadow.

It was longer now. Stretched out, and moving in a slow, awkward fashion.

Crawling.

Maybe he lost too much blood to continue his escape.

DeShear lowered his foot to the next step. It was shorter, and wetter, than the others. A smooth stone that had become wet and slippery in the growth of the jungle. The shadow kept crawling, so DeShear kept moving down the steps. One by one, he inched lower, never taking his eyes off The Greyhound. The steps were like ice, slick and wet. He'd easily fall if—

That's what happened to the killer. He fell, and he may have broken a leg, too. No way he'd stop running.

The hairs on the back of DeShear's neck stood on end. A cornered animal fights hardest. If The Greyhound had broken a leg, he'd shoot to kill for sure—if he still had the gun.

The roar of the water was louder now, impossibly loud for a river. It had to be one of the waterfalls—and a big one. In the darkness, it'd be hard to tell, but maybe the moon would show it. He crept down the last few steps, inching toward a flat, grassy area.

A faint white cloud swirled just past the edge of the clearing, a darker, more iridescent one churning below. The river was about thirty feet down a cliff, a wide, rushing beast, flowing out and off the edge of the world and down into the darkness.

At the edge, the shadow stood, a silhouette against the faint white cloud. He was tall and athletic, but slouching. DeShear stared at the figure, uncertain if the killer was looking at him or the rushing water below. A few feet away, the end of the earth beckoned. A cloud moved over the moon, but the vista was visible enough for DeShear to recognize it from pictures. Nungnung was hundreds of feet up, and recent rains had made it angry. Its dark water sped past, covering the visible distance in less than a second.

The shadow heaved its chest, its shoulders going up and down, just like DeShear's. He wiped the sweat from his brow. The runners' race was over. Only a victor needed to be decided.

The killer spoke, his words all but inaudible over the noise of the falls.

"What?" DeShear shouted, his gun trained at the man in front of him.

Limping along the edge of the cliff, The Greyhound raised his voice. "What now?"

Injured or not, DeShear kept his gun aimed at the stranger. He'd seen the act before, at the ambulance, and he had no intention of falling victim to it like the FBI agents had.

"Now we go back," DeShear yelled. "I take you in, and you go to prison."

The shadow shook his head, shouting. "You can't be on their side. You know what they've done. You've seen it for yourself."

DeShear saw no gun in the killer's hand, but that could be a trick. It could be in his belt, and it could be fired at any moment.

"I'm not on anybody's side," DeShear said, the roar of the waterfall eating his words.

"Killing me allows them to continue. You know that, and you know they have to be stopped. You want that as much as I do."

DeShear took a step backwards, keeping his gun aimed at the killer. The shadow was too close to the edge. One bad step could send him down the cliff and into the churning water below.

"You know I'm right," The Greyhound said. "You saw the graves. That's a part of your nightmare now, like it's been part of mine."

DeShear blinked sweat out of his eyes. "Let's go back to the hotel. Talk about it there. Plead your case to the press. Get some public sentiment."

The shadow shook his head. "I'm all busted up. Hauser took my arm." He took another step along the edge of the cliff. "Those steps did the rest. I can barely hold myself upright."

Strong guy, to be standing after all that.

"You won't shoot me," he said. "You can't. You see that I'm right."

"Let's not shoot each other. Deal?" The mist from the massive waterfall made the gun slippery. DeShear tightened his grip. "There are other ways."

"Like what, send them a sternly worded letter? I got a congressional inquiry, and they put the lead senator on their Board of Directors. They held all the cards until I started killing them. Your IRS trick sure isn't going to stop them. But my way works. It got their attention. And it will get other people's attention. This will make it stop. My way."

"That's not for me to decide."

"I didn't say it was." The Greyhound held his finger to his chest. "I made the decision. After all they did to me . . . it was mine to make."

The two men stared at each other in the darkness, the roar of the waterfall filling the air.

DeShear lowered his gun. "Come with me."

The Greyhound held his ground, unmoving, as clouds of mist floated up in the distance. Slowly, he nodded his head.

The clearing burst white with light, the crack of a large rifle blast booming through the night. The Greyhound jolted backwards.

DeShear dropped to the ground, turning in the direction of the gunshot. In the pale moonlight, soldiers from the Indonesian army came into view. Wading their way through the brush, they burst forward.

Twisting, The Greyhound's arms grappling for vines and leaves as he arched backward. His fingertips flicked over a few branches, then he disappeared over the edge of the cliff.

DeShear sprinted forward, staring at the water below. It raced past, a dark and powerful force of energy, rushing over the edge of the cliff and crashing into the black water below. He stood there, his heart pounding. No one could live through that. But if anyone could, The Greyhound would.

If we don't find the body, we might never know if he's really dead.

The soldiers came closer, shouting and waving at him.

DeShear turned to the water, and jumped.

The icy cold of the river shocked his system, but only for a second. The water threw him forward and over the edge. His stomach climbed to his throat as he fell, a roller coaster without cars, plummeting forever into the darkness, then the terrible crash and churning of the water below. He kicked and rolled, his lungs aching, fighting to find the surface, depleting himself as he clawed the water crushing him.

It lasted forever, fighting the dark water, his exhaustion turning his arms and legs into heavy bricks, but at last his lungs found air. He strained to push himself upwards through the water, breaking the surface again and again to greedily suck bites of air with his last ounces of strength.

The water past the falls was calm, a drastic difference from the churning monster above. The current pushed him to the edge where the river turned, and the sandy bottom met his dragging feet. With aching arms and rubber legs, he inched onto the riverbank and collapsed.

He lay there on his back, gasping, the moon staring at him through the trees.

Beyond him, a twig snapped in the brush. He mustered the strength to turn his head, spotting the shadow of a tall, athletic man, a silhouette in the moonlight, lumbering through the brush. The shadow stopped, seeming to look at him.

DeShear swallowed hard, panting as he lay on the wet riverbank. He had no gun, and no strength. He would lose any fight right now, and maybe the stranger knew it. He stared at the man, and the man stared back at him.

Then the stranger turned and walked away.

CHAPTER 38

The soldiers radioed for a Jeep, and within an hour, they'd found DeShear and gotten him back to the Viceroy hotel lobby. Lanaya wrapped him in towels and a robe, insisting a medic from the Indonesian army check him over while she asked a thousand questions. Camilla's team was scouting the grave site, sending pictures to her in the lobby—her makeshift command post—as she sat next to DeShear and guzzled coffee.

"Yes, it's possible he got away." DeShear shrugged. "My guess is, he drowned."

"The man you saw at the bottom of the falls," Lanaya said. "You claim he walked away—but The Greyhound was limping."

"Yeah." DeShear nodded. "But he could have been faking at the top of the falls." He pushed away the intern's hand and climbed off the couch. "Look, I don't know for sure. But I don't think he's a threat anymore."

"Why?"

"Just my gut." DeShear sighed. "He could have killed me in the jungle just by waiting around a corner and ambushing me. He had a gun, and I'd have never seen him until it was too late. He could have shot me at the top of the falls, too, in the clearing. The shots he fired when I was chasing him were to get me to stop following him. I think he missed on purpose. And if he really was the guy I saw walking away from the river, he could have dropped me right then and there. I was done, exhausted from fighting the river. I had nothing left, and it was obvious." He shook his head, his eyes focused on the floor. "He had me several times, and never made a move. And I could have killed him, too, at the edge of the falls. I didn't shoot him. We both just . . . I think we decided not to shoot each other."

"That's you." Lanaya knitted her hands. "What about me?"

DeShear patted her shoulder. "If he didn't kill me, he won't kill you. We're connected, you and I. And I think he gets that."

"Whatever goes over the falls is never seen again." The Special Assistant to the Prime Minister crossed the lobby, approaching them. "I hope you are recovering well, Mr. DeShear."

"Looks like he'll live," Camilla said to her. "I wish I couldn't say that about your special friend, Dr. Hauser."

Dina took a deep breath and let it out slowly. "It has been a long day for all of us, but as I said, Indonesia does not want trouble with our friends." She looked at Camilla. "Your press is fond of calling my country a semi-dictatorship. Well, in a dictatorship, the news is what the government says it is. So if we say Dr. Hauser's plane exploded on takeoff, then it did. And if we say he was not taken to a warehouse and executed, then he was not."

The small woman looked into the eyes of each of the three shocked faces in front of her. "Someone once said, 'Sometimes you simply have to do what needs to be done—and often the best choice is clear, but unpleasant.' I agree. Have a nice trip home." She strolled past the large Christmas tree in the lobby. "You may make it back in time to do some last-minute Christmas shopping."

Camilla stared at her long after she had gone from view, a hint of a smile on her lips. "I don't need to go Christmas shopping. I think I just got everything on my wish list."

Lanaya turned to DeShear. "What about you, Hamilton? Are you ready to go back home to sunny Florida?"

He groaned. "I am, but I'm not sure what I'll be going home to. My apartment burned with all my belongings."

"Well," Camilla said. "When Hauser's people were trying to make it look like you and your client torched your place, they paid your insurance premium first. It was probably to keep investigators focused on you two for the arson rap, but Harriman says Lanaya's flight schedule checked out and so did your alibi—so you'll be able to collect. I have a feeling that it'll all track back to Angelus, and I don't think they're going to fight that claim very hard. Their best bet will be to write a big check—if they have any money left after all this." She picked up her coffee cup. "And like Dina said, there are still a few shopping days before Christmas." Camilla crossed the lobby to the coffee machine, stopping to talk with her agents there.

"Wow," DeShear said. "Maybe I'll go on my Bahamas fishing cruise after all."

"Well, I will certainly be looking forward to getting home." Lanaya rocked back and forth, smiling. "It's been quite a while since I kissed my babies good night, and I *do* have some Christmas shopping left to do!"

DeShear sat up, toweling off his damp hair. "Next time you want to go on an adventure, schedule it a little sooner. I'm bad enough at buying presents as it is."

"I couldn't." The smile disappeared from her lips. "You were sick."

"Huh?" DeShear cocked his head. "What do you mean?"

Lanaya's hands dropped to her lap, one massaging the other again. "I'm afraid there's one last thing I need to tell you. I've been meaning to, but there was never a good time. This isn't either, I suppose, but . . ." She swallowed hard, glancing over her shoulders. "You remember when I told you about The Greyhound—about the Gammas, the genetic group he was part of. There are others." She lowered her voice. "You, for example."

"Me." DeShear sat frozen, the implications reverberating through his head.

"You were sick the week before I called on you. The flu, you said, but . . . it wasn't. We checked. And you are the right age."

His jaw dropped. "The sequence? But I'm fine—I just ran a marathon through the Indonesian jungle." A nervous laugh escaped his lips.

She lowered her eyes. "I think, in a few more days, that will very likely change." Taking his hand, Lanaya's voice fell to a whisper. "I'm sorry, Hamilton. Your records came to us like a lot of others. You weren't adopted. That was a cover story. You were born at the Arizona facility, as part of the program."

He looked at her, his mind racing, but the overwhelming pall of truth seeped through her words and settled in his gut.

I'm one of the Gammas.

Lanaya was many things, but not a liar. Not about something like this.

His heart sank. "So, uh . . . in a few days, I'll start in with all the symptoms." Her words came back to him about the months of suffering the others had gone through, and the slow death that followed. "I just—I spend the next year of my life in pain at a hospital, until . . . I die?"

Hearing himself say it out loud, when it wasn't about someone else, was strange. As a cop and a private detective, he'd delivered bad news to people before, but this was different. It seemed like a bad joke, but without a punch line—and no one was laughing.

"So, no cruise, I'm afraid." Tears welled in Lanaya's eyes. "You'll be ill for ten months or so."

Her voice broke as she spoke. "But—but Dr. Carerra says their latest tests have shown remarkable results." She wiped away a tear, forcing a smile. "One in five survived before, and with proper treatment, and the new meds, there could be great improvements. After what I've seen these past few days, you strike me as a fighter. You'll not only beat it, you'll lead the charge."

He swallowed hard, his eyes focused on the floor, empty inside. Learning of your own imminent death had a way of drowning out everything else.

"I'm sorry I deceived you, Hamilton, but working together has helped us connect with the very people who can help you." She sniffled. "They think there's a good chance you'll be fine."

"It's . . . not exactly the kind of news anyone wants to hear." He sat back, letting it sink in. He was part of the group, yes, but the drugs were available to possibly cure it now. If something like this had to come along, there were worse ways for it to happen.

And he'd learned from his friend, Harriman, how to fight such an illness. He'd been there for Mark; Mark would be there for him now, too.

He looked at Lanaya. "I . . . kinda wondered what made me so highly recommended."

"My self-appointed duty these past few years has been to seek out people like you. To make up for my role at Angelus. It was another deception I had to maintain until now. I'm very sorry."

He pushed himself to his feet and went to the window. The hotel lights illuminated the edges of the jungle. Palm trees swayed in the hot breeze. Beyond them, only darkness.

"Ten months." He glanced over his shoulder at her. "You skipping out on me until then?"

"Not in the least." Lanaya sat upright. "In fact, I have small children. I thought perhaps it would do them well to see what a real-life hero looks like, close up. Regular visits, perhaps. If you'd like."

"Lanaya and her kids." Deshear shook his head, a smile crossing his lips. "Well, if the illness doesn't kill me, that might."

"My dear Hamilton." She went to him, wrapping her arms around his muscular torso and squeezing him tight. "I have many friends. None but you have ever saved my life. In the end, it's life that matters. I owe you."

He sighed. "Okay, but no more deceptions. We're linked, you and I. Partners tell the truth to each other."

"Okay," Lanaya whispered, holding him. "I promise I won't lie to you anymore."

"Thank you."

"Unless it's absolutely necessary." She released him from her hug. "And in ten months, when you're all better, I'll have some more work for you."

"Ten months." He rubbed his chin. "You know, if there are other Gammas, there'll be other Greyhounds. Followers. Extremists."

"Indeed. And we shall need someone on our side to lead the charge."

DeShear nodded. "Yes, you will. Then let's talk in ten months. You have my number." He smiled at her. "And I'll be around."

THE END

Note to Readers

If you have the time, I would deeply appreciate a review on Amazon or Goodreads. I learn a great deal from them, and I'm always grateful for any encouragement. Reviews are a very big deal and help authors like me to sell a few more books. Every review matters, even if it's only a few words.

Thanks,

Dan Alatorre

ABOUT THE AUTHOR

International bestselling author Dan Alatorre has published more than 26 titles and has been translated into over a dozen languages. His ability to surprise readers and make them laugh, cry, or hang onto the edge of their seats, has been enjoyed all around the world.

Dan's success is widespread and varied. In addition to being a bestselling author, he achieved President's Circle with two different Fortune 500 companies, and mentors grade school children through his Young Authors Club. Dan resides in the Tampa, Florida, area with his wife and daughter.

Join Dan's exclusive Reader's Club today at DanAlatorre.com and find out about new releases and special offers!